The -ions

Book III of The Jarg Trilogy

TONY NUTTALL

To Liverpool, for giving me the tools I needed. A set of instructions would have been nice.

To Mum, Dad, Chris, The Nuttall's and The Bracey's, who must bear some responsibility for my thinking.
Pete, thanks for fixing the pump.

CHAPTER 1

NEW WORLD IS THE OLD WORLD

Consciousness crept in slowly, hearing then smell the first senses to respond, but disconnected, incoherent as they remained cut off from each other. I felt blank, probing for memories of what or who I was; wondering if I had existence or was now something different, something light, ethereal, a soul, dark energy. My mind was searching, straining to connect to hardware, re-booting, seeking sight, the optic nerve flickering, coming online as light emerged pink behind my eyelids whilst sound remained white noise, a gentle hum, flat, nothing, until a subtle movement reassured me I was something, somewhere.

I opened my eyes slightly, seeking its source, glancing around a white room, at a white ceiling, everything white, before stopping on colour, Judy, reading a book, remaining silent as I considered the machine I was connected to before closing them to lay still again, allowing memories to creep back, the first, Jacko, laying in the recording studio.

'Discombobulated,' drifted into my mind then back out again, like a feather on the breeze.

Further fragments appeared, finding each other before gathering in clumps, separate then gradually coming together, recollections filling in gaps like a jigsaw until I knew who I was though not where I was. Scenes played back, of The Temple, of the riot, then nothing, not a single thought or memory, as if I'd ceased existing. Looking back, I'd like to say there was a moment when something remarkable happened, that bright light, my mother appearing from a billowing fog in white floating gowns, giving a knowing smile before gently guiding me back, "It's not your time yet my darling;" or perhaps Jacko, "Alright La, bit fucking hot down there, you're booked in but you've got stuff to do first, the folder, remember?" But there was nothing, no dreams or visions, just a void, or perhaps a vacuum as I wondered what had been taken from me.

I was groggy, new thoughts difficult to formulate as I opened my eyes again and continued looking around, quietly wiggling my fingers and toes, rotating my ankles then wrists before working my way through my body, wondering why I was here.

Judy looked up, hearing a rustle, "Peter?" she asked, leaping forward, leaning over me as her book tumbled to the ground. "You're awake."

"Where am I?" I asked, my voice sounding strange, echoey.

"Broadgreen."

"What?"

"Neurology."

"What happened?" I asked, my throat dry, voice hoarse as I struggled to speak, trying to lift myself up as she gently placed her hand on my chest, easing me back down.

"The riots; you came in unconscious."

"Am I okay?"

"Few stitches, then a fractured skull and blood clot on the brain," she replied as vivid memories filled the void, his twisted face, the brick; must've been a decent shot. I raised my hand to my head and felt tentatively, finding it shaven, bandaged, the bumps of old scars.

"A blood clot?"

"Inside," she nodded. "You came close to being operated on, but the clot stopped expanding so you've been here resting and recuperating."

"Is it still there?"

"No, the doctor says your blood takes it away bit by bit, until it's gone."

"I've got to get up," I said, trying to sit up, swinging my legs towards the edge of the bed as a wave of dizziness hit me before she gently pushed me down again.

"You can't..."

"I've got to do Clarkey's funeral."

"Yoda did it."

"It's today," I protested.

"You've been here a week."

I remained on my pillow this time, staring at the ceiling, trying to comprehend how I'd lost a week of my life.

"Loads have been in to see you," she offered cheerfully, filling the silence. "Yoda, Migsy, Smiler, plenty from the estate, Said..."

"And do what? Just sit there looking at me?"

"Well, yes, they tend to have a gab across you. What are they
supposed to do?"
"I don't know," I groaned, starting to panic, "Why?"
"It's what people do, they go and see people in hospital."
"I know, it's just…"
I was thinking of them touching my body, looking at my scars, my
secrets as I glanced across at four bottles of Lucozade standing on
the bedside table wrapped in that orange film, taking me to Stan,
clearing the homes of dead people, vintage.
"How are you? How's the baby?"
"All good Daddy, despite what you've put us through," she replied
in that strange, squeaky voice they sometimes do, reaching forward
and clasping my hand as a wave of nausea hit me.
"How long have you been here?"
"As long as they let me, all day, every day."
I gave a gentle squeeze as a tear ran down her cheek. "I thought I'd
lost you. I didn't know who was going to wake up, if you'd be
disabled, if…"
"It's okay," I replied awkwardly, unsure of what to do as she leant
into an embrace, taking deep breaths as her body pressed against
mine; the succubus sat here, waiting, watching over me.
"Has anybody said anything about…"
"About what?"
"You know, you being here every day?"
"About us?"
"Well, yes…"
"They know," she said. "We couldn't keep it a secret for much
longer anyway," she continued in that voice, finishing with a shrug,
pointing to her bump.
"What did they say?"
"Nothing, plenty behind closed doors I'd imagine."
"Yoda?"
"Nothing."
"Nothing?"
I could almost imagine his face, blank, expressionless whilst
explosions detonated inside.
"Is everybody else okay?"
"Cuts and bruises, but it's gone bad."
"What do you mean?"

"The riots, every night now."
"Riots?"
"Yes, everywhere, it's terrible, fires, burnt out cars, shops, it's like a warzone."
"Christ…"
"They're guarding The Temple."
"What? Why? Who?"
"They've turned against each other."
"Who?"
"The rioters. They're fighting each other, as well as the police."
"But, I don't…why The Church?"
"They've been burning them down: churches, mosques, temples, you name it."
"I don't understand."
"Because of you…"
"What?"
She held up a newspaper showing fire, a silhouette, it's hand raised, pleading, as a blurred shape had already began its journey, launched from the hands of an assailant. HOLY WAR was written in red across the top.
"That's you," she said, pointing to the silhouette, "when they attacked you, the Muslims."
"No," I stammered. "That's not me, that's a policeman."
"There's a crucifix hanging down."
"I don't wear a crucifix."
She sat back and sighed, understanding the significance of what I was saying, "The world has turned," she began.
We spoke for over an hour before she left, of a country that I hardly recognised, a tipping point reached, institutions collapsing like dominos, one chain of events setting off another: prison riots that couldn't be contained; a police force that couldn't be trusted; hospitals reminiscent of war zones, a flood of broken bodies arriving as protesters from left and right set upon each other, distracting from the real story going on above.
I was doubting myself as I looked again at the newspaper; my memories were fragmentary, pointed shards, standing alone, like islands as the room went white and I was twisting, contorting, electricity running through my body until I blacked out, darkness.
Yoda was the next to visit though he was in business mode, cold,

striding in quickly, urgent, no small talk. "I don't even know what you were doing there, you just can't resist can you?"
"They've Photoshopped it," I said, waving the newspaper at him.
"Oh, come on Peter, really?"
"They weren't Muslims."
"You won't really be able to remember clearly…" he suggested calmly, trying to talk over me.
"It was…"
"We've given you time off, to recuperate," he continued, ignoring me. "I'll take over all pastoral duties."
"I don't want time off, I can't…"
"It's this lovely place on The Isle of Wight," he announced, a smile touching his lips as he pulled a folded pamphlet from his back pocket.
"I'm not going to the Isle of Wight."
"You have to…"
"Ibiza for clergy?"
"You have to rest, stay away from the protests, stay away from The Church."
"I have to fix it."
"You've done your bit," he said, reassuring me. "You need to stay away for a while, get better."
"I've done fuck-all, I'm being used…"
"There is something much bigger at play here, Peter."
"What?"
"We've been in decline for decades and now you've presented us with the opportunity to get back on top."
I took a double take, wondering if I'd heard him correctly.
"Are you mad?"
"It's the way the world is going. Countries are closing themselves off and religion is being reinstated into national identities."
"And I'm a pawn?"
"It's God's plan. We need to be there, at the top, now, shaping the future of The Church, of this country, and this is our opportunity."
"But we can't…"
"Don't give me that shit about religion and politics. Religion shapes policy in many countries around the world."
"Am I talking to the same Yoda here? What has happened to you?"
"Nothing," he shrugged. "I've always been a cunt."

"I need to talk to the press, make them stop. The protesters are turning on each other, burning temples, mosques, synagogues…"
"You're talking to no-one. This is good for the government, it's stopped the power-grab of the masses, and it's good for us, this is our chance."
"But it wasn't Muslims, they're deflecting."
"When the people get power, The Church loses power. They're like Bolsheviks. Is that what you want?"
"You sound like a Christian supremacist."
"It has always been this way. We started as part of the state and have never been otherwise."
"Protestantism, Secularisation separated The Church and state..."
"Don't you believe it. They get the taxes, we get the souls, both get power."
"Maybe a fundamentalist?"
"So should you be. Anglicanism is a combination of…"
"I know," I interrupted. "Ecclesiastical tradition, parliamentary legislation…"
"…and allegiance to the crown," he finished, jabbing his finger at me.
"A holy trinity?"
"If you like."
"That was centuries ago."
"We're still there, in the House of Lords, praying for the royal family in our services, but big-business has taken our place on the government's right hand, and we need it back."
"So, shouldn't you be on the streets with us? Protesting against big-business?"
"No, you're on the wrong side with all these leftie do-gooders. Religion doesn't survive on the left. You need to re-calibrate."
"I'll do no such thing."
"You'll see the truth eventually, Peter. It's big picture. These days people are all power and no fear, not afraid of gods, political power, bourgeois notions, nuclear family, blah, blah, blah. There's an allergy towards moral judgement of any kind, rejecting everything good as a model of being. They want to break free of any kind of shackle."
"Society has evolved, you can't take them back in time."
"You have a built in hostility to authority, which I completely

understand..."

"It's nothing to do with that, it's about fairness."

"We can only have influence alongside power. Surely you can see that?"

"But their protests are valid, we should be representing the people..."

"So what are you going to do? Write 95 theses, nail them on the doors, Luther?"

"Yes, it's a reformation, the country needs to be reformed."

"By some peasant revolt? Levellers? Diggers? You are clergy of The Church of England and you must do as your church requires."

"They are protesting about extreme inequality. We are Protestant, born from protest, against corruption, the clue is in the name. It's you that needs to re-calibrate."

"There will always be inequality; religion requires it..."

"Oh, don't go there," I groaned.

"Because in poverty" he continued, "people need someone to tell them that there's something better in the next life. We can bring them back to the truth. Don't you see? The biggest con is the belief that affluence is the key to happiness, to achievement, to a great life. They don't need money."

"They are protesting because there are thieves taking from them."

"Obey them that have the rule over you, and submit..."

"Hebrews? I could quote a thousand and one proverbs that would put The Church on their side."

"It doesn't matter anyway, it's moved on from inequality," he said, waving his hand as if swatting a fly. "It's a new war, they're fighting each other along religious lines, burning down places of worship. Even the Catholic and Protestant thing has flared up again."

"You're saying that as if it's a good thing."

"Just temporary, until we see how the cards fall."

"We're not Hugenots and Calvinists, there's no Habsburgs. We have freedom of religion, the country is built on tolerance."

"It's not what the people want. They are deciding."

"What does that mean?"

"They're on the streets, reshaping religion in this country."

"Based upon a lie," I repeated.

"You were just the spark, religious tolerance has gone too far."

"It's media spin, propaganda..."
"It's democracy. Let them make their own choices."
"I need to leave this place…"
"Be careful, Peter."
"I'm okay," I replied, unsure if it was a threat or concern for my health.
"Your Dad," he said, deftly changing tack, flipping me as his eyes flicked across to the machine with its red line jarring rhythmically to my pulse, betraying feelings as I reacted to his words, blood pressure rising, revealed in real-time.
"What about him? Is he okay?"
"Well…"
"They've been rioting in the prisons."
"He's not in prison."
"What?"
"He's not in prison," he repeated.
"Fuck. Did he break out? Do you know where he is?"
"He didn't break out."
"Well, where is he?"
"They've taken him to Ashworth, for assessment."
"No," I whimpered as my mind began to collapse around me, the red line trembling, becoming more erratic. "They keep serial killers in there."
"I know, I know, son, but…"
"They don't come out of that place…"
"He's not of sound mind," he replied, finding it difficult to say the words.
"They've kept him in solitary for so long."
"For his own good."
"How can it be for his own good? He's been sectioned."
"He's gone there from prison. It's not as if he's lost his freedom."
"They'll drug him up to the eyeballs, electric shocks…"
"They don't do that anymore."
"Lobotomies…"
"You're looking at it all wrong, they'll give him the care he needs."
"He'll end up dribbling…"
"He's sick, Peter," he said, raising his voice. "He's already dribbling."
"A cabbage…"

"Stop," he shouted, before taking a breath and the gentleness returned. "He's no longer locked alone in a room. He has a problem and they are going to fix it."
"It's my fault."
"Oh, here we go, self-pity city…"
"Always have to be the hero…"
"Stop."
"If I hadn't…"
"Stop," he shouted, angry this time, glancing at the wall, wondering if the room was soundproof.
"Can I see him?"
Yoda shook his head slowly.
"It's completely secure. Only God can see him."
As he left I had nothing to focus on but thoughts in this white, featureless cell. I wondered if I was also in Ashworth with Dad in the next compartment, looking at the same wall, Yoda and Judy maintaining a fiction as they filled me with drugs so The Church could continue its quest for power, without interference.
"Where's Peter?" I mumbled, searching my mind for the bogeyman, finding nothing, before switching to another tangent, wondering if I was in quarantine as some virus or pandemic rampaged throughout the world; mother nature, energy, God, shaking, cleansing it of humans. Perhaps I was trapped, a lab rat waiting to be infected, or maybe I was the infected, a carrier of pestilence and plague, bringing suffering and death to all I touched. That was it, that was me, pestilence, death, Azrael, Peter.
"Where the fuck's Peter?" I repeated, questioning whether the bang on the head had knocked a bit of sense into me, bumped Peter out to haunt some other unfortunate soul.
The doctor visited later that afternoon, interrupting my deliberations. He was not Josef Mengele and was not wearing a hazmat suit, knocking me off the tangent on which I was travelling as he shone lights into my eyes and asked simple questions.
"Who are you?"
That was a tricky one as I mumbled Peter, my body weak, head swirling as I tried to sit up, vision blurring, difficult to ascertain which way was up, leaving a feeling of motion sickness as he continued with my MOT, ignoring my stream of nonsensical dialogue as he ticked unseen boxes on a form.

"You may suffer blackouts, seizures, disorientation and confusion," he concluded. "You're free to leave in the morning."

Exhaustion ensured sleep as my body repaired itself, but still, I awoke periodically through the night when my mind would race. I felt almost locked in, a spirit that wanted to move with a body that couldn't as I stood for the first time in a week, staggering out of my cell along a corridor of doors, checking the name on each, looking for Dad as I felt my way along the wall, arse hanging out of my blue robe until finding the bathroom.

"You're supposed to press the button," the shift nurse gently reprimanded as I'd attempted to stagger back quietly, pinballing off walls then falling to the floor with a grunt where she found me.

"Not pissing in that golf club thing," was my curt response as she manhandled me into a wheelchair; what they all say, apparently.

My next steps came the following morning, the nurse helping me dress as Migsy put his arm beneath mine, providing support with his ample frame as I staggered around, legs buckling like a new born lamb. Earlier, I'd wanted to stand, run, but now I wanted to stay safe in my bubble, afraid of what I might find outside following Yoda's words. It sounded like I'd awoken into a parallel universe, where everything was the same, but different.

"Get back in bed," Migsy insisted, anger rising as we ended up in a heap in the corner of the room as I attempted to walk to the door.

"Keep going," the nurse countered over her shoulder.

"He's not ready."

"Somebody else has booked it," she mumbled apologetically, giving a shrug as she stripped the bed for the next incumbent.

"I'm alright, just get me out."

"You're fucked."

"Just get me out," I repeated as he bundled me into the corridor, then the lift, nausea rising as it lurched and started descending before opening up into Bedlam, Hell, the corridors filled with beds, their occupants lying still, sedated, watched over by relatives, or screaming, filled with agony and rage as staff ran from complaint to complaint, on the verge of breakdown.

"What's this, Aleppo?"

"NHS," Migsy replied. "It's a three tier system, you pay to go upstairs. Business Class for you kidda."

"And these?"

"Bronze package, free healthcare."
I slumped across the back seat, glancing out of the window as we travelled through the city. Life appeared as normal though people seemed to be quieter, walking at a faster pace, their minds pre-occupied. The pervading smell of fire was the only suggestion that something was amiss until the first burnt out building came into view like a grainy photograph from the war, just a shell, scorch marks travelling up the elevations above empty black openings as daylight illuminated it's charred insides. The flames had hollowed it out, a patch of timber and slate clinging on around the chimney the only suggestion that there used to be a roof.
"Have you been involved?"
"Nah, steered well clear, small time."
It was quickly followed by others as we approached the centre, husks standing silent and mournful, an apocalyptic backdrop to the running battles of the night before. Bricks lay scattered between burnt out skeletons of cars, wheelie bins and barricades. It didn't seem real, like an art installation, a different place, a different time as volunteers brushed away debris, sweeping neat piles of broken glass across scorch marks and battle scars gouged into the tarmac.
"I can't believe we've ended up like this."
"It's changed so quickly, people are furious, the whole place is falling apart."
"They've been furious for months but it was peaceful."
"We've reached a tipping point, thousands were dumped out of their jobs, just last week."
"Where?"
"Everywhere, the outsource companies have collapsed. The City's been shorting the shares, made a shed load out of it."
"What's an outsource company?"
"Most of your congregation work for one," he grinned. "All the public services, NHS, schools, prisons, railways, rubbish collection, benefits, everything the government is supposed to do, you name it."
"It can't have just gone."
"It has, the whole structure has collapsed. There's a few still going in, but the others have no employers so no jobs. They've got families to feed, mortgages to pay."
"So people are angry."

"So people are angry," he agreed. "They've also done the usual and left a nice big pension scheme for us to pay out."
"So, what's the government doing?"
"They don't know where to start, it's too big to fix. They've fucked it, every sector of the state has ceased functioning, apart from the military."
"It sounds like chaos."
"The problem is there is no way to stop it. Markets are collapsing, shops are being looted, Deaf Eddie got on the front of The Echo carrying a telly."
"A good one?"
"Yes, 48 inch curvy one," he grinned. "They keep issuing statements but nobody believes them anymore."
"Stay Calm and Carry On?"
"Pretty much. They're blaming rioters for everything, but they caused the whole thing, what did they expect?"
"What about the police?"
"They're all over the place, they don't know what side they are on. Half of them are striking, the other half are not, they're fighting each other."
"So?"
"So now the army's been deployed. Last night was supposed to be the start of the curfew."
"Curfew? You're joking?" I groaned, as I remembered Said's words, the military on the streets.
"No joke, curfew. No chance of working like, red rag to a bull, there were way more rioters last night."
I glanced out of the window at more fire damaged buildings. It was the Mosque, Brougham Terrace.
"Was that your lot?"
"Probably."
"Shocking."
"I don't know why you're getting arsey, they nearly killed you."
"It wasn't Muslims."
"It was, the news said…"
"Oh, come on, you're better than that."
"Somebody saw them do it. How would you fucking know?"
"Because I saw it."
"Serious?"

"Serious."

"Do you know them?"

"Yep."

"Fuck, who? The Nightman?"

I jerked upright, remembering. "The Nightman, in the riots…"

"Lucky said he was after you. For a second I thought it was him, before they told us about the Muslims."

"I nailed him, in the riot, on the plaza, left him on the ground…"

"Nobody else saw him," he replied, shaking his head.

"It was him. The guy watching when we first arrived, big lad, hoodie…"

"Oh fuck, that's not The Nightman. You did that?"

"What do you mean?"

"That's The Leatherman. The Rip had him watching you."

"Does nobody have their own bloody name in this place? Who's The Leatherman? It's like Gotham City."

"The Rip."

"Is he okay?"

"Still on a ventilator, they're keeping him unconscious."

"Fuck," I shouted, punching the seat in front of me. "Sounds like a nasty bastard anyway, The Leatherman…"

"Nah, it's because he's a useless tool, thick as shit, only good for keeping dixie."

Sickness rose as I remembered his palms raised in submission, before dropping to his knees, streaked with blood. My hand covered my mouth as I closed my eyes, hearing that squelch as I stamped down on him, enveloped in smoke, surrounded by screams of madness.

He pulled up outside the house and the door opened, Ginny holding it ajar whilst Judy peered out from homely comfort behind. The world seemed to have broken down into parallel realities. They'd always been there but the differences seemed more pronounced, the disparities more extreme.

"Alright love, your Judy's here," Ginny shouted, excitedly.

Migsy glanced across. "A little mouse tells me that you, err…"

"Yes," I replied, after a long pause. "Early days."

"A few months, maybe?" he grinned, arching an eyebrow.

"A few months," I agreed, watching his face as the words registered and a huge smile broke out, spreading across his features as he leant back and pounded me on the shoulder, knocking me flat on the seat, far more enthusiastic about it than I was.

"Go'ed mate."

As the door closed behind me, I entered a new reality, familiar but different. Ginny was like a yo-yo, the sounds of her footsteps fading as she took the dishes away before reappearing an hour later, the light tap on the door announcing the next delivery of an endless supply of scouse. Then she'd sit, watching, until I finished the bowl, giving encouraging soundbites with each spoonful:

"Put hairs on your chest that lad…"

"Vikings loved it, no such thing as a skinny Viking…"

"You be careful girl, scouse used to make my Terence horny as hell…"

"This one's blind, you've ate all my mutton…"

I'd eat then lie down and drift away, my body switching to stand by in order to digest and heal.

Despite circumstances, I felt content as Judy and Ginny clucked around me, a new experience as I lay there trying to understand the feeling, absorbing it, breathing it in. I was helpless but they were there, fixing me, healing, nurturing, scouse for the soul as I lay listening to the television confirm everything people had said, watching cities erupting across the country. It wasn't just here, the world seemed alight as the newscaster switched from a burning Australia, through to California and on to Europe, all man-made as different causes created the same effect. It was as if fire had lain dormant, waiting underground until conditions permitted before spreading as scenes from Paris, Brussels, Marseille, Berlin and Athens now filled the screen, their skies orange, filled with billowing smoke as waves of advancing protesters crashed against walls of police, armed with batons and shields.

The internet was the tinderbox as continuing revelations added to the fury. They'd stopped blaming Russia as their oligarchs threatened to withhold party donations, instead calling out generic intelligence agencies for destabilising countries, or China, for manufacturing pandemics to destroy global economies, Covid-28, or whatever they were up to, though nobody could figure out why. But that was just noise, a distraction to avoid scrutiny, a tactic now so commonplace, it had lost all value. It was the parties that had come apart, their unified fronts shattered by infighting as they

fractured then re-formed on the basis of ideological purity towards
out-of-date belief systems. They were power without responsibility,
sending bile and death threats spinning through the media, trying
to promote their versions of truth, always heady cocktails of
sentiment and rage as they attempted to unite the public behind
their cause, leaving a trail of social debris.

To some it was a blip, to others the beginning of the end, a collapse
of civilisation completely understandable with hindsight, all that
social stratification. The only real debate was how quickly it would
happen, the Mayan or Roman model.

"Basically the canary in the coal mine were countries like Syria," a
tinny voice suggested, chipping away at another fault line. "Volatile
societies collapse leading to a mass movement of people who then
destabilise the next country, then the next…"

"Don't let them in then," the Gammon suggested.

I reached over and switched it off, casting the room into darkness,
hearing loud and excited voices passing outside, a helicopter and
sirens in the distance. Judy was asleep, her breathing the only
sound in the room as I lay still, bracing myself, waiting for the fear
to rise. But, the old fear did not arrive, it was replaced by a new
fear, a normal fear as I realised it wasn't just me anymore, feeling
the warmth and gentle moving of her body, the small bump
pressing into my lower back.

∞

Heads shot up as I entered the hall, climbing up from their yoga
mats and crowding around, reaching forward for handshakes and
hugs. Even Gabe floated over, hugging me tight as I felt a tear drop
from his cheek. I could immediately feel The Temple drawing me
in, embracing me, blocking out the outside world.

"You look fucking awful," Mary said, pulling me in towards her. It
struck me how important these familiar faces now were, a surrogate
family to cling onto, after a violent storm.

"Been eating scouse for days," I replied with a smile. It felt good to
be here amongst them; they looked genuine, relieved.

Lucky grabbed me by the shoulder. "Sorry I left you mate, I feel
fucking terrible."

"No need to apologise. You didn't leave me."

"What are you doing here? It's too soon," Margaret chided.

"I've got to do the service," I replied, feeling courageous, heroic.

"You're so thin," Elvis said, appearing alongside.

"Like an x-ray with clothes on," Libby shouted over, the alcohol not quite bridging the distance as the front line of contortionists flinched.

"What's been happening?" I asked, trying to sound decisive, getting down to business.

"The usual. No club nights though, because of the curfew," Mekon Don declared mournfully.

"Curfew? Never thought I'd see that. Even for religious ceremonies?"

"Yes, they've managed to close that little loophole."

"It's great," Ivy shrugged, red and sweaty from her exertions. "We never used to go out but we're out every night now."

"What's all that stuff in the road?" I asked; It looked like somebody had been fly-tipping.

"The barricade," Stan declared proudly, puffing out his chest like Jean Valjean. "Protecting the church."

"From who?"

"The Muslims."

"This wasn't Muslims," I sighed, pointing at my shaven head.

"The Nightman?"

"No."

"Then who?"

"It can wait, more important things to sort out first, like taking down those barricades. We're a local resource for anyone to use, don't care which team you support."

It was the strangest service as Elvis approached me with an idea that I somehow agreed to, no doubt vulnerable and eager to please. The chapel was full as they sat quietly, heads tilting in various directions behind their VR headsets. All I could see were mouths, half of which hung open as they forgot the real world, becoming totally engrossed in their new environment. Yoda was sat at the end of the first row, tilting his head back before reaching his arm out in front, waving into thin air, 'Bono' leaving his lips.

"Elvis said he'd set you all up in St. Pauls," I suggested, as heads switched towards me, though some were wearing headphones, so remained oblivious.

"Didn't have time," Elvis mumbled, focused on something unseen.
"Oh, so where are you all?"
"State Penitentiary."
"In orbit."
"New York."
"Jurassic Park."
"On an iceberg with some penguins."
"Intestines."
"Palestine."
"Jungle."
"Dagoba."
"Great Barrier Reef."
"So none of you are in St. Paul's?"
"No," came the reply from random shaking heads.
I spent most of the service guiding them back to their seats as they stood up and walked into each other. Willo let out a wail and appeared to be headbutting something.
"Zombies," he yelped, "Fuck off," as I guided him back, only for him to stand up and run into the wall as Crystal vomited into her lap then started crying.
"Sorry, get motion sickness."
I sang the hymns alone, the odd voice joining in with the chorus as they couldn't see hymn books, then wondered if any of them heard a word as I gave a sermon about peace between the different religions.
"Great service," each said, with the exception of Crystal as they passed on their way out of the door, removing phones from their headsets as they handed them back to Elvis.
"Keep it for a tenner, keep it for a tenner…"
"Can you lend me 68p?" Yoda asked, holding out a palm full of slummy.
"Have a pound," I replied as he grinned, placing the headset in his carrier bag.
"What are you doing with the rest of the day?"
"Nothing, just resting," I lied.
"Good, good," he mumbled before shuffling off, leaving Discharge remaining alone, headphones on and hand to his groin.
"Is he watching porn?" I asked Judy as she stood next to me.
"Of course he is."

"It's a bloody church," I complained, recalling the Over-65 swing.
"What do we do?"
"Just leave him," she sighed, turning me out of the door. "Probably
can't walk at the moment anyway."
I walked into the back of a stationary Yoda as I left The Chapel,
finding the congregation still there facing a crowd standing before
them, hundreds of faces silently studying us. I wondered if they
were real, if they were friend or foe, if time had paused as nobody
moved or made a sound as I wandered into the space between
them.
"What's this?" I asked, my voice echoing through the hall.
A voice began to reply before being hushed as I glanced back to
Yoda who answered with a shrug, as confounded as I was.
Migsy stepped forward, my purple surplice hanging off the end of
his finger.
"What's this?" I asked.
"Yours if you're up to it. They've missed you."
"But we can only do services on a Sunday morning, the government
has stopped everything else."
"Sunday morning looks a bit like Saturday night to me," he said,
looking around the hall.
I glanced around at the faces, looking back expectantly as I
remained in no-mans-land, "But, they'll hear, they'll come…"
"Put these on," Migsy instructed, holding forward a pair of
headphones.
I placed them over my ears, finding God is a DJ blurring out as my
eyes shot up to the DJ platform, finding Crab Scratch bouncing
before the curtain.
"Wagwan fam," he giggled, his voice overlaying the music coming
through the headphones.
"Wigwam," I mumbled in reply, glancing around as dancers started
appearing on the other platforms, still, waiting for permission to
perform. Further people were clambering along the rigging as the
red silks dropped, waiting for bodies to cascade down them.
Migsy's mouth was moving as I removed the headphones, "What?"
"A silent service," he repeated. "This is your church, there's your
congregation, are you going to do a service?"
"I've just done one."
"That was the warm up."

"I'm fucked…"

"They've been waiting for weeks."

I reached forward and took the surplice, emotionally blackmailed, feeling its smooth texture as it slipped over my head. There was a hum of excitement then silencing hisses throughout the crowd as arms were flung into the air and they started to dance as their headphones came online. It was a surreal experience, the only sound the hiss of smoke machines vomiting clouds and the rustle of bodies moving as lights stuttered then disappeared, sending the place into darkness before strobes and lasers took over, sending graphics spinning, transforming the place into something abstract, beyond description.

I walked through to the staircase, finding Willo waiting, his foot tapping gently to the music as he held out his offering, a path to another world.

"Would you care to join me?" he asked.

"Where are we going?"

"On an exploration of reality, the dark side of the moon."

"An expedition? To find God?" I replied with a grin, hesitating before reaching forward, feeling my energy rising as my fingers touched the pill, accepting my ticket to another place in my search for the almighty.

The experience felt stronger, perhaps due to my weakened state. They appeared frenzied, their pent-up tensions finding release, shaking off the troubles of the world, as we forgot everything, lost in the here and now, whatever, wherever that was.

"Feds at the barricade, innit," brought an abrupt halt to the proceedings as Crab Scratch's voice came from nowhere, like an omnipotent God. Everything and everybody stopped, frozen statues, before the lights came on, thawing them out as they started rushing forward, forming lines in a well prepared drill. Everywhere was activity, Plan B, as people rushed to set up tables and chairs in Red Molly's as she hurried around, handing out cups of tea and taking orders. The silks performance had turned into a silks lesson, whilst the platforms of dancers went into practice mode as they gathered around, slowly repeating a sequence of moves. I appeared to be the only one out of the loop, staring open mouthed as colourful shapes floated through my vision. I started swaying, then dancing, unsure of what else to do until Migsy appeared at the side of the stage.

"The surplice, give me the surplice," he called, holding out his hand.

"What's going on?" I asked, pulling it over my head and throwing it towards him. "What do I do?"

"End of a service."

"What?"

"It's a fucking service, say a prayer," he hissed before disappearing behind the folds of the curtain.

I glanced up to see a sliver of light appear, then enlarge as the entrance doors began to open.

"…and lead us not into temptation, but deliver us from evil," I preached into the microphone as the door opened fully and the police entered, pausing, looking around, smelling a rat.

"For thine is the kingdom, the power and the glory, for ever and ever, Amen."

"Amen," they chanted back in unison.

I walked down through the crowd, still in rows, smug, chatting, as the police watched me approach, their body language oozing suspicion.

"Hello Brian, come to read The Riot Act?"

"It's a gathering of over twelve persons," he replied, knowing he'd lost the argument before it began.

"It's a religious service within the allotted time."

"Why aren't you doing it in The Chapel?"

"Have you seen how many worshippers we have with us today?"

"You're the next Billy Graham, are you?"

"It's not me, they love God, what can I say?" I shrugged.

"Wonderful service father," Margaret said as she shuffled past.

"Why is there smoke everywhere?"

"Atmospherics, get them in the mood, closer to God."

"Up on a cloud?"

"Yes, that sort of thing."

"Great service father," Stan and Ivy interrupted, shaking hands as they passed.

"Did you come to pray?"

"Don't get smart arse with me lad."

"Well, what do you think is going on?" I asked, turning the tables.

"An illegal gathering…"

"Doing what? Did you hear music? Were the screens on?"
"No, it was silent, but…"
"A giant fucking mime class?"
"Lovely service father," Big Jim called over as he was leaving.
"You're up to something, it's full of kids."
"And pensioners," I pointed out, waving to Lucky and Mekon Don as they passed. "They're all doing different classes or visiting Red Square."
"They were all together, the nightclub…"
"Is that what you're suggesting? Pensioners and kids, having a disco? A bit of Nat King Cole, Margaret? No love, go for the Skrillex."
He let out a sigh as more holes were punched into his argument. I thought he was finished, but he rallied, clutching at the last few straws.
"You're eyes are fucked and you're sweating like a bitch on heat, have you been taking drugs?"
"I've taken all sorts of drugs," I confessed. "I was nearly dead last week. I'm rattling the amount of pills they've given me."
"I can have you tested."
"Test away," I replied, calling his bluff. I'd been easing off my medication, supplementing with a daily microdose, finding an equilibrium. I was in a good place, Willo had taken me to a better place.
"I'm putting an officer on next weeks service," was all he had left. "See if you get a similar turnout."
"You're going to police a church? Bit quiet with all the riots?"
"Not officially. They love God, what can I say?" he shrugged, returning my sarcasm before glancing across at Yoda who was in the lobby wearing his headset, his hand lifting as he tried to touch a different reality.
"What have you done to him? It's a fucking cult," Brian groaned, shaking his head before leaving with his silent entourage.
Bob Sponge was waiting as I returned to the office, grinning as I entered. "You look well, considering."
"Feel like shite, enjoyed the service though."
"That one won't be making it to the papers."
"Did you manage to speak to your mates, about the press release?"
"They're not interested."

"What do you mean they're not interested?"
"Half of them have had their accounts suspended, they can't work."
"By who?"
"The government."
"They've taken control of the media?"
"They've taken control of plurality in the media. Banned fake news, supposedly."
"They are the fake news."
"Exactly…"
"And they've accepted this?"
"Why do you think billionaires and oligarchs own newspapers? They're all part of the same system."
"So you don't know anyone?"
"No-one that'll go off script."
"So, what do we do?" I asked, throwing the newspaper down in front of him. "They're still pushing this image and it's complete bullshit."
"We don't need them," he replied. "Go around them, social media. Nobody listens to them anymore anyway," he continued as we set up the video camera in The Chapel, the crucifix over my left shoulder as I faced the lens, fully robed, to explain my truth to the world.
It took three takes as I sat, trying to sound wise.
"What's up with you? Nervous?"
"No, just still not right."
"You're shaking like a dog having a shit."
The next was stopped after two minutes, "Will you stop saying erm."
"Sorry, I didn't realise…"
"There's more erms than a Stevie G-La interview."
It was short and to the point, discrediting suggestions that my attack was based upon religion, becoming a mini-sermon as Bob stood behind the camera giving thumbs up as my mouth took over.
"We are a secular society, where all religions should be treated equally, where people choose to believe or not. Religion shouldn't affect policy, placing one religion in an advantageous position over another and should not be used as a basis to disenfranchise any section of society, including other religions."
I had a mental image of Yoda exploding as I continued.

"Religion should not be used as a tool for governance, just a choice an individual makes, one of the many facets that goes towards making a person," before finishing as all good sermons should with a message of peace and reconciliation.

"Nailed it," Bob said, typing frantically on his laptop before we recorded another, aimed this time at the far right.

"Send that through to your Alt-Right mates please Migs."

"Who?"

"You know, the Fourth Reich…"

"You're sure?"

"Worth a try," I shrugged. "Nobody else is speaking to them. Might find someone with a bit of sense."

"Better chance of Stevie Wonder finding Wally."

Bob was becoming tense, making me tense as we packed the equipment away. I'd hoped it had gone away, so much had happened since our last conversation, the world had changed, I'd changed, but I could feeling it getting closer with each minute of silence as my mind offered a range of probabilities, none of them positive.

"You OK?" I asked, ensuring Migsy was out of the room before closing the door with a quiet click.

"No," he replied. "It's about the other business…"

"Go on."

"I started making a few discrete enquiries."

"And what did you find?"

"Nothing, but…"

"But what?"

"I got a call."

"From who?"

"Inspector John Taylor, apparently."

"What did he say?"

He remained quiet for a second.

"They asked me why I was looking into the death of Colin Best."

I felt a wave of goosebumps rise then fall, betraying the fear inside.

"So?" I panicked, pushing my seat away from the desk, standing, as if it made a difference. "Did you bullshit?"

"Yes, of course," he replied, sounding slightly insulted, "but then…"

"What?"

"He asked why I'd been investigating the other three."
"Fuck," I shouted as the goosebumps returned, swathing my body,
my skin feeling tight. "I thought you'd tip-toed around this, I
thought…"
"I did. I used anonymous names and email addresses, VPN's;
they're different constabularies, no way of linking them."
"So how did they know?"
"I don't know," he shrugged.
"So, what did you say?" I asked, raising my voice, increasing the
tension.
"Nothing, I just put the phone down."
"Well, have you looked into Inspector John Taylor? See who he is?"
"Yes…"
"And?"
"There is no Inspector John Taylor."
"Fuck," I shouted again as another wave of panic set in.
"Fuck indeed," he replied.
"You need to back off, forget about it."
"But, what if…"
"It's not, it's just because the people were from around here.
Parishioners asked…" I lied, as he stood in silence. "Leave it,
destroy the cuttings…"
"But…"
"Or that's it, no more stories," I threatened, the only weapon in my
arsenal.
"Okay, we'll leave it," he replied calmly, after a long pause.
"Probably a waste of time anyway."
I could sense the reluctance in his voice as behind my smile, panic
turned to dread, paranoia. I'd gone nuclear on him too soon, giving
myself away without a word being said as I'd threatened to cut him
off. He'd picked up the scent, knew there was more, but he was
there and could be managed. It was the unknown onto which my
mind now fixed, Inspector John Taylor, a blank face, waiting to be
filled, a shadow.
I'd been caught peeking.

∞

As curfew approached, Lurkers streamed excitedly down the hill towards the battleground of the city centre whilst my life was going in a different direction, away from chaos, towards 'home for dinner' normality, laying down, watching television.

Peter was still missing, I was becoming normal.

Routine and ritual in The Temple also appeared as normal as it could be in the circumstances, classes going ahead despite their being no evening shows to prepare for, running smoothly without me as I'd arrive each morning, hanging around Red Molly's or the office waiting for reports from the front line.

"Mad last night, la," Smiler declared as he walked in, arms aloft, still high on adrenaline.

"You're eyes are fucked, have you not been asleep?" Migsy asked with a grin.

"Tear gas."

"Christ…"

"No bother, stings like fuck though."

"They're cranking it up a bit then?"

"Trying to, but they've got no chance. The police and army are trying to work together, gaps everywhere, half of them look embarrassed to be there."

"Still, it's the army, on the streets, against their own people."

"They're not the only ones upping their game. Did you see the news?"

"What bit? There's so much at the moment."

"The Little People uploaded details of a certain retailer's tax-dodging escapades."

"The Little People?" I asked, as another faction appeared.

"Hackers."

"That's every day isn't it?" Migsy replied, sounding bored. "It's become normalised. They're not arsed anymore."

"They also released a list of associated addresses," Smiler continued excitedly.

"So?" Migsy shrugged, still not getting it.

"Each address has been cleaned out, torched."

"In Church Street?"

"In every city; even a couple of houses down south. They're on a website, ticks appearing next to the assets when they go up. 'Level Complete' starts flashing when they all got ticks."

"And what?"

"And they'll release another one each day, every day. Quite exciting waiting for it."

"They won't like that up them," Migsy warned, slowly shaking his head as he suppressed a grin.

"More Cobra meetings," Smiler shrugged. "The protests are focused now, not just smashing things up."

"They'll soon stop that, be baton rounds next."

"They can't stop it, it's all encrypted. They've asked the tech companies to stop encryption but they told them to do one. There are Little People in every city, all co-ordinated on social media, mobile, so they can't catch us. They end up chasing shadows then taking it out on the peaceful protesters on The Plaza, big crowds thanks to you," he said, turning towards me.

"Thanks to me?"

"Your video, explaining how they'd lied…"

"It's not supposed get more people on the streets."

"They're fucked off, lied to again. You've refocused them."

"Any more religious buildings attacked?" I asked, unsure if the video was a success or disaster.

"Not last night, all focus is on The Little People now."

"A few on the far-right forums actually agreed with you," Migsy added. "You've pointed them in the right direction for the time being."

"The war of religion is hopefully over then?"

"You do seem to connect with them for some reason," Migsy suggested, shrugging, shaking his head.

"Cos' he fucking looks like them," Smiler agreed. "Better with a mask on; head like a celeriac."

"They've taken your video down, stop you causing any more trouble."

I opened the laptop and checked, finding it deleted, "Bastards!"

"Doesn't matter, it had over a million views," Smiler said, almost smiling again. "It's been copied and pasted so many times, they'd have to turn the internet off to stop it."

Yoda had a different view on it as I answered his call, putting it on speaker as Migsy and Smiler chuckled quietly.

"What were you thinking?" he screamed.

"Telling the truth."

"Have you seen what's happening?"

"You can't put that on me."
"I can't protect you if you are going to do this."
"They were burning down churches."
"I'll pay for you to go to Ibiza myself if it means you'll fuck off somewhere else."
I glanced across at Migsy who was creased over, his laughter silent as tears ran down his cheeks.
"They were using me, it was a lie."
"You're going to get fired. You're fighting The Church."
"I haven't heard The Church taking sides."
"Because it can't publicly."
"Then they can't sack me publicly."
"They'll find a way. Don't do anything else stupid…"
"I won't…"
"You said that yesterday and look what you fucking did. I just can't trust you," he shouted, finishing with, "knobhead," before slamming down the phone.
There was no chance to join in with the laughter as shouting began in the hall. Things were moving fast, difficult to keep up with in this new reality, my mind still not functioning, unable to comprehend the many facets of the club, the world, my life, battling on all fronts. Migsy leant out the opening, calling down to the art class, "What is it?"
"They're coming," Shaun replied in his Mancunian lilt.
"Who?" Migsy asked, "Who?"
But Shaun had gone, scuttling across the dancefloor towards the doors.
We stood, looking at each other, before bolting at the same time, clanging down stairs and across the now deserted hall, between portraits on easels, abstracts staring at nothing.
"Man the barricades," came a shout as we emerged, blinking into the light. People were stacking furniture again in the middle of the road as tyres were rolled out and stepladders erected behind chaotic structures. Children were arranging bricks into neat pyramids.
"What's this?" I asked Migsy, standing in the doorway as people busied themselves, appearing well drilled, each with their own role. The furniture was coming from the workshop, passed along a human chain before being stacked haphazardly, one upon another.
"Don't think it's a drill…" Mary said, coming alongside.

"Drill for what?"

"An attack, the Muslims."

"Oh, for fuck's sake, it wasn't the Muslims. I'll go and take a look," I suggested, taking a step forward before Migsy pulled me back.

"No, stay here until we know what it is."

"The religions aren't fighting anymore, and even if we were, why would we be hiding behind a barricade? We could talk it out."

"It's not just Muslims," Migsy replied.

"Hare Krishna's going to kick off? It's all going to get wrecked," I moaned, pointing to the furniture which was still being passed from the doorway.

"Get more for it after a battle," Migsy grinned, "looks vintage, shabby chic."

"You sound like Stan," I replied, as Degsy strode past in full military fatigues before climbing to the top of the structure. It wobbled violently as he stepped off the ladder, onto the top, achieving some sort of equilibrium, getting a cheer from his comrades as he faced forward to see who was approaching.

"Why's he dressed like that?" I asked.

"He's commander of the wall," Migsy grinned, planting an elbow into my ribs.

"Our John Snow?"

Voices went silent, the atmosphere tense as we waited, listening for any sound, heads bobbing up from a crouch to peek over the barricade. I was feeling slightly empty, missing a part of me, Peter, who would be prowling at the moment, chomping at the bit for the battle to come.

"Will he be alright up there?" I whispered, nodding at Degsy who was stood still, like an abstract meerkat up an abstract tree.

"Fine as long as you don't make him laugh, piss everywhere."

A vehicle could be heard slowly approaching, diesel, heavy and cumbersome by the sounds of it. Whispers started circulating, rumours rife as levels of excitement began to rise.

"It's the army," Mary whispered, dropping to a crouch then running to a pyramid of bricks, ready for action.

"The army, what are they doing here?" I asked, turning to Migsy.

"Be a warning for the videos, letting you know they are there."

"Really? The army?"

"You didn't expect them to do nothing, did you?"

"I didn't expect anything," I replied, as Yoda's admonishments came back to me, 'you never do.'

The barrier looked flimsy, unable to withstand the force of a skateboard, never mind an armoured vehicle as brakes squealed and the truck stopped, followed by the sound of the doors opening and booted feel climbing out before slamming shut. Small hands were picking up bricks as others whispered put them down, stay quiet, as Lucky ran across, hunched over.

"What's he doing that for?" I whispered.

"Snipers," Migsy smirked.

"It's not the fucking Somme," I complained, trying to stand up as he pulled me down again.

Lucky stopped at the bottom of the structure. "Thee-yaa lad," could be heard in the silence as he passed up his megaphone to Degsy.

"We need access to the building, come down please," the first voice announced, not from around here.

"What for?" Degsy replied into the megaphone as fingers went to ears; they must have heard him up the hill.

"Jesus, can you put that thing down?"

"I'm not Jesus," Degsy shouted into the mouthpiece. "Why are you here?"

"We have orders to seize computers."

"On whose behest?"

'Behest,' I mouthed to Migsy, arching an eyebrow.

"The government."

A hand reached forward, grabbing a chair, trying to pull it out of the barricade, causing the whole structure to sway, sending Degsy' arms cartwheeling as he tried to maintain his balance.

"Stop," the commanding officer shouted.

The design was perfect, its weakness was its strength, each piece interlinked, joining onto others, an analogy of society, complex and unstable, ready to collapse should a single piece be moved. There was no way for them to get through without causing injury.

"I joined the army when I was young," Degsy announced to his captive audience. "Without direction, without anything and it gave me a way out, a career, an identity, respect and a sense of meaning, fighting for a noble cause."

Their tone changed as they realised they were powerless, aware of the mobile phones pointing at them, filming their actions. "If you

could just come down, we could have a sensible conversation…"
"But the heroic idea of defending your country was a lie. We were
just an army for hire, oil in Iraq, pipelines across Afghanistan and
Syria…"
"Come down immediately."
"You'll shut up and listen, I'm a higher ranking officer."
"You've retired…"
"We fought in Iraq, killing and maiming underequipped guys,
soldiers and civilians, creating widows and orphans…"
"Come on grandad, step aside."
"Now look what you're doing for those very same people."
"Just following orders."
"Exactly, just following orders. All that nationalism and patriotism
manufactured to exploit you. All that regimental history, flags full
of bullet holes so they can sell their shit to foreigners."
"Look, come down before we take you down."
"And what about the next country they send you to? To kill their
people and steal their assets?"
"Sir…"
"When does it stop? I look at my grandchildren and wonder if
they'll be consumed by fire sometime in the future, explosions
ripping through them, for greed, profit, shareholders."
"Point taken, now if you could…"
"Their dad, my son, was killed in Afghanistan for shareholders. I
sent him to die, sacrificed him, but they didn't build a religion
around him or me, just a business class flight to Brize Norton."
Migsy cast a sideways glance, confirming the last barb may have
been directed at me.
"And this, look at yourselves," he said, opening his arms wide,
sending the structure swaying. "Will they use the military against
their own people, to maintain market share?"
"No Sir, we are just here to maintain…"
"No, you are here to enforce, not maintain. How long till they put a
gun in your hand, tell you to point it at us?"
"It really won't come to that…"
"Will you just follow orders then?"
"Sir…"
"Delegated responsibility?"
"We're getting nowhere…"

"Will you pull the trigger?"
"Could I speak with somebody else?" he shouted as we all remained silent.
"Is Father McKay there?"
"Sounds familiar, what does he look like?" Degsy replied.
"Don't take the piss, is he there?"
Again silence.
"Okay, could you please advise Father McKay he must hand in his computers by sixteen hundred hours today or face arrest."
"Take a serious look at yourselves, embarrassment to the history of the uniform and the honourable men that have worn it, catspaws..." he boomed into the megaphone, his denunciation turning into a rant.
"Just let him know."
The chatter rose around us as the vehicle pulled away, some thrilled by the exchange, others disappointed that it didn't lead to anything else.
"Arrested?" I hissed, turning to Migsy, eyes wide. I was feeling sick, thinking of Dad.
"Don't worry, they're just putting the frighteners on you."
"It's worked."
"You've done nothing illegal."
"That doesn't usually matter."
"If they wanted you, they'd have come and taken you."
"But still, I've got to give them my computers."
"Well we'll give them your computers," Migsy grinned as he put his arm across my shoulders.
Hacker Packer sent down an old ZX81 which was promptly packed and couriered to the central police station. Meanwhile, he was setting up firewalls around our existing computers, taking it upon himself to build his own digital barricade.
"You're email has been hacked," he revealed down the phone. It was the first time I'd spoken to him, he sounded stoned.
"What?"
"An external agency is watching your email."
"Who?"
"I can't tell you that, but they has been for some time, years."
Their next attack was more blatant, more aggressive, as Ginny threw the red top across the table to me the following morning,

"You again."
Apparently, they hadn't found the ZX81 funny.
BLOOD ON THE STREETS filled the front cover as I read
apprehensively, thankful to find it was referring to financial
markets and not The Leatherman, laying bloodied in the riots,
another skeleton, or soon to be skeleton, in my already overflowing
closet. I flicked through until stopping at a two page spread
revealing a different skeleton, the girls in the village with their tops
up, breasts exposed as I was sat between them, gawping gormlessly
ahead under the heading STRIPPER VICAR. Their faces had been
pixelated, their identities hidden, though the bodies were
undoubtedly young. The words said nothing, no quotes, nothing
libellous, just assertions, directing the reader to certain conclusions.
I was furious.
"Bastards," I shouted as I tried to explain myself to Ginny and Judy,
the words garbled, tripping over each other as they came out of my
mouth.
"It's not what it looks like, I had no idea..."
"I don't care what you did before me," Judy shrugged.
"But I didn't do anything, I was watching the match."
"Looks terrible," Ginny said, stiffly.
"It's to undermine me, especially around here with the last priest..."
"They're basically calling you a paedo..."
"They'll believe it," I shouted in panic. "People will fucking believe
it."
"I don't," Judy said calmly, placing her hand on my knee, as if that
could make it all better.
"But you're not them. They'll fucking lynch..."
The doorbell rang and we paused, staring at each other before
Ginny struggled up out of her chair, walking gingerly towards the
door. I could hear voices, a brief conversation before the door closed
again and Ginny shuffled back in.
"That was Big Jim," she announced solemnly. "You've been
summonsed for an extraordinary meeting at The View at twelve."
There was a stunned silence, we all knew what it meant.
"The View, they never go there..." I mumbled.
"They're gonna fuck you up," Ginny said cheerfully, "I've seen this
so many times."
"It's got no windows..."

"They're not going to kill you," was Judy's attempt at reassurance.
"They will…" Ginny countered.
"They will if they think I'm a paedophile."
"Chop your cock off," Ginny cackled.
"You're not helping."
"Dry bum you."
"Ginny!" Judy scolded.
Big Jim was standing outside the door, arms crossed, unmoving, following me with his eyes as I strode towards him, trying to keep the walk casual and relaxed but feeling self-conscious, uncomfortable under his gaze.
"Alright Jim, what are you standing outside for?" I asked as cheerfully as possible, though his expression didn't change.
"To stop people coming in."
"I'll best be going then."
"Apart from you," he growled as he reached behind to his back pocket, unfolding the newspaper in front of me before opening the pages.
"I've seen it," was all I could say as humour dissipated and my stomach dropped. He leant across and held the door open, nodding his head, a command to move and I moved, feeling like a condemned man as I crossed the threshold and he stepped in behind me, his body pressing into mine in the tiny lobby.
"You're coming as well?"
"Wouldn't want to miss it," he replied, nodding towards another door. "This has been coming for a while, was only a matter of time."
I paused, looking at the featureless plane of wood. If it was an enemy on the other side then I'd have no problem entering, but these were friends and I was terrified, not of what they may physically do but words they may say that could tear down everything we had built here. They'd always been wary, accepting but waiting for me to fail and I'd been amateurish, giving them the excuse that they needed, reckless, handing it to them on a plate, sending out stupid, childish videos. I could hear Yoda's voice in the back of my mind as I scolded myself, "We don't go against power." The barman glanced across, not trying to sell me a Segway this time as he shook his head slowly, my fists clenching and unclenching as I reached forward and pushed the door open, stepping through gingerly as faces turned towards me, finding them all dressed in

uniform black as they remained silent, staring as I backed into Big Jim.

At that moment I couldn't decide if I was missing Peter or not, I needed his courage but also needed its opposite: calm, diplomacy, tact.

"What are you going to do?" I asked, hearing a tremble in my voice as they said nothing, standing as one, as if about to attack. There was something cultish about it, like a secret society with their secret livery, secret rules, secret ceremonies, secret means of disposing of a body. I tried to push backwards before noticing their white collars.

"You bastards," I shouted, "I've been shitting myself all morning." The room collapsed as one, Lucky bent over, almost retching with laughter, they were in hysterics, "Your face…"

"I was terrified…"

"You, you…" Stan was braying, pointing at me, stamping one foot, tears running down his cheeks.

"I thought you were going to kill me…" I exclaimed as the laughter continued, an attack of a different kind, one that I welcomed.

"Why are you all dressed up as vicars?"

"Cos' you get all the birds," Mekon Don shouted between breaths.

"Figured it must be the uniform, because you're an ugly fucker."

"Big lump of scar tissue with a collar and a mouth," Willo giggled. "Cheers."

"How can you be so ugly with just one head?" Elvis shouted.

"Alright, alright," I said, holding up my palms in surrender, laughing along at my own expense.

"Not mingers either, fit ones," Discharge continued, holding up the opened newspaper.

"That's not true," I argued, perhaps a little too defensively. I'd been running through scenarios all morning, none of which fitted the current situation.

"We know, soft lad," Lucky said affectionately.

"I didn't even know they were doing it."

"They're trying to stitch you up," SpongeBob said, stating the obvious.

"I was watching Everton."

"Now that is obscene."

"I've been literally shitting my pants all morning."

"There is Judy though," Discharge said, arching an eyebrow.

"Yes," I agreed, after a slight pause.

"I'd love to shag her," he continued, doing that pelvic thrust thing whilst slowly shaking his head, eyes closed, teeth clenched.

"Thanks Discharge," came a voice from behind, making him stop mid-thrust as his cheeks turned scarlet, sitting down quickly to everybody's amusement. I turned to find Judy with Ginny next to her in a wheelchair.

"You lot bummed him yet?" she chirped.

"You were in on it?"

Judy gave a shrug and innocent smile whilst Ginny creased over, teeth falling onto her lap as she laughed, all gums and watery eyes. I could see Alf, crawling in the chapel.

"If he had any more sense he'd be an idiot," she shouted before creasing up again.

"Bastards," I mumbled. "So, what's this all about?"

"A show of support with our own unique slant."

"Plus, it's Margaret's birthday."

"And I'm the present?"

"The gift that keeps giving."

"Why here? We could have used the club."

"In case the rozzers turn up."

"They won't come here," Stan said.

"SAS wouldn't come here," Mary added.

We drank and laughed, leaving me swaying as I pee'd into the sink as the urinal was blocked, dwelling on kindness, coming from the most unexpected of places, people with nothing giving all they had, their friendship and humour.

Talk was political, like a Speakers Corner or a house of drunken lords, though most remained awake as they took centre stage. Some applauded whilst others heckled, hit by flying sausage rolls.

"Any movement for change needs to come from the bottom," Lucky shouted. "Do you think the middle-classes are going to change anything whilst being drip fed a cocktail of comfort, fear and hate?"

"But the middle-classes are rebelling," came the counter. "It's not about us anymore."

"People don't give a shit," Lucky continued. "They're too busy with celebrities, television, the next Iphone, Strictly and Bake-Off.

They're self-centred, they know these tax dodgers exist but couldn't give a monkeys as long as they're alright."

"It's not us on the streets anymore. They've been mugged off; they
are taking their money, have been for years but now they see it's not
benefit cheats or immigrants..."
"Hear, hear," they shouted, clapping or slapping tables as they
lifted their drinks, our own 1922 Committee, banging desks like
juvenile idiots as Stan took the imaginary lectern.
"The standard of living for the young is falling. Uneducated or debt
ridden, unaffordable housing, insecure employment, minimum
wage, zero hours contracts, no youth services, it goes on and on," he
shouted. "There is no benevolence from the government, just cut,
slash and burn. We have now reached a tipping point when the
young provide their own version of cut, slash and burn..."
"Hear, hear,"
I realised that I had found a place where I truly belonged, it had
been here all along, home. There were no itchy feet, no ever
repeating pattern of moving on, at least none that I could detect as I
sat amongst what had become a surrogate family.
Like a family, they came as a package, complete with eccentricities:
embarrassing uncles and touchy aunts, irritating cousins with
prejudice and baggage, young siblings with their machismo and
phobias, but here I was, amongst their blemishes and imperfections,
wanted. Perhaps it was relief, only hours earlier I'd been convinced
they were going to ostracise me, pack your bags, hit the road Jack,
but now the pendulum was swinging towards acceptance,
belonging. For the first time I could see myself settling, that point
where a nomad stops, deciding this is the place, hanging up his
shoes and walking no more.
Judy was excused, no place for a pregnant lady, as the air filled with
Margaret's special blend, the buffet demolished before it landed on
the table. Serious chatter continued, talking about the park, the
riots, the state of the country, becoming raucous as the alcohol
flowed, a room full of faux-vicars soaked in beer, cackling and
braying, swearing like navvies through the thick smoke. It was our
island, our shelter as the country continued to pull itself apart, but
the outside world was imposing itself, the newspapers, the military;
perhaps we all felt its temporality as our hedonism took us through
the afternoon until dusk, when I left, staggering down the hill,
Ginny, my surrogate grandma snoring in her wheelchair as pin-
pricks of light flicked on in the city below, the Welsh Hills just a

silhouette as my feet crunched on fragments of barriers,
unanswered questions, scattered on the ground.

∞

My re-calibration of religion, of God, continued as we attempted to
outmanoeuvre the emergency laws, entering a game of cat and
mouse, hide and seek, as we sought creative ways to work within
their restrictions. Everything was shifting, different fronts in
different realities as we found our loophole in education.
"Are you sure?"
"Definitely, probably," a drunken Jamo, our legal eagle, slurred,
taking his second job of official taster more seriously than his first as
Der Kaizer tested his latest Golden Ale on him before releasing it for
public consumption.
I'd reached out to the universities before the riots and they were
keen to get involved. They practically lived here anyway, their
buildings and student accommodation encroaching towards the
estates as cheap land resulted in shiny towers full of cell like rooms
clad in modern glass and metal panels, housing inhabitants from all
over the country, all over the world.
There were two distinct populations living in the same space, both
completely ignorant of each other. The astronomy night, despite its
negative outcome, had convinced me that there was an opportunity
to bring these disconnected people together, whilst also helping The
Temple in its battle to exist.
The students had been enthusiastic about everything, which I'd
found slightly disconcerting. The idea of debates, activities, yes, yes,
yes, giving the impression they would say yes to anything. I'd
asked them to choose the subject matter of the first debate, my way
of tying them down to continued engagement.
"The history of God," came their reply after much huddled
discussion, a banana skin, intentionally thrown my way as they all
looked on in anticipation for any sign of discomfort.
"Agreed," I'd replied enthusiastically, happy to disappoint. The
subject didn't matter to me, The Temple could open.
The night had arrived and despite my laissez-faire approach, I was
feeling slightly nervous talking about religion to an academic
crowd. It wasn't the war on religion that concerned me, nor cynics

or atheists, it was those from different factions of Christianity, looking to score a point before their peers.

The Bible was the problem; for most viewpoints, it offered an alternative interpretation somewhere within its text, Psalm X says this or Y says that. Arguments and counter arguments had gone back and forth for hundreds, thousands of years without agreement. Wars were based upon them, hundreds of thousands killed by this splitting of hairs, and that was just Christianity. For other religions I was even less confident, knowing the bare bones of each, a shallow understanding of the concepts but scratch beneath the surface and there was little depth to my knowledge.

Yoda was skulking around the office, still angry, wondering why I was lingering.

"I thought you'd be locking up?"

I shook my head, "Students coming tonight, first debate."

"Bloody hell, you're not allowed."

"Educational, with the support of the university," I smiled.

"What about?" He frowned, the furrows running deep.

"The history of God."

"Trying to catch you out. What are you going to say? Do you want me to write it?"

"No, I'm going to go pre-Christianity, before Abraham."

"That's giving them plenty of ammunition."

"It's not a battle, the war of religion has ended, remember?"

"On pause," he reminded me, shaking his head.

I nervously watched from the office window, waiting for the police but surprised to find locals arriving first in dribs and drabs, carrying bags loaded with bottles and cans, all looking up into the space as if there for the first time. Plato and his bearded entourage arrived followed by a few Wraiths remaining a step or two behind the chatting groups, on the fringes, but there. It was already looking busier than expected.

"What are you going to say?" Yoda asked, nervous, fishing.

"Wait and see," I replied, still angry with my religion, the way I'd been used, the way they'd attacked me, attacked others. I was starting to feel disconnected, cut off, Yoda my only connection to a body that appeared to reject me.

"Don't do anything stupid," he warned.

"Of course not," I mumbled. He was hating this, sensing something about to happen, out of his control.

The students arrived in a glut, maybe fifty to seventy, an invading army of academic intellect finding safety in numbers. Some were carrying trays of beer whilst others looked like they'd already drank one, introducing themselves as I left the office to mingle, finding a couple of lecturers I'd met before, PhD students, a professor and an endless entourage of students studying a wide spectrum of subjects. Red Molly was making a killing, pouring her home brew vodka into metal cups as students queued to buy a token snack. Out of date Wagon Wheels were the cheapest item that qualified for a double shot as the line became a closed loop as the front of the queue linked onto the back in a continuing cycle of Wagon Wheels and shots. As the ever increasing circle kept slowly turning, everybody else was standing in groups, islands of chatter as I signalled to Crab Scratch to fade out the background music. The sound of conversation gradually took over, becoming more pronounced as I closed my eyes for a few seconds and just listened. It was perfect, everything The Temple should be.

Tapping on the microphone, the conversation slowly diminished as faces focused on me whilst taking up the limited number of seats. The rest were standing behind or sitting in front, though the two groups remained separate, like oil and water, the home and away end, only coming together when they had to.

The lights lowered and the screen next to me illuminated a tree like diagram, full of symbols and branches.

"Talking of religion and God is talking of evolution," I began, pausing to listen to my voice echo around the hall then the whisperings that followed as I'd immediately put those words in the same sentence. It grabbed their attention as I watched heads jolt and eyes look up at me, not quite brave or comfortable enough to shout out at this early stage, but still, everybody had something to say; we could have stopped the presentation and started the discussion there and then.

"The story of religion closely follows the evolution of man from hunter gatherer through to the lives we live today."

"It was invented by man," a local voice called out, slightly hostile of course.

"Correct," I responded with a smile, "As a means of understanding the world."

I glanced over towards Yoda who was staring straight ahead, eyes fixed on nothing.

"The world and religion did not start with the Birth of Christ, just like the universe didn't start six thousand years ago."

More murmurings.

"There are no hard-line creationists here, I take it?"

The murmuring stopped, replaced by silence.

"The first records of religion come from around eighty nine thousand years before Christianity appeared," I said, pointing to the bottom of the chart.

"Christianity is up here, a relatively young branch on Religion's evolutionary tree; we've had just over two thousand years since the birth of Christ. The first evidence of any sort of religious inclination has mainly come from archaeological exploration indicating certain rights had been followed by man and Neanderthals, certain ceremonies, suggesting a belief system."

"Neanderthals?"

"Yes, excavations of Neanderthal graves suggests ceremonial rites, excarnation for example…"

"Excarnation?"

"The removal of flesh and organs from the body before burial."

"Probably just hungry," I heard a voice mumble.

"So, you're saying a species distinct from humans also carried out religious acts?"

"Well, we are closely related…"

"But still?"

"Yes"

Mutterings.

"Communities were nomadic at this stage, small tribes of hunter gatherers, their religion based upon Animism and Shamans with their own rituals and symbols such as part-human, part-animal sculpture."

"Zoomorphic," an Irish accent called out, standing left.

"That's the word," I replied, smiling into the darkness. "Some forms of Animism and Shamanism still survive today, Plains Indians or Aboriginal belief systems, for example."

"Dreamtime," another voice called out from seating right, the thick accent suggesting it was a local resident this time.

I pointed to the width of the tree. "As man populated the Earth, different religions formed in different areas in exactly the manner evolution works, created by and adapting to local conditions as a response, an explanation of the natural world. Some died off and some evolved through time to become something else. This is why in different areas of the world we still have many different religions today, each with very different versions of God."

Only the occasional crack of a ring-pull was breaking the silence of the room as Yoda continued staring straight ahead.

"The majority of religions at this time followed the same evolutionary path, from Animism into Pantheism, the idea that God is present in everything; in essence, the universe and everything observable in it is God. Over time this evolved into Polytheism as they tried to understand different aspects of the environment, with different deities often representing different aspects of the world, forces of nature, for example the Gods of Ancient Greece, Rome, the Norse Gods."

"And Hindus?" An accentless voice called out. "They've got shit loads."

"That's a common misconception," Tejel interjected. "They have one God, Brahman…"

"They have millions: blue, loads of arms, an elephant's head…"

"They are all different deities, different aspects of life, pathways to Brahman, the primordial one."

"During the Neolithic revolution," I interrupted, "the human population exploded and religions became organised along with the foundation of the first cities and kingdoms, rulers often aligning themselves with gods and religion to reinforce their position, establishing temples or shrines for communal worship with their associated rituals. Theocracies…"

"Like the Church of England you mean?" Stan called out.

"Well not quite…"

"The Queen is the head of The Church, government and state."

"Point taken," I smiled. "But we have a state religion which is not really that powerful in this country. Decisions are not made based upon religion, we are very different from those theocracies of the Neolithic period…"

"No human sacrifice?"

"Not officially," I grinned.

I went through a whole list, spread across the globe: Celtic, Norse,

Druidism, Vedic, Hinduism, Buddhism, Sikhism, Taoism, Mayan, Incan, Aztec, countless religions, a richness threaded through humanity before pointing to a thick bough in the centre.

"Christianity grows from the Arabic Semetic branch of the tree," I began. "Starting with Pantheism, we evolve over eleven thousand years, through Mesopotamian, Canaanite and Babylonian Polytheisms until we arrive at Judaism, the first of the Abrahamic religions and a monotheism which is important, a belief system based upon a single God in opposition to the multiple Gods of before."

There was a nervous shuffling as we got closer to home.

"With Judaism there was no room for any other Gods. Abraham was promised a new land for his people by God but the land was already occupied by various peoples, including the Canaanites. This decree was enforced with the massacre of every living thing they encountered in accordance with God's command."

"And there lies the problem with religion," Miriam complained in her flat monotone.

"Still doing it to The Palestinians," a young student called out with a bit more passion.

"We'll save that subject for another discussion," I smiled before continuing. "This God was named Y-H-W-H, as Hebrews didn't write with vowels, but is now known as Yahweh which makes it a bit easier for our purposes, or HaShem. Without going too much into the detail of Judaism, a number of important things happened. First of all, as we have said, the worship of the existing gods was banned, there was to be only one God and all had to worship Yahweh indicating a conflict in ideologies. Second, one of the first religious books, The Tanakh was produced, changing over time as their relationship evolved with God before it was canonised, the text fixed. The book set out rules by which you should live your life, the Covenant, the agreement between God and the people, a precursor to the Old and New Testaments and The Quran."

"Just a means of making people governable," Mekon Don mumbled.

"Opiate of the masses," Plato called out.

"Third was the creation of a temple, to focus worship of Yahweh. This was met with derision by followers, suggesting there was no need, he was a God of the wilderness. This is important because

they established a 'House of God' and here we can draw a linear
connection from that temple through the many synagogues,
churches and cathedrals to this Temple we are in today. With the
building came the high priests, rituals and ceremonies, the
accumulation of power and wealth that comes with it, and the idea
that the priest-king or high priests were somehow God's
representatives on Earth, conduits or messiahs who inevitably failed
to live up to their title."
"He's not the messiah, he's a very naughty boy," a local voice called
out for a few cheap giggles as Der Kaizer emerged from the
darkness carrying a tray full of sloshing pints, the Golden Ale
passed the test it seemed as Jamo appeared next to him carrying
two.
"Pound a pint," I could hear him whispering as he stooped down,
the plastic glasses passed through the crowd whilst payment came
the other way as he tried and failed to remain inconspicuous. He
may as well have shouted, wolf nipple chips and otter's noses,
joining in with the Monty Python recital which appeared to form
the basis of religious education in these parts.
"Despite the failings," I continued, fighting a tide of disinterest, "the
people never gave up their belief in a future messiah who would
establish God's kingdom on Earth, which leads us nicely to
Christianity, one of the branches that grew from Judaism, one of
many interpretations of the Covenant with God, how to live in
accordance with God's decree, which came about of course with the
arrival of Jesus of Nazareth."
His name didn't quite have the desired effect as they continued to
mutter and mumble, pound a pint.
"He was one of a number of so called wonder workers around at
the time: Appolonius of Tyana, Honi the rainmaker, Theudas,
Eleazar, The Egyptian were some amongst many, travelling around
performing miracles, exorcisms, healing the sick, divining and
interpreting dreams."
"One minute I'm a leper with a trade, next minute my livelihoods
gone," a high pitched voice called out. "With not so much as a by-
your-leave!"
"You're cured mate, bloody do-gooder," came back from the other
side as Monty Python proved contagious.
"Is that you Moat?"

"Affirmative," he replied. I could just make him out, wearing a toga.

"Detractors called him a magician," I continued, trying to stay on track. "But, for his followers, by linking his miracles with the prophecy of Isaiah, he was the messiah. God born in the likeness of man."

"Thank God Paul Daniels wasn't around then," Lucky joined from a different angle as he reached forward and took a pint off Der Kaizer's tray.

"Jesus was giving a different interpretation to the people of how to live in Covenant with God. As with religion today, there are hardliners and more liberal interpretations of a text. Jesus offered a liberal interpretation, basically the Kingdom of God is open to those who turn to God and love thy neighbour as you love yourself. He preached that people who do good will be rewarded and those that do evil will be punished. He brought forgiveness."

"Pint?" Der Kaiser whispered, crouching before me, as if waiting for the Eucharist, the body and blood.

"Thanks," I mouthed, as the offering came the other way, sweat and tears, reaching forward to receive my pint before continuing.

"Palestine was a place of rebellion at the time due to the Roman occupation: the Zealots, the Essene, The Sicarii. The country also had a long line of so called messiahs before Jesus: Simon son of Piraea, Simon son of Kochba, Judas the Galilean, Hezekiah, who were all killed by Rome."

"Pound," Jamo whispered, hand outstretched with a pint tucked under his elbow.

"What?"

"That's a pound," he repeated, nodding at the pint.

"F-f-fuck," his wife shouted from the crowd.

"Jesus was also executed for his words and actions, challenging the existing and only true dispenser of power and religion at the time, the authority of the Temple," I continued, feeling around in my pocket as Jamo patiently waited, going nowhere. "Only the Romans had the authority to put criminals to death so he was handed over to Pontius Pilate, then crucified."

"Biggus Dickus," one of the students whispered to a few quiet giggles, finding common ground with the locals. I was beginning to wonder if most were here for a piss-up; I felt like an RE teacher, facing a class of bored adolescents.

"So we come to life after death, the resurrection, where people witnessed the direct actions of God in the form of a miracle, as Jesus came back to life. It symbolised the defeat of death, superseding the penalty of the Old Testament, imposed on man for the indiscretions of Adam and Eve, the original sin, the fall of man. It was atonement with God, people and God at one again, the destruction of death, suggesting eternal life and everything that goes with it."

I glanced across to find Red Molly following Der Kaizers lead, going in the opposite direction, anti-clockwise, her tray laden with Scampi Fries, Wagon Wheels and the all-important vodka. Heads were tuning, wondering which way to look.

"Is anybody listening to this?" I asked, getting frustrated, though most were too distracted to answer the question.

"Yes," Judy replied.

"It's good," Willo nodded as Yoda gave a non-committal shrug, counting his change.

"Since the Old Testament, Christianity has continued its evolution through the New Testament before breaking off into separate smaller branches: Protestantism, Roman Catholicism, Anglicanism, Anabaptism, Eastern Orthodox, Oriental Orthodox, Assyrian Church, and these break down into smaller branches again, adaptations of adaptations, much like natural selection."

I pointed slightly further up the diagram, "The other great branch from Judaism is of course Islam, Christianity's younger sibling if you like. Islam began with the prophet Mohammed, the last messenger of God in the early seventh century, but for Muslims this is not entirely true, they believe it began with creation and all religion since then had been a false understanding of God and Din which embraces all aspects of life and by which all people should live."

The word Muslim appeared to refocus them as murmurings came from the darkness. Red Molly had stopped and was looking at the screen.

"With the belief that God was beyond human understanding, Mohammed rejected the idolatry of other religions and went alone to a cave on Mount Hira seeking the real God or alHaqq, the True. Here God transmitted through Mohammed the final revelation, The Quran. It is not believed to be written by Mohammed but through him, the pure uncorrupted words of God which became the foundation of Islam. Before Mohammed delivered the Quran, it is believed that previous messengers of God, the prophets, had also delivered The Quran, including Adam, Noah, Abraham, Moses and Jesus. They believe however, that the message was misunderstood in certain instances, or relevant to the time and place and was corrupted with other stories, therefore not the pure words of God. Over time many religions were altered by conquerors and empires. With regard to the Bible, they see the words of Jesus, a prophet, a man, and not the direct words of God."

"Surely Mohammed was a man?" Lucky asked, back on track.

"Always a bloody man, isn't it," Red Molly protested.

"Yes, but he only wrote the words received from God in the Quran. His own thoughts and words went into a different book, the Hadith."

"Do you all worship the same God?" A brummie accent asked.

"Who?"

"The Jews, Christians and Muslims?"

"No, the Muslims worship Allah," an authoritative voice called out.

"Allah is the Arabic word for God," I corrected. "The answer is yes, we do worship the same God, but that is my opinion, there are many others who say no. The Quran acknowledges that we all worship the same and emphasises the positive relationships between the faiths, we are all 'People of the Book'."

"Then why all the fighting?"

"Different franchises," came a voice from my right.

"Why did the Muslims attack you?" Smiler asked.

"They didn't attack me, that was a lie," I replied, glancing down at an unmoving Yoda.

"You're just saying that," Smiler insisted. "All that forgiveness."

"It was invented by the media, trying to distract, setting religion against religion. It was a power-grab," I continued, publicly berating Yoda as he glanced back defiantly.

"Imagine how peaceful the world would be without these religions," Red Molly stated, forgetting about sales, seeking confrontation.

"You really think so?" I asked as the mutterings started again. "It's man that uses religion as a justification for terrible things."

"Really?" A student voice called out. "When their moral guidance is full of racism, violence, genocide and hatred."

"The Quran?"

"All of them, The Bible included."

"To be read allegorically, not literally. The books were written long ago for predominantly illiterate or poorly educated people to understand. The world is constantly changing and the texts are fixed in time. Also, they cannot cover every feature of human life, therefore they require translation and interpretation by people which can lead to various meanings. Most religion based trouble in the world comes from the differences in the various interpretations of these religious texts. We have discussed the branches of Christianity but with Islam we have a similar story, the main divisions are Sunni, Shia and Sufi, then within these there are further branches still, up a hundred and fifty other sects aligned with the teachings of different schools of Sharia and their interpretation of the Quran.""

"Religion is a man-made fictional story that has been used to justify the death of millions and the world would be a better place without it," Red Molly replied, her tone suggesting that was the end of it.

"Has been used is the key phrase there," I answered, before pointing to the top of the tree. "Various man made movements have replaced religion in recent history. Abstract concepts like fascism, nationalism, communism, liberalism, socialism, lots of isms that have created ideological clashes also killing millions. Darwinism, evolution and survival of the fittest were key tenets of Nazi ideologies, for example, leading to the Holocaust. God gave man free will and what they do with it is up to them. Now the next great man made fiction, money, is the true justification for killing, whether cloaked beneath religion or nationalism. Look at a map of the world and most war is where natural resources are present. It's a chase for wealth usually riding in on the back of one of the isms we've mentioned."

"Capitalism also kills indirectly," Red Molly agreed, "profit at whatever cost."

"How so?" I asked.

"The slave trade…"

"The Great Bengal Famine," Tejel shouted out, standing up, as if in parliament. "The British killed two million Bengalis…"

"Two million?" Elvis called out, doubt colouring his voice.

"Killed by taxation, money, 'humanitarian hysterics' the British called it. Your Churchill is no hero to us."
"Well, Gandhi was a racist," Elvis replied defensively. "Look at his words during his time in Africa."
"We are all multiple truths," Plato shouted, "all hypocrites."
"Hang on a minute," Poison Ivy hollered from the darkness, with a hint of anger. "You say that man is at fault, but at worst man condemns his victims to death."
"Well that's pretty bad," I replied.
"Your God condemns them to an eternity of torture and pain. Whatever terrible things man does, it's nowhere near the cruelty meted out by God."
"Darwin believed the same, a damnable doctrine he called it," I mumbled in agreement, speaking without thinking as Yoda placed his face in his hands.
The mutterings got louder as conversations blossomed simultaneously.
"We're on a tangent now, that's another discussion," I suggested, trying to get back on track again, noticing how whenever The Quran was mentioned the conversation inevitably went to war. How we were primed to instantly think of violence as I waited for it to peter out before continuing.
"As with the Bible, the Quran reveals what people must believe and how they should behave. But in the Quran God creates everything, all possibilities in life then it is for the individual to choose the right path based upon their knowledge of God. It is the different interpretations of the right path where friction between the divisions occurs."
"We are right and everyone else is wrong."
"But that's the only way a religion can survive," Poison Ivy called out. "It has to be exclusive, us versus them."
"They can't all be right," Discharge mumbled.
"So," I said, putting an end to the presentation before the discussion continued its trajectory towards war and violence. "This has only touched very lightly on the religions, but hopefully we have given a broad outline of the history of God and our understanding of God for the purpose of discussion."
There was a general round of applause as the lights slowly lit up the space, anonymity fading as their faces became visible again, sitting

in rows.

"Do we have any comments?"

Voices rose almost immediately from all sides, different questions on different aspects of the talk. I managed to quieten them down somewhat but there were still plenty of small conversations going on as I took a big drink of my ale before pointing to a random raised hand.

"You have Atheism at the top of the tree. That's not a religion, it's the opposite of religion."

"I put that there, with a question mark, I might add, to get the debate going," I smiled. "But, I do believe there is an argument for it being there."

"I'm an atheist and I don't believe in any sort of gods or supernatural being," came the reply. "I don't worship any sky fairies, it's not a religion."

"Depends on how you use the word religion. I think the meaning of the word has evolved," I replied. "It's not just about believing in a God, it can mean following a set of beliefs upon which a number of people agree. We've already mentioned a number of isms."

"Buddhism doesn't have a God," Plato called out.

"Correct, some religions are also guidelines on how to live without the supernatural influence, but atheism does believe in a concept about God based upon faith and not proof. Does that not make it a religion?"

"No, there is only the material universe, no Gods, no afterlife…"

"It has its own orthodox beliefs like a religion, its own evangelical preachers, its own narratives it bases its beliefs on, the big bang where nothing exploded and created everything for example."

"Science has explained all of these."

"Only to a point, and science is not the exclusive property of atheism. It fits in comfortably with many religions, including Christianity."

"There is no church, there are no rituals, it's just supernatural shite, the biggest scam in the history of man," came the student's slurred reply, sounding slightly offended, providing a good point to change tack.

Locals and students were now talking where they came together in a free for all, layers of multiple good natured discussion happening simultaneously to a backdrop of beer cans cracking open and laughter.

"Your linking of religion and evolution in your opening sentence was an interesting one. As you suggested, through natural selection the weakest die off and the fittest continue evolving."

"Yes."

"In society, the gap between religion and real life is getting wider by the day, at least in this country, it is becoming irrelevant in most people's lives. Do you see a long term future for The Church?"

"It does have to evolve to survive, I agree. But, there are debates currently going on, issues like same sex relationships, for example."

"The House of Clergy just voted against it."

"Oh," I replied, stumbling a bit. "And, look at this place. That's The Church over there within this secular space," I said pointing towards the structure. "We are evolving but possibly not quick enough."

"But surely the Bible will only let you evolve to a certain point, then its message becomes diluted, a twisting of doctrine purely for the survival of The Church. Institutional Christianity as Kierkegaard called it?"

"I think the basic tenets of Christianity are compatible and relevant to society without becoming diluted. There is scope for change if The Church is brave enough to do it, but it is a fine line to balance the theology with society."

"Does God even want The Church to survive?" Another voice asked. "You said earlier about protests at the temple to Yahwah."

"Ye ma," came a thick scouse accent to my right, Discharge with a valuable contribution.

"Do people need to attend a church to connect with God?"

"No, I don't believe you do need to go to church to connect with God, but we create a place, an environment with different values, where people come together, closing out the outside world of money and aggression, and talk of love and friendship, morals, goodness, feelings and emotions. Look at what we are doing now."

"I don't know a single young person that goes to church," Poison Ivy informed everybody.

"We nearly didn't come because it is a church," a student added from the other side of the room.

Smiler stood up and raised his hand.

"Smiler," I nodded surprised.

"I hate Muslims, but didn't know anything about them, so thanks for that."

"Oh, right, okay," I replied as he sat back down, probably still hating as he attracted glances from around the room to which he seemed oblivious.

A well-spoken voice came from the left. "Just looking at your diagram there, a tree of religion, the tree of the knowledge of good and evil if you like," he said, sounding a bit like Prince Charles. "Given the massive numbers of religions there are and have been, how can you believe in any of this?"

"You either believe in one of these hundred thousand gods or you don't," I replied with a shrug. "The great thing about all of them is a belief in something remarkable, beyond our capacity to understand, a wonder at existence that the world seems to have lost."

"But it's just a meme that has spread and mutated over time, changing to survive. We have evolved out of religion, now science and technology have liberated us from this enforced ignorance."

"As we evolve, so does our relationship with God. It doesn't go away because the same questions remain unanswered," I replied. "The fact that religion evolves doesn't make it any less real, meme or not."

Margaret was putting her hand up at the front, her hair like a cloud of candy floss.

"Your religion is an accident," she declared matter-of-factly as some of the younger people passed comments behind hands and giggled.

"Sorry Margaret, can you explain?" I asked, hoping she hadn't noticed the mocking. She either hadn't or didn't care.

"If you live in a certain part of the world in a certain time then you will follow one of these many religions," she said, pointing towards the chart.

I nodded as she paused.

"How can that be fair? You don't go to heaven because you happen to believe in this or that religion?"

She gave me a grin and a half-wink, she had me and she knew it.

"John 14:6, No man comes to the father but by me Jesus said," she continued. They were quiet now. "Isn't it unfair that people are going to Hell just because they were born into the wrong religion?"

John tied me down, stopped me from going to where I wanted the conversation to go, the idea of religions opening up to each other, respecting each other as different paths to the same place.

"You are correct," I said, smiling at Margaret, "in that whilst talking of inclusion and love, there is exclusion at the heart of religions as they seek their monopoly on God. But we have so much in common, and, in my opinion, it is that commonality we should surely focus on, not the differences. I represent the Church of England and that is where my beliefs lie, but we are all just trying in our different ways to know and understand our existence and God."

I looked around and everyone was silent, "I'll leave you with this, somebody else's words, Desmond Tutu," I said, wary of not getting into a sermon. "God is not a Christian, nor a Jew, or Muslim, or Hindu."

"Blasphemer," a lady shouted out angrily. "How can you say he's not Christian?" Her chair fell over as she stormed off into the darkness, towards the exit.

"Who said God's a he?" Miriam called out in retaliation.

I began to turn before stepping back to the microphone.

"Oh, and next week's discussion," I paused and pondered as the voices went silent and faces turned towards me, "is religion and war."

There was a long pause before a wave of sound filled the space with excited chatter. They seemed pleased with the choice which hopefully meant a good turnout next week.

"Sorry about that lover, couldn't resist," Margaret apologised as I congratulated her. "Had to show them students we've got a few brain cells between us."

"Thanks for coming," I smiled.

"Nothing on the telly," she shrugged, rooting around in her bag; I was dreading what she was going to pull out, a joint the size of a fire extinguisher probably, so made my excuses and continued through the crowd, stopping and shaking hands with various people.

Conversations continued long after as people left their seats and started mingling around the hall, music taking the edge off the individual voices and sudden shrieks of laughter, unifying them into an even background of sound. It was starting to feel like we were sliding into a club night but with a different cast, the divide between the groups blurring, facilitated by drink as cans were opened and snacks offered as again, food broke down barriers. Plato was in deep conversation with a couple of the lecturers whilst Discharge was trying his luck with another group of students who were politely responding to his banter. They appeared unimpressed to my unqualified eye but he'd no doubt tell me different.

"Another drink?" It was Judy. I looked at the bottle, split, on a high but wary, expecting something negative must surely happen.

"Go on then," I replied, finding it difficult to say no to her, spineless as usual. "I'll just take it easy."

My instinct proved correct as Yoda strode towards me minutes later. I glanced up, finding police filing through the doors, waiting as a dark mass, like a malignant tumour.

"Did you call them?" I asked, more accusation than question.

"No."

"They just turned up did they?"

"There are people everywhere or they may have their own people here. I'm not sure where this paranoia is coming from, but at the moment I'm keeping you out of a cell."

"But, it's a lecture…"

"Was a lecture, quite a pro-Muslim lecture, which finished two hours ago. It's now an illegal gathering."

"So, why are they waiting there?"

"Because I've asked them to, despite your little lecture."

"I was trying to be impartial."

"You're not supposed to be impartial, there are sides."

"After what they did to me?"

"Did for you. You just don't get it," he said, shaking his head solemnly.

Crab Scratch left the DJ booth as the hall returned to silence and people filed out quietly, affronted but not quite drunk enough to riot. I understood why the police had remained by the door; all it needed was a spark.

I kept my distance, watching Yoda in discussion with Brian, lips moving with the occasional glance across, accentuated with random hand gestures as they waited for the hall to empty before following the stragglers out through the double doors.

We walked towards the office, moving from one dark mass to another, discovering Kooky and crew waiting in the stairwell as I eased Judy behind me. It seemed appropriate, the dark side of The

Temple greeting the new me at long last. He'd been the missing piece, and in a strange way, I'd missed him.

"Coookeee!" I shouted in a poor impersonation of a Sesame Street favourite. He was too young to understand, though no doubt understood disrespect.

"You midnight?" He sneered.

"What?"

"Midnight?"

"What?"

"Midnight mass?"

"I haven't got a clue what you're rabbiting…"

"Midnight Mass," he said, getting frustrated. "Grass?"

"Well speak fucking English; it's like talking to Chas and Dave."

"Did you?"

"Speak to the police? I had to," I shrugged.

"You know the rules."

"Your rules."

"Everybody's rules," he said, leaning in before stepping back again, memories still fresh.

"I didn't tell them."

"Good boy."

It sounded ridiculous, he was ten years younger, a reversal of a pensioner calling me father.

"Where is Uncle Knockout?" I asked. I hadn't given him much thought, despite his actions.

"Out of town for a bit."

"County lines in some little village somewhere?" I mocked. "He's not made for your world, too lightweight."

"Did a good job on you."

"Not good enough," I replied, remembering his twisted face, the brick leaving his hand.

"Let's go, Peter," Judy whispered, tugging on my sleeve.

"It's not about being hard enough, it's the extremes that you'll go to."

"And what extremes will you go to?" I asked.

"I'll finish the job that he didn't."

"You're a shit house, a child killer…"

"You do what you have to do," he shrugged. "You know, you could have avoided all of this if you'd just paid your taxes."

"He wouldn't have thrown the brick?"
"Your card was marked."
"Then I agree."
"What?"
"I agree," I repeated, knocking him off balance.
"First payment by the end of the week then…"
"There's a curfew, so ten percent of fuck all is fuck all," I said dismissively before walking up the stairs, nudging Judy in front of me.
"How's your Dad?" He asked, stopping me as we turned on the landing.
"What?"
"Your Dad, how is he?"
"Somewhere far away from you."
"Far away from everyone I've heard, in his own little world. Nobody is far away from me."
I took a step back towards the stairs as Judy's hand gripped my arm tightly, surprisingly tightly considering her tiny frame as he took a step back. One of his goons flicked open a knife whilst the other was digging around in his jacket pocket before slowly pulling out a long machete which was unexpected to say the least. He looked surprised himself, obviously a new toy.
"Police are outside," I warned, wishing Peter was here, so much better in these situations.
"There are consequences you know, for your actions," Kooky continued, sounding more confident with reinforcements.
"As there are for yours."
"God gonna get me?"
"He's in the queue."

∞

Last night's release was all over the news, another high street mogul whose stores were burning, the police spread too thin to respond whilst the military were busy guarding key institutions, surrounded by the flowers and dancing of peaceful protest.
He was missing, somewhere on his yacht in the Caribbean, but the contagion had spread from island to island, the people of Tortola having no stake in the wealth buried there, living in poverty, hand

to mouth since hurricane whoever. Fire was their weapon of choice, affordable to those with little, leaving mansions burning on the hillsides, marinas breached and designer shopping arcades now ashes on the ground. Offices of enablers were being sought out, their computers and files taken, kept safe and handed over to those who could unlock their secrets. The scenes were apocalyptic, scuttled boats almost completely submerged against a backdrop of smoke hazed paradise, the beaches still white, the sea a crystalline blue as they rid themselves of parasites. It was captivating, the whole nation, the world, tuning in and glued to their screens at the same time every night, waiting to discover who would be next. The government remained silent as it was Davos week, whilst opportunist strong men attempted to fill the void, jostling for position, switching politics like chameleons, delivering the soundbites they thought we wanted to hear. But their words were hollow, for the morality had gone, taken piece by piece by the takers, thinking their magic money tree could go on forever.

"They're not real," I shouted, nursing my whiskey to keep the hangover at bay as I placed another microdose on my tongue, watching whole city blocks in flames, dancing across the screen. It was a eureka moment, my thoughts spinning and colliding as I stared at the events unfolding, considering the protesters, politicians, police and the army, all players in a make believe game, wrapped up in layers of delusion.

Plato was right, they were living in a simulation, an artificial world of intelligent design, a society just made up, real but not real, where fictions were indoctrinated by flags and anthems, letterheads, oaths and rituals, created like magic spells to support the story as titles, buildings and uniforms attempted to make the fairy tales real.

Everything was about money, the fighting, the protests, but money wasn't real, just pieces of paper carrying the printed portrait of a fiction.

"It's all bullshit," I giggled, "Capitalism, countries, political systems, social systems, the law, man-made illusions." For a society so bent on proof and science, I was surprised they accepted it, for there was no scientific truth, it was constructed from fantasy, make believe. They called it culture, an invented reality, creating invented behaviours, engineered desire, buy this, think that, a debtors prison. None of them were free, the whole of human civilisation tied down

with webs of shared fictions, its inhabitants so caught up surviving the day to day that they couldn't see what was real anymore.
"It's so fucking obvious," I whispered to Judy's sleeping body before pacing around the room, taking another tablet, unsure if I'd already had one.
"An altered reality."
I had the television and radio on together, overlapping, hearing the voices of the young as they rejected the narratives, the past superseded, as they imagined a new world where the priceless becomes the new worthless:

"Gold's just metal…"

"What's the point of a diamond?"
"Champagne's just fizzy wine…"
"The Mona Lisa's shit…"

"It's Middle-Earth, Peppa Pig World," I giggled quietly, joining in. Throughout history, the story was the same, exploitation of the majority for the benefit of the minority, the narrators continually reshaping their creation, ensuring their position on top as they reminisced about Churchill and Dunkirk, shoring positions, awarding themselves MBE's, knighthoods or a berth in the House of Lords. They were nimble, always passing on the cost of mistakes, but now, within this Disneyland, all these truths and fake truths were running wild; no wonder people were angry and confused.
"How do they know who they are?" I whispered to my unborn foetus as another Molotov cocktail exploded in Nottingham, illuminating the room in orange before the adverts came on as I lay twisting on the floor.
It wasn't a blackout, but a whiteout, a loss of control and I'm trembling, jerking: the walls are white, the ceilings white, my body soaked with sweat, I'm restrained.
I'd thought of sharing it, discussing my revelations with Lucky or Stan, perhaps Willo, but from birth they were shaped by these stories; it was the only tale they knew and they wouldn't understand. I could rant and rave at them, scream from the lectern, but the fact that my beliefs were different would have no effect. It would take the beliefs of thousands, millions, to change before society changed with it. I did have my part to play however, not in

protest but by doing what I was supposed to do, the path before me clear and righteous, unfurling across the floor and through the wall as I reached out to touch it, wondering how many microdoses I'd taken.

I'd been used to drive a wedge between religions, people pulled apart and pitched against each other in my name. It was a guilt that lay heavy, the images of burnt out mosques and synagogues flicking through my mind as I lay awake, thinking of the days I'd spent travelling around the city, observing everyday life offset by this new reality: roadblocks with soldiers, checkpoints requiring ID, thirty minute walks now taking two hours as they imposed control for our own good.

"Why me?" I whispered to God, to no reply.

My chosen path led me to burnt out structures, places of worship now blackened walls and acrid smells, something I was familiar with. They were surprised to find me there, most unsure of what would happen next, their religion on hold as they looked for temporary accommodation though offers were sparse for fear of further attack. I'd introduce the idea gently to gauge reaction, offering an option, their only option but it was radical, different than anything they'd experienced.

"I don't know," was the usual response, alongside a nervous shuffling of feet, but as the world was collapsing around us, I was dreaming, caught up in the idea and how it might work, rooms with a religion to each, the ideal shape a panopticon, Strangeways, redeveloped into a spiritual centre with a big dancefloor at its heart.

"Dad," I grinned to the naked doctor who was keeping me company, the first I'd seen since my rebirth.

"Got to keep it secret," I whispered, placing my finger to my lips. I showed the Pandit, Rabbi, Shia Cleric and Imam Khatib around at different times, each visit clandestine, not speaking about the others as we inched closer to a yes. There was disagreement within them, young and enthusiastic, wanting to move forward and be a part of the idea but held back by their traditions. They were followed by the Sikh Granthi, Buddhist Bhikku, Hare Krishna and Ras Tafari priests who were less troubled with the idea of a shared space. The closer the sibling, the more difficult they were to persuade. Catholics didn't need my help, whilst Methodists, Presbyterians and Lutherians responded with an instant no, sounding offended by the idea. Others were slightly more open, but only slightly.

A phone call revealed that religions do speak to each other, as Yoda screamed at me manically.

"Slow down, slow down," I said, "you sound like a fucking Dalek."

"You cannot do this," were the first words I understood, amongst the garbled rage.

"Who told you?"

"The Jehovah's Witnesses. They're made up, keep babbling on about the battle at Armageddon."

"Ah shit," I groaned.

"First you do that stupid fucking internet thing, then your bloody lecture, and now this."

"Their temples, synagogues, mosques were burnt down because of me..."

"Though of all the stupid things you've done, I didn't see this coming. You've got imagination, I'll give you that."

"I've got to fix it, make it right..."

"Why didn't you just go to the Isle of Wight? You're not thinking straight, bang on the head's knocked you stupid."

"So that's what I'm doing, fixing it."

"Doing what exactly, Syncretism? Trying to combine all of the religions, cherry picking the best bits?"

"No, no..."

"Cao Dai? Unitarian Universalists?"

"No. I'm not changing the religions, they're just going to be under the one roof."

"Gods R Us? What about Anibus and Ra? Did you invite them? Hope you didn't forget Osiris..."

"It's the right thing to do."

"They'll close you down."

"Who?"

"The Church. You're embarrassing them, going crawling to all these other..."

"I'm not crawling to anyone. I'm offering help, as I should. What would Jesus do?"

"Oh fuck off with your 'what would Jesus do' rubbish, it's not relevant."

"Of course it's relevant."

"It's Fucking Mormons, suppose you've invited them too."

"Forgot about them, I'll speak to Norman."

"Norman the Mormon, this is no time for taking the piss."

"Mormon Norman," I corrected. "He lives behind Greaty Market."

There was a long pause, his breathing heavy down the phone as he considered whether I was taking the piss. I was. "They'll close down The Temple."

"They can't close it down."

"Of course they can."

"They don't own it, I do."

"Well, no…"

"Their church is the one they just sold at the top of the fucking hill."

There was a long pause which I refused to fill as reality stuck.

"Please Peter," was all he said, floundering, realising the conundrum they were in.

"I'll think about it," I lied.

It had taken four hours for us to reach agreement, sat in a circle like an AA meeting in the middle of the dancefloor, illuminated by a single beam of light from above. Each was surprised to see the other sitting there before them, looking confused, unsure if they had been duped, whether they should be angry.

We all came to the centre of the circle, touching elbows in a post-pandemic hand shake as we agreed there was no time like the present. We decided not to make a public statement or grand announcement, wanting to keep our secret that little bit longer, wanting it to feel as normal as possible, no big deal, gauging reaction as people glanced up from their activities as deities and furnishings started passing them. Some had been hidden away and preserved, foresight saving them, others were damaged from the riots, charred or dented, limbs missing like the ancient roman gods that had faded into mythology; perhaps this was the fate of all gods. For a place where change was the norm this was something new, they were something new, they didn't live on the estates. They were disrupting the balance as even the High Rip kept their distance. But despite the diversity, they were surprisingly easy to accommodate, no need for a panopticon, just one room stripped of all iconography, transformed between services.

Heads turned and silences ensued as new groups arrived for the first time, looking around apprehensively at the activities around the hall before making their way to the chapel, temple, gurdwara or synagogue, whatever its latest avatar may be. Some fitted in with their stereotypes, items of dress or physical appearance giving them away, making them self-conscious as their personalities and physical characteristics disappeared behind their religion.

"Do Jews have pews?" Migsy asked.

"Think so," I replied, an informed guess.

For the Jews, the pews could remain. They had no idols, but a makeshift ark containing Torah scrolls that weighed a tonne. Migsy and Smiler were the only people that could lift it, grunting and cursing in a most unreligious manner as they shuffled it into place.

"I thought you two were supposed to be fit," the Rabbi chided whilst placing a Menorah on top, "Grunting like a rutting aardvark."

Kippah's were the only item that gave the congregation away. There were no wide brimmed hats, shaggy beards or twirls of hair, unorthodox apparently.

The Ras Tafari also kept the pews but decorated the walls with swathes of bright green, yellow and red fabric, the Lion of Judah carrying a golden sceptre forming a focal point at the front of the room before an Ethiopian Flag. They were instantly recognisable and not just by the colour of their skin. Hair was their symbol, dreadlocks, left long and natural, like Nazarites, a look that had been appropriated by fashionistas, diluting its original meaning of protest.

Margaret knew a number of them, particularly the elders, their heavily wrinkled faces breaking into beautiful wide smiles, knocking twenty years off as they spotted her walking towards them, arms spread in a welcoming gesture.

For the Sikh's, the pews were removed and large, heavily patterned communal rugs laid out. They had no iconography, just an equally heavy Takhalmmlolt replacing the ark with a copy of the Guru Granth Sahib laying comfortably, like a prince, on top of pillows and brightly decorated fabrics. They arrived turbaned, smiling through their beards, instantly comfortable in the new surroundings, making an effort to touch elbows with everyone they came across. They did not walk straight to the chapel but spent time mingling, looking at artworks being painted, watching the acrobats practicing on the trapeze whilst also dropping off a large donation to the food bank.

For the Buddhists, different rugs were laid out along with flowers around the perimeter of the room. Three large golden Buddha statues were placed at the front, each with a different hand gesture in an apparent state of bliss. Saffron was dominant as they swept through the hall, bald and permanently smiling, a blaze of colour distracting the jugglers as they threw flaming clubs into the air. They'd disappear into silence before a gentle "Ommm," would gently fill the space, like a vibration in the air.

The Hare Krishna's had heavily decorated Sita Rama figurines surrounded by turquoise curtains, flowers and gold ornaments, lots of gold ornaments. Their chants echoed through the hall causing people to glance at each other and grin before continuing with what they were doing to the backdrop of voices. Even Red Molly could be seen tapping her foot behind the counter, her lips unconsciously forming the words. Some had shaven heads with little ponytails trailing down their backs, dressed in orange, waving joyous hands and banging drums, tambourines and cymbals as they made their way out of the chapel and did a circuit of the hall, bystanders dancing along as the procession passed.

Everything was removed for the Muslim services and prayer mats laid out, cutting diagonal across the room, giving it a different dynamic as they pointed towards Mecca. Beautifully decorated texts from the Quran were placed on walls, sweeping lines of silver, curving, forming indecipherable words of art. They dressed normally, just the white Taquiyah's the men took out of their pockets and placed upon their heads whilst the ladies lifted shawls before entering the chapel or mosque as it had now become.

It was the Hindu services that required the most change, again bright communal rugs laid out then strings of yellow and red flowers hung. Various deities appeared for different services: Ganesha, Krishna, Shiva and Kali, all taking turns on centre stage where devotees placed offerings, Puja of flowers and spice, coconut and incense.

Word of new arrivals brought a group of Syrians to the hall, The Eastern Orthodox Church of Antioch. It was Said who came across and shook my hand warmly, "You know, we are an offshoot of the Catholic branch?"

"We're all part of the same tree," I shrugged. "It really doesn't matter."

"Then we would like to use the space if that is possible."
"Great, though you understand there are many other religions using The Chapel."
"Beggars can't be choosers," he smiled. "This is important, another chapter in our settling here."
"How's that going?" I asked.
"Some are fine, some not, which is hardly surprising," he shrugged. "Those struggling are receiving counselling, but for others the break down hasn't arrived yet."
"If there's anything we can do?" I asked, waving my hand in the direction of the hall.
"It's me that should be asking you that question," he replied.
"Then please start joining in with activities, start some of your own, teach us."
"I'll ask around, though some are slightly reticent. It's the soldiers on the streets that some are finding hard to grasp. They think it's starting again, that we're cursed."
"The riots? Have you been okay?"
"A few youngsters throwing stones, shouting this and that, but nothing serious. There are a few that would like to go out and engage, but we keep everyone indoors."
"I'm sorry about that."
"No need for you to apologise, idiots are a global phenomenon."
It was like a conveyor belt of religions, some going out whilst the next came in, like a stage-set changing between scenes. The effect of this coming together was unexpected, a revelation, similar to the lecture, putting them into context. I found it amusing how we observed the other religions as if watching fairy tales, with their own quirky idols and regalia, whilst we considered our own as infallibly true. We were all doing the same thing, weaving intricate webs of meaning.

All the furniture and idols were hidden when not in use, separate, not touching, behind the giant curtain hanging behind the structure. Lord Ganesha was looking over the crucifix whilst Krishna and Kali were having a staring contest as Buddha sat calmly between them. I knew who my money was on. It was an analogy of the hall itself as the people gradually came together, arriving early or hanging around afterwards at the most unlikeliest of places, Red Molly's tea shop within the Red Square of Atheism, her communist flags defining the space.

It started with the food as always, donations to the shop in exchange for a coffee or a chat, which Molly, an expert in everything, was more than happy to accommodate. It was perhaps because all Gods were equal in her space that they came here and discussed their different religions, attracting others, Plato turning up regularly, even Discharge was there, speaking passionately to a Hindu lady.

"We are here to fuck, that's it, nothing else. To fuck as often and with as many different people as possible."

"I'm not sure if you come from the Heffner or Dawkins school of thought," she replied in a slightly sarcastic tone.

"We're nothing, our lives as meaningless as bacteria in the grand scheme of things. There is no such thing as right or wrong, good or evil in nature. They're man made ideas that will disappear when we do. It's just reproduction."

"Hence your obsession with sex?"

"That is my religion."

"Fucking?"

"Yep, all the rest of it," he continued, "culture, jobs, hobbies, religions, football, drinking, fishing, knitting, languages, whatever, is a by-product, just detritus, meaningless."

"Do you not think you are a result of the fetishisation of sex by society? They've created this taboo, about the most natural thing in the world. I bet it's all you think about."

"It pretty much is," he confirmed.

"Perhaps The Father could let you have your own service," she suggested, "as it's a religion?"

"Most guys pray alone," he smiled, after a little consideration.

I thought of intervening but she seemed to have the measure of him, either humouring or possibly even interested in this new religion, sipping and smiling into her Chai.

The offerings had diversified from her traditional communist fare: Challah, Hummus, Falafel, Ital, Halal. A whole range of meat, vegetarian and vegan dishes started to appear, different each day as people headed straight to Molly's to see what was on offer. I ate there most days, chatting as people became more familiar.

The diversity of activities was normal but this diversity of people was something new. It wasn't just me, I was a piece in a much greater game as a number of disparate parts had come together to make this possible. The Temple had evolved into something breathtaking, beyond imagination, beyond even the club night as everything was clicking into place. Somehow, the religions had decided on the moves independently, taking a chance, not only in services and ceremonies, but also buying in to the idea of the club. I wasn't sure what they'd told their institutions, maybe something, maybe nothing, but it was working, the people were talking, realising that we're all the same: laughing at the same jokes, watching the same movies, eating the same food, protesting about the same politicians. They seemed ecstatic about it, excited by the discovery that the labelled people were actually normal and were interested, not insulted by the differences between them.

"This is what The Temple is for," I mumbled to myself, revelation arriving as I watched from the office window, realising that even the drugs had purpose, taking me beyond my human limitations, seeing past cultural boundaries.

Gradually, they stepped across the borders of Red Square and started taking part in classes, joining and bringing their own cultures to the club. Holi arrived at the perfect time, ending any doubts about the course we were taking. It was joyous, everybody wearing white as the streets turned multi-coloured along with the people, any trace of race or nationality disappearing beneath colours; we were all different but the same, laughing as we behaved like children.

"It doesn't come off," Migsy exclaimed, striding in, his head still green. "I've had three showers, it doesn't fucking come off."

Smiler strode in behind him, he was blue and golden.

"I always suspected you were pro-European."

"Fuck off. Does this stay on forever?"

"Think so," I replied with a smirk. "You're all multi-coloured anyway with them tattoos, don't know what you're bothered about."

"You look like Papa Smurf," Migsy grinned.

"Fuck off Shrek," he retorted as he strode out for another shower.

Once the success of our project became apparent, the institutions found themselves unable to stand by and watch. It became obvious that they were being pulled in different directions at our weekly round table meetings as pressure was exerted upon them, telling

them to walk in line, bow down, dampening their initial enthusiasm
for the project as they tried to balance conflict within themselves;
determined to keep this thing going but at the same time heading
towards the inevitable point when they would come up against
their institution, where they would be called naïve or misguided
and an answer would be required, a yes or no. It was a subtle
intervention to begin with, an understated violence, soft power,
using the weight of history and tradition to correct those that were
deviating slightly from their path, compelling us to climb back
behind the walls that separate us. But we didn't want to go back, we
wanted to continue stepping forward, together, as we'd seen
something fundamentally good on the other side.
Additional protests had started outside, other religions offended by
the sharing of space joining our original protesters who still turned
up occasionally, more for the social aspect. The separate groups
would frequently stand next to each other, not sure where their
allegiances lay, shouting at the building then half-heartedly at each
other. Again, with familiarity, then food, they came to some sort of
compromise, realising they were not that different after all,
frequently forgetting to protest as they chatted and exchanged food
and drink.
Yoda delivered my message personally. It was the first time I'd seen
him for weeks as he entered, just as the Hare Krishna's were
finishing their lap of the hall.
"Alright?" I asked as he came striding purposefully towards me,
pulling me into an embrace, though the scowl remained as he
watched the chanting group enter The Chapel.
"We need somewhere private to talk."
"Yeah, fine, the café?" I suggested, pointing towards the hammer
and sickles.
"No, private," he repeated, nodding his head towards the office.
"Crab Scratch is over there," I said as we walked across the hall,
"doing a class. He's been asking about you."
He seemed to lighten up for a second, glancing over through the
window, before focusing back on the office.
"I'll speak to him later," he murmured, the determined look
returning to his features.
"It's good to see you," I said, as the door closed behind us. "Despite
everything that's going on, please don't be a stranger."

Yoda just sat down, pinching the bridge of his nose between his fingers.

"What is it?"

"You've been suspended."

"What?"

"You've been suspended, pending an investigation."

I slumped down into my chair, legs empty. "They can't, it's working…"

"I tried to warn you…"

"But take a look outside, it's…"

"But you just carry on, ignoring…"

"It's working, look outside," I shouted, standing up behind my desk. "It's so narrow minded, they're so…"

"It's not that," he said quietly.

"What do you mean?"

"It's not that, but, reading between the lines, it probably is that."

"I've done nothing wrong. I'm doing my services, all my duties…"

"Conduct inappropriate to the work of a clerk in holy orders," he declared, as if reading off a memo.

"What does that mean?"

"You have abused spiritual powers."

"Spiritual Abuse? I'm helping others in a time of need. Just because they are different religions…"

"No," he said, holding up his index finger. "You have abused your position with a vulnerable member of your congregation."

"Abused. What do you mean? Abused?"

"To engage in sexual relations," he finished.

It felt like a blow to the stomach as I fell back down into my seat, just white noise in my head as emotion took over thought. It was anger, embarrassment, shame.

"She's not vulnerable."

"She's a recovering drug addict."

"How can you say that? To me? Abused?"

"Because that's what they're calling it," he replied sternly, never one for sugar coating. "Did you think nothing would happen?"

"I'm not, it's not…" there was nothing I could say.

"From the outside it looks like predation."

"But. It's not. It's an accident. It's consensual."

"She may believe it is, but she is vulnerable, easily manipulated, hence the investigation."

"No, no, you don't even know her."

"It paints a picture…"

"She's not…"

"The Church has to act decisively with any hint of sexual impropriety, you understand that."

"Like Father Williams in his penthouse?"

"You might get a penthouse, each case is different."

"You make me sound like an offender."

"Maybe you are?"

"You don't believe that do you? Do you?" I pleaded as I dropped to my knees behind the desk.

"Of course not Peter, but it's not me you have to convince."

"They make me sound like a fucking paedophile."

"Not paedophile, but they may consider sexual abuse or even rape." I grabbed for the bin and vomited into it, my stomach churning as it emptied.

"I'm innocent," I stammered as a line of drool connected me to the bin. "We can have relationships, we can…"

"You're not innocent. You've got her pregnant," he shouted, his turn to stand, "Before marriage. Even if you are innocent, there are certain standards The Church requires you meet. Can you imagine how this looks to them?"

I curled over and started to cry. It was uncontrollable, my body heaving as Yoda made the picture clear to me. He was right, I had failed, blinded by myself, my ego.

"So what now?" I asked.

He handed over a letter, "I'm afraid you're suspended with immediate effect, I'll take over the services here for the duration of the investigation. I'm instructed to take over all of your duties, also to stop this ridiculous thing you've got going with these other religions. They've got to clear out."

"This is what it's all about, isn't it?"

"Probably, but you've made it so easy for them, Peter."

Shame washed over me again, I wanted to beat myself, hurt myself.

"I've told you again and again. I'm on your side, but you just don't listen, you go down these fucking tangents."

"I'm sorry," I said, shaking my head. "I didn't realise."

"You're like a child playing big boys games, making ridiculous mistakes."

"I'm sorry," I repeated. "Why aren't the papers all over it? They could destroy me."

"Because yours truly is protecting you, as usual."

I crawled over and placed my forehead on his feet, my body shuddering as the emotions coursed through me.

"Thank you," was all I could think to say, again and again, "Thank you."

'Have you missed me?' Peter whispered, as my head rested on his knee.

CHAPTER 2

THE PASS-

"You are not," she shouted, before slapping me across the ear with her bony hand, sending my head ringing.

"I've got to, there's nothing here for me."

"The Isle of Wight? That place is too old for me and I'm a hundred, for fuck's sake," she shouted before slapping me across the other ear.

"Ginny, I've been suspended."

"So what? You just walk away at the first sign of trouble?"

"I don't know what else I can do."

"Show a bit of backbone," she shouted as I ducked out of the way of her bony knuckles flying towards me. "Stand up for what you believe in."

"They're calling me a sex offender."

"For what? Having a relationship?"

"I'm not allowed…"

"So you're walking out on her? Just packing your bags and fucking off because some arsehole sent you a letter? That's proper shit house behaviour."

"No, no," I mumbled before sitting down, realising that was exactly what I was doing. "I don't know what to do."

"Don't throw it all away. You've brought them all together, you're in a relationship, having a kid, what are you thinking?"

"But, they're putting a stop to it, Yoda's taking over."

"They're taking us back in time, to the bad old days."

"Of what?"

"Anger, hate, sectarianism. It's history repeating itself, attacking holy places."

"This has happened before?"

"We were the Belfast of England and right here is where Roman Catholics and Protestants clashed, in Everton. Great Homer Street was where the two communities came together, poor Irish Catholics near the docks, and Protestants up the hill, all in slums, poverty, ripe for manipulation. It happened every day, they hated each other. St. Paddies day and twelfth of July was murder every year. The Cats were treated like the immigrants of today, scapegoats for everything bad: falling wages, crime, prostitution, as if we'd been a Garden of Eden before they arrived. The press did their bit, creating stereotypes."

"Same as they do now," I murmured, sitting, my momentum gone.

"Same," she agreed. "You still get the 'Irishman walks into a bar' jokes because the media in them days told everyone the Irish were stupid. Then the politicians jumped on it, the Conservatives were partnered with the Protestant Party. There were riots, Juvenal Street."

"That's near to the club."

"So there's no better place to fix this thing. Maybe there's something in the water, in the ground around here. One of them ley lines or something?"

"What stopped it?"

"All sorts of things, fighting side by side during the war, slum clearances, then a better standard of living."

"Religion doesn't seem so important then," I mumbled, echoing Yoda's sentiment.

"Then a larger identity subsumed them."

"Which is?"

"Scouse."

"I'm trying to bring them together, it's working."

"You have to, because if people like Yoda have their way, they'll close themselves off from each other. Then there's the others that won't like it, the Orangemen…"

"There's plenty that don't like it." I replied. "They've all got protesters outside now, Muslims, Jews, Hindus, their own versions of Orangemen."

"Well, fuck them."

"I didn't know you were so into it, this multiculturalism."

"Why? Because I'm old? We've got the two cathedrals, Paddy's Wigwam and that other big fucking thing, linked together by Hope Street. Can't see any reason why there shouldn't be a mosque, synagogue, temple or whatever on that street as well. Do what you think is right."

"Half of them are going to jump ship anyway."

"They certainly will if you do. Let them do what they are going to do, but you lead by example." She said prodding her bony finger. "Look at the life you're building here, and you're ready to throw it away for a few words."

"They're not just words."

"Of course they fucking are, twisted words, corrupted words from some nomark in an ivory tower. The people around here know they're not true. If you run away you'll lose everything, most of all the respect and belief of the people, and that's the only thing that's important."

"You're right," I mumbled. It seemed I was being swayed by each person that spoke to me, perhaps they were all right.

"Sorry for hitting you, but some people can only learn important lessons by being hit," she continued.

"At least your husband didn't get involved this time," I replied, glancing across at the urn.

"Now you're sitting, I'll make you a cup of tea. Run away while my back's turned and I'll hunt you down and cut your balls off."

"I'm staying here," I mumbled, too confused to laugh at the thought of a hundred year old lady hunting me down. The funny thing was, I didn't doubt that she would.

"And put that bag away before Judy sees it, she doesn't need to know. I'll have probably forgotten by tomorrow, so your secrets safe. Fucking Alzheimers."

She was right, I couldn't run away anymore, the old modus operandi was over. I'd packed everything back into the drawers and wardrobe when Judy came in from work, guilt and embarrassment running through me again as I realised what I'd been about to do, leave my unborn child, a knee jerk reaction placing me with the lowest of the low.

They were equally understanding in the club as I explained that Yoda would be taking over the services, looking down on the crowd below as Smiler held me over the edge of the platform by my feet.

"Drop him on his head, see if that helps him think straight," Mary shouted, full of contempt.

They wouldn't accept it, the outrage causing all activities to stop as the people crowded around. The Knowalls arrived one by one as word got around, dropping what they were doing to attend the latest emergency.

"I've got no choice," I explained, my face bright red, throbbing.

"Why?" Voices were shouting up. They didn't understand.

"I've been suspended."

"We can see that."

"No, from my job."

"What for?"

"Is it because of the religions thing?"

"No."

I saw Lily down there looking up at me, her hands covered in clay from the pottery class.

"They've accused me of Spiritual Abuse."

"What the fuck's that?"

"I think they mean sexual," I stammered. At that moment I wouldn't have minded if Smiler had let go and I'd gone crashing to the ground, but I just hung there in the silence.

"What have you done?" Lily shouted.

"What have you done?" she repeated, her face bright red with anger.

"Judy," I replied, feeling humiliated. "And she's pregnant."

"And that's it?"

"Isn't that enough?"

"Let him down," Lily said with a sigh, her anger abating.

The crowd shouted no at the same time as Smiler looked perplexed, wondering whether to let go. It was like pantomime as I hung there swaying.

Lucky arrived as Smiler was about to put me down, prolonging my torture as he dangled me over the edge again.

"What's going on?"

"He's been suspended, so he's letting Yoda take over his services."

"Is he fuck."

It was a scene repeated as each of The Knowalls arrived separately, beginning with the same question, "What is going on?" followed by an "Is he fuck."

My face felt purple by now; I could sense Smilers arms trembling as my weight took its toll. If he dropped me I'd explode like a blueberry such was the amount of blood in my head. The pins and needles in my limbs has stopped long ago as I wondered if I'd ever feel them again.

"I'm going nowhere," I whispered, then shouted in submission, as
the Hare Krishnas joined the Ras Tafari and Sikhs, looking up at me
in disbelief.
"What?"
"I'll stay."
"I knew you'd see sense in the end," Lucky grinned. "Bring him in."
"Thank fuck for that," Smiler mumbled, laying me on the platform,
his arms appearing twice the size as I waited for circulation to
reincorporate my limbs.
"I just can't see how it will work," I explained, trying to backtrack
once I'd descended to the dancefloor.
"What can't you see?"
"If I don't go through the process, they'll just fire me."
"So?"
"What do you mean, so?"
"You can still be our Priest."
"I can't. I won't be part of The Church anymore."
"So..."
"So?"
"So we don't care if you are a part of The Church or not. You're still
our priest. You'll still do the services and all that."
"So, if I'm not a priest, I can still be your priest?"
"Exactly. Who gives two shits about them?"
"But I'm a Church of England…"
"You're a Christian first and foremost though, right?"
"Suppose…"
"Christianity is not The Church, that's a religion."
"Now hang on…"
"Christianity is a belief in the teachings of Jesus, the son of God.
You don't need The Church to continue being our priest."
"But…"
"Your sermons will be as relevant whether you are connected to an
institution or not. It's a personal thing, The Protestant Reformation,
the freedom to interpret the Bible in your own way."
I didn't know where to begin with that logic. It was like arguing
with a child when they say something infallible yet naïve. There
was no way to counter their point, it was a challenge in a way, an
ultimatum, putting me on the spot with a scenario that I could
accept or deny. But, he didn't know what he was asking, the

personal difficulty of me stepping away, standing alone as I looked up and saw Yoda in the doorway, a dark unmistakable shape, just his eyes catching the light, wet, twinkling.

"How long have you been there?" I asked as all heads turned.

"Long enough," he replied. "You've got to tell them to leave," he continued as he stepped closer, flicking a finger towards the religious groups stood in a semi-circle behind me.

"Oh dear, he's not very PC," Said mumbled behind me. They were similar in many ways, never shying away from strong words.

"Small man syndrome," he whispered, his half-inch height advantage qualifying him to make such a comment.

"I'm not asking them to leave," I said, hearing somebody else's words come out of my mouth.

"Peter, we've discussed this…"

"I'm so sorry."

"Then why are you doing it?"

"Because I'm confused. Because you're all right," I said, turning back to the silent audience before returning my gaze to Yoda.

"This place is me, I'm nothing without it and whatever happens I've got to accept the consequences."

"What do you have that you did not receive?"

"Corinthians? You're right, God has placed me here for a reason…"

"You're a priest, in the service of The Church, and you move on, you always do."

"Like a sex offender? Moved on every couple of years? History covered up? Not anymore."

"You're not moved on."

"What?" I exclaimed, in words thick with surprise. "Oh come on, every two or three years…"

"You've done that to yourself," he interrupted. "We've never moved you anywhere."

"But…"

"We've never moved you anywhere," he repeated calmly. He was right as we stood there glaring at each other. He had the upper hand. He always had the upper hand.

"Come on, we know you're not a sex offender," he offered in a conciliatory tone, breaking through the tension. "Stupid perhaps. Naïve. They'll just take you through the motions. I'll be with you all the way."

"I'm not prepared to go through the motions," I replied quietly, a revelation to myself. "I'm not going through the system," my skin going cold at the thought of The Church and its processes and procedures, giving myself to a vast, blank network of faceless officials with structures and policies, various stages, each separate and corruptible. Once within, they could make up anything.

"I…I know you have an aversion for systems, but…"

"It's not anger, or rage," I replied, quietly. "I just can't."

"It's an irrational phobia."

"Irrational?"

"We can manage it."

"They're asking too much."

"This is the easy path Peter, the coward's way."

"This is…right."

"So, you'll just throw it all away?"

"I'm in an untenable position. Throw all of this away or throw all of that away."

"Lose your career? Your calling? For this little project?" he continued.

"I shouldn't have to lose anything, it's the Church that have put me here."

"You put yourself here, though in hindsight, perhaps it was predictable. Your loyalty to The Church is based upon debt as opposed to belief. Perhaps that's why you're so susceptible to these other religions."

"You're questioning my belief now?"

"You've always been in soft parishes with stable congregations. Now you're somewhere radical and you've absorbed this place and gone off the rails. We should never have brought you here."

I glanced around at the faces surrounding me, appearing to take Yoda's comments as a compliment.

"We were always going to end up at this point," I concluded. "It was the whole reason for it. Do something radical, have a go."

"Not necessarily. It's your personal failings that have got us here, sexual improprieties."

My skin went cold as he spoke the words in front of everybody. The S-word, not a word to say in public as I glanced around.

"I seem to recall Bishop Gordon also had his suspicions in your last parish," he added, raising an eyebrow.

I opened my mouth, but nothing came out, it didn't need to as I saw Yoda visibly flinch.

"Will you fuck off," Lily shouted, stepping past me.

He looked momentarily repulsed as he recognised her.

"There's no impropriety in what he is doing," she continued, pointing her pointing finger. "It's a normal relationship, between a man and a woman."

"We have policies on this," Yoda stated calmly, standing his ground as he switched into a different mode. "It's the life he chose."

"Has Judy complained?"

"No, but we have to act on information. She's vulnerable. I'm sure you of all people can understand that. Did Danny complain?"

There was a sharp intake of breath all around as the room remained silent. He'd crossed a line and didn't give a shit. I could see how this would progress, she'd challenged him, his authority, he'd take passive aggressive to another level as only an elderly man of God could.

I tried to intervene, "Please…" but I was no longer the focus of the crowd.

"What Father Williams did to my son is sexual impropriety, rape," that finger poked. "How dare you put him in the same box."

"He's not in the same box, but he's being investigated for something similar."

"They're not even related."

"Sex is sex, abuse is abuse," he shrugged matter-of-factly as he crossed more lines. Mutterings were emerging from the crowd as people could no longer bite their tongues. The air was electric with tension.

"How dare you," Lily shouted.

A voice came in from the leftfield. It was Molly. "Does anybody want a cup of tea? I've got a vat full of Masala Chai and nobody's drinking the fucking stuff."

"No, no," came the urgent replies and groans as she appeared, as welcome as adverts, her approach unnoticed, despite her mop of bright orange hair.

"Sausage rolls?" she continued, "sausage rolls?"

"No."

"Fuck off…"

"I'll have a sausage roll Molly," Elvis said.

"Ok love…"
"Have you got any Spicy Nik-Naks?"
"No love."
"Onion rings?"
"Yes."
"Will you fuck off over there and order food," Lucky snapped.
"I'm hungry," Elvis shrugged as everybody remained on pause.
"It's kicking off and you're ordering fucking Nik-Naks."
All eyes turned back to Yoda as Molly walked away, wondering
what to do with the Chai. He didn't disappoint.
"You'll be glad to hear, Father Williams is responding to
counselling and is well on the path to recovery," he baited, like a cat
with a mouse.
"What?" she screeched, responding as he wanted, defeated by her
own emotions.
"He's no longer deemed a threat, which is of course good news for
everybody," he said cheerfully. He was pummelling her, his words
fists as he stood there, stoic in front of a baying crowd, laughing at
them. I loved him, despite his words, his self-belief, his arrogance,
his complete inability to read a situation as she leapt forward and
punched him in the eye. I saw it in slow motion, too slow to react,
grabbing her fist as she moved to follow her excellent jab with a
haymaker.
"No, no," I shouted, pinning her arms to her sides, pulling her back
as she struggled to get free, her face red, hair flailing as she became
savage, jerking violently.
He looked smug, she had lost control and he had won, like a
puppeteer, controlling with words, but this was a distraction, taking
us away from what was really happening, that should be happening
behind closed doors, out of the public arena. They were moving to
get past me as I struggled to maintain my grip on her. She was
screaming now, the words incoherent, animalistic, appealing to the
deep primitive emotions of the pack as one of their own was
attacked.
"No, no," I shouted as they eased forward, his collar the only thing
creating doubt, making them hesitant as he stood there defiant.
"You need to go" I said to Yoda between screams.
He gave a nod then didn't move.
"You know, there will be consequences, if you don't comply."

"I know," I wheezed as an elbow planted itself in my ribs.

"It puts me in a difficult position. You are against The Church."

"I know," I repeated as a heel ran down my shin. It felt like I was vomiting the words, barely coming out as they caught in my throat.

"We are on opposing sides."

"It doesn't have to be…"

"Of course it does, we have boundaries that we live within. They want to tear this place down, The Temple…"

"And do what? An evangelical pop-up?"

It felt like he had contracted out the physical violence to a third party supplier as she threw her head back, catching me on the cheek.

He replied with a shrug, his dislike of the Evangelicals stronger than any he had for this place.

"Metaphorically of course," he mumbled. "Tear down the Temple."

"They are looking at the wrong place. This is only The Temple by name…"

"It's a place of corruption, debauchery, prostitutes and money lenders," he replied quietly as he glanced around the room, unable to resist as his eyes picked out sinners.

"It's a place of God, of peace and compassion, equality," I countered. "It's the institution where the corruption lies. That is the true Temple, Lambeth Palace."

He shrugged, apparently tired of the game. "Whatever happens, I still love you, like a son."

Guilt washed through me.

"I love you too," I responded, without embarrassment, as if it were just the two of us in the room.

"And they love you," he said lifting his arm towards the crowd that was gathered behind, wanting to kill him. "I do understand that."

"I know."

"Please remember, I am just the messenger, whatever they decide to do."

"Don't shoot the messenger," I replied with a nod as he turned and walked out of the hall, his shadow shooting towards me, cast long for a short moment, turning him into the giant he was as he opened the door before disappearing into the black as it swung closed quietly behind him.

I remained still, feeling exposed and lonely, the crowd behind seeming to sense this as they turned back to what they were doing, just a couple of pats on the back but no words, I had no words, I felt alone.

"Here's your sausage roll love," I heard Molly say as I walked back towards the office.

The letter came by courier two hours later, confirming my suspension and probable expulsion due to refusal to comply with due process. There was nothing regarding the accusation which was a relief to me, it was still only spoken, just wind, gossip and rumour, nothing compared to the power of the written word. Although surrounded by people, the loneliness came flooding back. I'd turned my back on the thing that had given me meaning.

I felt vulnerable but also anger at The Church, for its lack of understanding, its narrow mindedness. They'd cut me off, like an abuser isolates their victim from friends and family, leaving them alone, without any support structure. I felt wretched for it was ego, I'd lost myself in this place, to these people. Where there should be humility, there was none, just narcissism, gazing at this place as a reflection of me.

'Fuck humility,' Peter whispered.

CHAPTER 3

TRIALS

"Fucking kite on that," Migsy said, holding open the pages.
"Looks like he smokes fireworks," Smiler mumbled in agreement.
"Face like a Pepperami," Mary contributed from behind her newspaper.
"The hot one, all red and angry," Smiler agreed, almost grinning.
The newspapers were again the first predictable method of attack, though thankfully Yoda had managed to keep Judy out of it as I whispered a thank you to him under my breath.
The first headline simply said EXTREMIST, with a picture of the usual scarred head and a few grainy photos of men in turbans entering the club.
It was a relief, a fabrication suggesting I had gone rogue, preaching poison, stirring up hatred and colluding with terrorists. I almost laughed. Ordinarily, I'd be outraged, but in such remarkable times its effect would be minimal, tomorrows chip paper as fast moving events overtook and buried it. People had stopped believing.
They'd overplayed their hand, making them little more than comics, mouthpiece of the comedians. I heard laughter filling the hall alongside the chink of Molly's cups as newspapers were passed around.
"Think they spelt that wrong," Willo giggled from behind my desk, showing me another with CULT written above a photo of the quickly erected barricade with the army vehicle parked outside. It continued onto the next pages, where they'd formed a link with the picture of the girls, suggesting improprieties, all hot tubs and cocktails going on behind closed doors. I grinned, appreciating their creativity as I turned the page, showing me next to David Koresh then something with roman numerals, NXVIM.
The reality was stranger than they could imagine as life went on as normal within our bubble, where acrobats flew above painters at their easels; dancers practiced routines on the platforms whilst

glimpses within structures revealed a wider variety of activities; Stretch showing the old peoples home his Boa Constrictor to gummy giggles and kiss me quick humour, offset by the constantly changing religions throughout the day. As usual the adverse press was having the reverse effect, a siege mentality creeping in, reinforcing the tightness of our group.

Their second mode of attack was less predictable, taking a second to register as 'account frozen' flashed up on the screen as I tried to pay salaries.

"Fuck," I shouted, jumping up, sending my chair spinning to the ground.

Migsy glanced up before looking down at his papers again. He didn't seem to care, though I'd been having panic attack after panic attack, so was probably tired of my mini-meltdowns as my mind careered from one disaster to the next.

"We're fucked for money," I announced with as much drama as I could muster, trying to catch his attention. "They've closed our accounts."

"Of course they have," he mumbled.

"What do you mean 'of course they have?'" I replied, mimicking his voice.

"Doesn't matter, let them," Migsy shrugged.

"There's no money, they're strangling us," I shouted, then, "bastards," for added dramatic effect.

He remained still, bored.

"We don't need it," he replied, monotone and flat after a long pause.

"Don't need it?" I was going the other way along the octaves, high pitched.

"Don't need it," he repeated. He was playing a game, knew something I didn't and was taking great pleasure in stringing me along behind that poker face.

"Have you found Prince Rupert's stash under the hill or something?"

"No, just careful investing."

"You?"

"Yes, me," he shrugged, looking up with a slight smirk on his face. "You need to know these things in business. Can't be walking around with cash all over the place."

He glanced up when I didn't respond.

"What are you looking at me like that for?"

"I just didn't see it coming," I replied, wondering if he was joking.

"Better not be drugs."

"Way more lucrative than that, and legal."

"But everything's tanking, the world is fucked. What have you done with it? Jingles?"

"Cyber currencies," he replied, arching an eyebrow, trying to look professional.

"Are you taking the piss?"

"We've been using them for years, way ahead of the curve. It's just second nature now, I suppose, authorities can't get near them, they're anonymous, so suits us fine."

"But we've got accountants, DP and Emma do them for us."

"There's those accounts and then there's the other accounts," he explained, all smug, using his hands to explain the concept of two accounts clearly.

"Why didn't you tell me?"

"Because you're not in the slightest bit interested."

"It's not dodgy money?"

"No, it's our money. I've just been diverting some away from you before you piss it up the wall. Hacker Packer's our unofficial accountant, does all of the buying and selling."

"We can't have that much in it."

"We've got more than you can imagine," Migsy grinned.

"But it can only be a few grand. You can't have been skimming that much off?"

"The value has gone through the roof. Companies are collapsing so the markets have tanked. Gold is going the same because of the 'useless metal' mantra going about. All that money has got to go somewhere and with a bit of manipulation the sheep buy into it. Our few grand is worth millions."

"Fuck," was all I could think of to say, but in a positive manner, such a useful word. "So we're okay?"

"We're okay," he grinned.

"Divine intervention."

"Nah, just basic human greed," he shrugged. "We're in our own little parallel world, religion without The Church and money without the bank and tax man. While we're at it, it's probably a good time for this," he said, unlocking his filing cabinet and handing me three small, plastic wrapped parcels.

"What is it?"

"Insurance."

"You do insurance as well?"

"Another habit I've picked up."

"What...?"

"Bank accounts and identities," he said, with a whisper.

"We can't do..."

"Hopefully you'll never need it, but the world's fucked. Just split them up and hide them away somewhere safe. Don't tell anyone, not even me."

"But..."

"Not even me," he repeated, serious face on as I placed them into my desk, taking the easy path without further argument.

Their next attacks were physical as the good news kept coming, SpongeBob striding into the office like Yoda, determined, something on his mind. "You're looking very serious, what's up?"

"Lock the door," he ordered, looking around the room anxiously.

"You're making me nervous, what's up?"

"Sit down," he said, no small talk, just bullet points, commands, as he took a package out of his bag. He was trembling slightly.

"What's that?" I asked, feeling concerned, seemingly innocuous envelopes the most dangerous weapons these days, giving no hint to what's inside, information the new power.

"I've been busy," he replied as he opened the end and tipped its contents out onto the desk, a cascade of newspaper cuttings and articles fluttering down, some falling off the edge before continuing their meandering journey to the ground.

I knew what they were instantly. I was terrified, full of rage.

"What have you done?" I shouted, knowing full well what he had done.

"Look at them," he instructed quietly.

"I thought I told you to..."

"Look at them," he repeated forcefully. "There's over fifty."

I felt winded. "Fifty," I muttered, dropping back into my seat.

"All..."

"The home."

"All..."

"Dead," he nodded.
"I told you not to touch this," I shouted, my anger reignited, driven
by fear as I leant over and grabbed him by the lapels of his jacket.
"You've got to see this," he shouted back, grabbing my arms,
holding them firmly.
"They're watching you…"
"They're not. It's impossible. I was smarter this time. Impossible."
"I told you not to do it," I groaned.
"I had to, I had a responsibility…"
"Responsibility," I spat back at him. "To who?"
"To you."
"I asked you to leave it, that was your only responsibility to me,
fucking leave it."
"They are killing you."
"What?"
"They are killing you all."
"You can't prove that. Who?"
"I don't know who, but you don't get this many deaths of young
men by accident."
"Coincidence."
"It's not a fucking coincidence."
I sunk back into my chair, burying my face into my hands. I was
feeling sick.
"Why couldn't you just leave it?" I moaned.
"Because there's not many of you left."
"It doesn't matter, I told you…"
"You started me on this path."
"It was a mistake."
"It was not. You're afraid. This is your way of speaking out."
"Don't give me that subconscious shit."
"It was a different version of you then. You're all over the place, I
don't know which version I'm going to get these days."
"I expressly asked you to…"
"Then why did you tell me in the first place?"
"Like I said, a mistake."
"I found something then you told me to leave it alone, forget about
it."
"So why didn't you?"
"I'm a journalist, I have a responsibility to report. They'll be coming

for you next. I couldn't let that happen."
There was no hint of doubt in his words, completely believing in
what he was saying.
"Fuck," I shouted, thumping the desk before glancing down at the
slips of paper, seeing words and blurry faces looking back at me,
faces I'd probably recognise if I wasn't so afraid to pick them up.
"You had no right."
"They-will-kill-you," he explained, slowly.
"Then why haven't they killed me already?"
"Who knows? Because you're in the public eye, maybe?"
"I haven't always been. I've been sat on my arse in villages for
years."
"We don't even know who's doing it. Who knows their reasons?
Because you're a priest?" he shrugged.
"Oh, they must be deeply religious then."
"What happened in that place?" he asked, changing tack, deflecting
my attempt at sarcasm.
"I can't say."
"You've got to talk."
"No, I physically cannot say those words."
"I can take an informed guess," he suggested, raising his eyebrows.
"Abuse? Sexual abuse?"
I gave a slight nod, wanting to put my fist through his face, break
bones. He'd picked the locks, entered my darkest rooms containing
my darkest secrets. I felt like an offender, wanting it concealed,
buried for ever.
"Fuck, I'm so sorry…"
"You haven't told anyone about this, have you? The police?"
"Not yet."
"What do you mean, yet?"
"You're not the only survivor. There are others, living normal lives,
completely unaware of what is coming towards them."
"The past is in the past."
"It's not, it's caught up, it's here and now, and it's killing you all,
one by one."
"The press?"
"I'm going to submit it to a secure third party."
"No, you must need my permission."
"It doesn't need to mention you, you're John Doe."

"They'll make links."
"It's strictly confidential, nothing goes ahead without my say so."
"This isn't about me, or about them," I said as it dawned on me.
"This is about you, and your ambition, to be a real journalist."
"Somebody is killing abused children on a massive scale, burying evidence. My guess is it's somebody very powerful. This could be one of the biggest stories in history."
My thought went back to the folder, its pages filled with faces, names, addresses. Somebody wants them killed.
"Is that it? An exclusive?"
"No. There's you, there are the other innocent people. Lives can be saved."
"It's your ego," I said, shaking my head slowly, "dreams of a Pulitzer Prize."
"They can be bought to account."
"You've been using me."
'Fuck me, you get it at last,' Peter groaned.
"No, I've been helping you."
"Leave that there and get the fuck out."
"No, I'm here…"
"If that story see's the light of day, I will kill you."
"You can't say that, you're a…"
"I swear to God, I will find you and I will kill you."
'Hallelujah!'
I believed every word I was saying. He appeared bigger than any threat he may have uncovered, the revealing of secrets, for the world to know, to gossip and laugh about. I'd rather be dead.
"I'll come back tomorrow, when you've had a chance to calm down."
"I won't…"
"You've got me all wrong…"
"Swear to me you won't publish."
'Pinkie promise?' Peter mocked.
"I'll…"
"Swear to me," I hissed.
"I swear," he conceded, sounding shocked, crestfallen as his mental constructs of how the revelation might go dissipated. He'd no doubt been dreaming the universal dream of doing good, being the hero.
"Leave," I instructed.

"I'll come back tomorrow, and I'll keep coming back until we can have a sensible conversation."

"Leave," I repeated, the last word I ever spoke to him, he was dead that evening.

"Hit and run," Migsy announced, ashen faced the following morning. He'd never really liked or trusted him, but had gotten used to him being around. The same as me, I supposed, as feelings of guilt were overcome by relief, for he had deceived me, betrayed my trust, but, for now, my story was safe.

'Keep telling yourself that,' Peter whispered.

"Do they have any idea who?" I asked.

"No, a dead zone. No cameras, nothing. A car lost control, skidded off the road and hit him, then buggered off."

"The car?"

"Burnt out, left it up the hill."

"By the church?"

"Yes,"

"Jesus," I replied, as links were forming in my mind, lines going from conspiracy theory to conspiracy theory, shooting off in all directions, spiralling out of control. I tried to slow it down but it was already past me, the current too strong. I couldn't formulate a thought as images flashed before me. They were closing in, tightening the net, I felt my eyes rolling, the room going white.

"Fucking hell," Migsy said, grabbing me, directing me towards my seat. "Are you okay?"

"Yes, yes," I muttered, but my head was still full of white noise, restraints, white walls, flickering images too fast to see, letting out a groan before quickly coming back into focus, jumping up as the cold water hit me, finding Migsy standing with an empty glass across the desk.

"You were sliding."

"I'm okay," I replied, waiting for my brain to reboot. I felt slow, lethargic, as I slumped back down, my legs empty.

"You looked like you were going to pass out or something."

"I'm okay," I repeated, not sure if I was, reaching for a drink to steady my mind.

"You're not linking this to us are you?"

"It's a warning."

"No, no, it's coincidence, an accident. It's lawless out there of a

night, all sorts of things happening."
"They're coming for me."
"They leave burnt out cars up there every night."
"They're coming for us," I said, my eyes opening wide, glaring at him, starting to slip again.
"Oh, come on man, snap out of it. You're in shock or something."
I pointed across to my filing cabinet, the key still hanging in the lock. "There…"
"What?"
"Bottom drawer."
"What is it?" he asked apprehensively, sharing my fear of papers and documentation before taking a step towards it, turning the key as metal rubbed on metal, screeching as he pulled the drawer open. He didn't give his usual WD40 comment as his hand emerged, grasping a bunch of coiled up papers, the furrows in his forehead disappearing as he jumped back, dropping them on the floor.
"What's that?"
"The dead," I replied, seeing my panic mirrored in his face.
"I didn't give you that many."
"The reporter," I mumbled.
"You told him?"
"Yes…"
"You fucking told him," he shouted, launching himself across the desk, grabbing me by the throat.
I felt him squeeze but offered no resistance, my airways tightening as his fingers dug in. Through watery eyes, his features were screwed up, teeth bared, eyes raging, still young, still in The Pit. All I felt was shame, 'I'm sorry' coming out in a wheeze as I started to fade again, welcoming the spots appearing in my vision, staying, joined by others as consciousness slipped away. He dropped me too early as I missed the chair and landed on the floor, gasping, filling my lungs as I remained there, wondering what might come next, the kicks? Stamping? Maybe the chair? But, nothing arrived, I could hear his breathing, heavy as he stood looking down on me. "Why?"
"To get proof."
"Of what?"
"What you suspected."
"It was just a stupid feeling."
"There's over fifty."

"Good God," Migsy said, slumping down into my chair.

"I told him not to. I told him to stop."

"You shouldn't have done it in the first place; it's personal, it's ours…"

"I don't know why I did it. Why the fuck did I do it?"

"At least we know now. The Nightman's been doing overtime."

"It's my fault, that he's dead."

"Going for glory I take it? Reporter of the year?"

I nodded in response, "Something like that."

"Never trusted him," he mumbled, shaking his head as he leant down and pulled me up. "You and me against the world again, it seems."

"Looks like."

"You strong? Can I count on you?"

"Yes, I'm good."

"Never go down like that again. You fight, whoever it is. You win." I could hear Jacko in his words as his finger hit my chest, opening a door in my mind, allowing a memory past its repression, taking me back to The Pit and a pep talk following a fight, one of brutal gouging and choking, the gloopy wetness of an eyeball still on my fingers, too exhausted to stand.

"Somethings coming," Migsy continued, sensing my mind was elsewhere.

"I know," I murmured in response, still in The Pit.

"Are you ready?" he asked, giving my cheek a gentle slap, refocusing me.

"Ready," I nodded, unsure what he was asking, feeling the opposite.

Our mood was like the weather the next day as dark clouds hung low, their drizzle limiting visibility, keeping our view to the immediate, as if the rest of the world had not been rendered, did not exist. The reporter was in my thoughts as he had been all night, flipping from anger to remorse to panic about what copies of the story might be out there. Maybe his death was coincidence, impersonal? A result of the lawlessness, the anger, the recalibration of society as the big picture was changing in a violent evolution. Nobody knew what the other side looked like, apart from the Jehovas Witnesses.

I'd drunk half a bottle of whisky by breakfast, trying to keep the hangover at bay, using it to knock back pills as I read the news, looking for distraction. The government was collapsing and the fault lines in society widening, pried open by malignant or beneficial forces, nobody knew. More mansions and yachts were burning, whilst emergency legislation allowed residents of Kensington, Chelsea and parts of Surrey to employ private armed security companies to protect them from the masses. Most were ex-special forces based in Hereford, though American and Israeli companies were knocking at the door.

One innocent man had already been killed, but this was deemed acceptable as fear warped morality.

"What was he doing walking down that road?" Marcus of Weybridge asked the TV reporter.

Migsy looked as grey as the clouds when he approached with a newspaper. A mint humbug was clattering around my teeth as I tried to conceal my breath.

"What have we done today?" I asked, expecting a joke in response but the furrows were back, deep across his brow as he pointed to a small article on page twelve.

"Not much then?"

"It's serious."

"What does it say?" I asked.

"Members of the Liverpool underworld are concerned about the impact of The Temple on their trade, blah, blah, blah,"

"That's pretty tame compared to the usual."

"It is," he agreed. "Almost pointless with everything going on, so why is it there?"

"Dunno," I shrugged. "Is it true?"

"I've arranged a parlay but word on the street says the club is not a problem."

"Then why? Lazy reporting?"

"Come on. You're usually good at piecing these things together."

"You said there was no link, I was being paranoid."

"The reporter, the Nightman…"

"You think?"

"It's either a warning or your card's marked, the clock's ticking."

"Tick-tock, tick-tock," I grinned.

"It's not a fucking joke."

"And you call me a drama queen."

"If the reporter was right, The Nightman has been killing and now he's coming for us."

"Last night you were all coincidence, don't worry," I said, waving my hand dismissively.

"They've set it up with this," he explained, tapping the article.

"Set what up?"

"Your death, you've got to be careful."

We were interrupted by the phone buzzing across my desk, relief flooding over me, seeing his name flash up, hearing his voice.

"He's back in prison, they've let him out of Ashworth," Yoda reported, his words without greeting or warmth.

"Dad?"

"Yes."

"Can I see him?"

"Yes," he replied, "this afternoon, I'm heading up there."

"Can I come with you?"

"I'll meet you there," he replied after a long pause. Probably the right decision. What would we say?

My heart was racing, filled with excitement as I strode through the streets towards the charred city below, passing familiar faces, no time to talk, head down, waiting impatiently at every checkpoint as they spoke to a little man in their chests, eyes flicking over me, up then down. The people and the city were different, glances seemed sinister, full of mistrust.

As a person of interest, I was recognised as I lowered my hoodie, causing them to tense up, all cheer dissipating as their hands subconsciously fingered the Heckler and Koch slung across their chests. Emotions were amplified, joy replacing dread as I was begrudgingly allowed to progress to the next, then the next, until I was eventually sat on the train seat, impatiently waiting for its departure, watching others climb on, looking for clues as they took their seats. Would they put a person on me or rely on the CCTV that had undoubtedly followed every step of my journey? I grinned, glancing up at the lens pointing down the carriage, thinking of the hoodie I wore and how it offered some sort of protection from the prying eyes. Peter's invisibility cloak.

The doors took an age to hiss then close with a bump before the first shudder racked through the carriage as I recollected the last time I'd made this journey, a different time, a different universe. How innocent it all felt, how trivial the problems, how I yearned for those days as city was replaced by the green of the engineered countryside streaking by.

Yoda was waiting for me as I entered the visitors lobby. I paused, unsure of how he would react until he held his arms open and I fell into them as they locked around me and pulled me in tight. There were no words, no need for words, I felt safe as I rested my chin on the top of his head.

We didn't go via the usual route as he hooked his fingers around my arm and pulled me into a side room, through a door I hadn't noticed before.

"This a shortcut?" I asked to no reply as we walked down a corridor before entering a small room; it looked like an interrogation cell, just a wooden table with plastic chairs scattered around.

"What's this?" I asked apprehensively. "The Chaplain's office?"

He turned, facing me, raising his hand to my cheek.

"Peter," the only word he said.

"What is it?" I asked more urgently.

"They found the body of your father this morning."

"Body?"

"He'd been attacked. He was dead when they discovered him in his cell. There was nothing they could do, I'm so sorry."

"What do you mean? But, no, he can't..." I gasped, finding it difficult to breathe, to inhale; the air felt thick, I was underwater, drowning, my lungs filling with water as I scrambled for air, gasping, not enough air.

"I'm so sorry," he repeated, pulling me back into him as the water disappeared and I was dry, trembling, panting, back in the room.

"I don't understand, he's locked in a cell, they can't..."

But deep down, I knew that they could, as guards turned the other cheek. Less paperwork.

"It's got all the signs of a contract," Yoda continued below me, talking to my chest.

"No, it's not true, it's not true," I repeated, knowing he was wrong.

"I'm so sorry, Peter."

"But how could they? It's impossible. It's a mistake. He's locked in a cell."

"No, Peter, I've seen it."

"Can I see him? I want to see him."

"No."
"No?"
"No, they've got to clean him up."
The door opened and a police officer entered, closing the door behind him, placing a folder on the desk before looking up at me almost mechanically.
"I'm so sorry for your loss," came the words, delivered without emotion, his eyes blank, staring forward, bored, like he went through this routine every day. I watched him as his features started to melt before disappearing, leaving just an oval and a mouth which continued moving, though no sound appeared to come out.
"What did they do to him?" I asked, still sure they had made a mistake.
"Shanked him, multiple stab wounds, a frenzied attack."
"He died quickly?"
"No, he bled out."
I gagged, then vomited onto the floor as Yoda manhandled me onto a chair, resting my forehead on the edge of the table as he rubbed the back of my neck, up and down, up and down.
"Deep breaths, deep breaths," I could hear him saying through the ringing in my ears. It felt as if time had stopped, was glitching, as his words and actions continued to repeat as the ground was shifting beneath us.
"I can guarantee, we'll do our utmost to catch the perpetrators," the officer was saying from a well- rehearsed script, the opposite of emotion as he looked down on both of us.
"Do you know of anybody that may have wished to hurt your father?"
"Oh just fuck off, will you," Yoda lashed out. "This isn't the time."
"No," I lied, as Kooky flashed through my mind, hearing his words, 'nobody is far away from me'.
'You've killed Clarkey, Bob Sponge, and now your father,' Peter giggled.
"Sorry?" The police officer asked.
"No, I don't know anybody that would want to kill him," I confirmed, looking up before reaching out and flicking open the folder before me.
I only saw it for a second, probably less as they both leapt forward, a photograph of a word scrawled across the wall, FROGIVE in

smeared blood that had dried brown, the letters a new font, haphazard, rushed, panicked as his body lay slumped below the misspelt word, eyes open, revealing his final thoughts at the point of death. It was me.

"What are you bringing that in here for?" Yoda screamed, wrenching it from my hands then ripping it and ripping it again until he could rip it no more.

"He's lost his father, you can't fucking show him that."

"He wasn't supposed to…" the officer started but Yoda cut him off.

"Get out. Get the fuck out," he roared, at a volume he saved for special occasions, but the image was branded into my mind, 'forgive' seared forever, although I knew I couldn't follow his final wish. I had to get out, I had urgent matters that needed to be attended to.

"Got to go," was all I could say, "Got to go," like a broken record, three simple words, on repeat, repeat, operating on auto-pilot as time shifted to fast-forward, walking down the corridor, back into the waiting room then outside, empty, unable to think, overwhelmed.

'Won't have to go there any more,' Peter whispered, the only coherent thought that entered my head as we walked across the carpark, towards a Capri.

"New car?"

"Yes, I thought fuck it, you only live…sorry."

"It's okay."

"Come home with me."

"I'm okay."

"You're not, come with me," he pleaded. I wasn't sure if it was a request or instruction.

"I need to be alone."

They were the only words spoken for the entire journey, repeated at certain points. I was turned away from him, staring out of the window, looking but not seeing as my mind was filled with rage, thoughts of violence, until he dropped me at the front door where Judy was waiting, sitting on the steps.

"I'm here for you," he said as I pulled on the lever, opening the door. "Forget everything else that's going on. I'm here for you."

"Thank you," I nodded, unable to muster a smile. "I just need to get my head around it."

"Alone?"

"Got company," I replied, nodded my head towards Judy before gently clicking the car door closed, then yanking it open and slamming it shut, fucking door.

As Yoda departed the black Range Rover arrived, Migsy sitting behind the wheel, staring forward, waiting as I walked back out past a panicking Judy, her grasping hands and sympathy left unrequited. He had that familiar look, the glazed eyes, the slight smile, there were no words, he understood.

His role was chaperone and observer, ensuring the level of retaliation was just as we found The Rip in dark corners, Migsy accelerating, sending them sprawling across the ground, limbs twisted, bones broken for me to take over, pulling me off before life left their bodies, preventing murder as I pummelled them, interrogating their broken faces.

I was Peter, raw, violent power as we descended upon the alleyways like Shiva, Apep or Perses, deities of destruction, striding through the estates, driving rats out of the sewers. Nothing else mattered, just revenge as Peter cackled, driving me on. They were fish in a barrel, arrogance ensuring they didn't flinch as we approached, protected by reputation, untouchable till touched, as fists struck, breaking bone, tearing skin and interrogation began.

"Where is he?"

"County lines…"

"Fuck off, county lines," as I returned the blade to its owner, sinking it slowly into his cheek then drawing it across as he let out a scream, repeat, repeat.

I was becoming increasingly brutal as frustration crept in. He was nowhere to be seen and word had travelled. They were harder to find, though the occasional tip off came our way. Sirens were closer in what had become a game of cat and mouse as we moved cautiously, trying to avoid detection.

"It's armed response," Migsy whispered, "we haven't got long."

I looked down at my hands, finding them covered in blood, waiting for revulsion but it was the opposite, exhilaration that set my heart racing with the thrill of it all. I turned to the side and licked the metallic taste off my fingers, connecting to something deep, a primal, truer version of me. This was Peter at his finest, predatory, as Migsy sat in frustration, banging on the wheel, we'd been through nine of The Rip but no Kooky, my father unavenged for now. Peter's work was done for the night as he faded, leaving me calm and accepting of my actions, tired and emotionless, as we pulled into a basement.

"God wasn't with us tonight."

"I'm not sure God would have approved," Migsy replied.

"They were the actions of a son," I declared, suggesting there was something honourable in my actions, seeking justification.

"They were righteous," he agreed, his language mirroring mine as we spoke like Eighteenth Century nobles. "An eye for an eye, only, we didn't get our eye, he's still out there."

"He'll run far away if he has any sense."

"Maybe, or he'll be consolidating."

Smiler was waiting with changes of clothes and a packed lunch of energy drinks and snacks, as if we'd just finished a charity run. It felt surreal as I opened the Tupperware to find a Bakewell tart in the corner of my box as if left there by a loving mother.

"Swap the plain for salt and vinegar?" Migsy asked, waving a bag in front of me.

"Whatever," my reply as he handed over a half-eaten pack, cheeky bastard.

"Good night lads?" Smiler asked as his latex clad hands took our clothes and placed them in a black bin bag. Somebody else was already in the car with wipes giving off a strong alcoholic smell, whilst another was inspecting the damage to the front.

"Could've been better," Migsy mumbled.

"Getting rusty?"

"Getting old," Migsy agreed.

"A few of them are in dock, in a bad way, sounds like fun."

"They speaking?"

"Nothing. I've sent a representative along to remind them of the etiquette in this situation."

"Great, can't tell with these kids. Police onto anything?"

"Nothing."

"Good. Eyes and ears, we need to find Kooky, finish the job."

"Will do."

"If the police get to him first, then tell them to stand off. We'll sort it out."

"They'd do that?" I asked, surprised.

"If we ask nicely," Migsy grinned.

We entered a dimly lit stairwell through a plain white door, climbing up the worn carpet of noisy step by noisy step before arriving at another door, this one padded with a gaudy fabric. A pale, skinny guard opened the door after three tiny knocks, fitting in with the décor and low lighting in his maroon velvet jacket and winkle picker shoes, screaming out cancer as he appeared to age before me, the wrinkles sinking deeper, multiplying across his sallow features. 'Lads' was his only word as Migsy handed over his phone before removing a silver handgun from his inside pocket. No shock registered on his face. He looked more concerned by my appearance as I stood still, waiting. I didn't know where we were. It didn't matter.

We entered a room of maroon flock wall paper, the strata of cigar smoke drifting through the air. It felt like a scene from the prohibition, the attendees decked out in smart tailored suits, speaking to each other with politeness and respect though there was tension as they walked tightropes, a wrong word here could cause violence for years. Sean from the funeral was the only face I recognised, though the others were similar in many ways, anonymous, middle aged and unremarkable, the unlikely heads of the criminal underworld.

We were the last, our arrival sending them to the large table at the centre of the room, each approaching a chair before looking over. "Sorry for your loss," was their means of introduction, travelling around the table as their masks showed the depth of feeling of an old family friend. This was the parlay, an event I'd wished to take no part in, however here I was, sitting amongst them as they studied the hands placed before me, still covered in blood.

They continued chatting, full of smiles and laughter as they discussed buying in the troughs and selling at peaks. Cybercurrencies had made them all traders as they discussed short and long game strategies, where to place your stops.

"You're very popular all of a sudden, sunshine," Sean began.

"What?"

"Contract went out on you last night."

"Who by?"

"Dark web, confidential," came the reply.

"How much?"

"Twenty-five."

"That's insulting."

"Some skaghead will take it on."

"Who?"

"Who d'ya think?"

"Kooky?"

"Small fry."

"Who runs him?" Migsy asked.

"You tell me," Sean replied. "He's one of the independents that appeared, after Jacko popped his clogs."

"Which means the Albanians, trying to get a foothold."

"They're knocking on the gate."

"How is this happening?"

"Things have changed since Jacko died. It's become atomised, difficult to control."

"So anyone can set up and start selling, phone the nearest Albanian?"

"To a degree."

"And you think that's alright?"

"Profits are fine and the place is quiet, the kids are just shooting each other."

"Or killing my father," I interrupted, causing all heads to turn in my direction.

"Kooky doesn't have that sort of reach," a man with pinched features declared, sounding bored. There had been no introductions though some of them were infamous, household names around the estates. This was Beak, I assumed.

"They killed him last night."

"There was a contract on him."

"From who? Where?"

"Dunno, dark web, McGinley and Farrow did it."

"Who?"

"Two on a long stretch. They aren't getting out so probably did it for their kids. Honourable really."

"Honourable?" I replied angrily.

Migsy's hand landed on my wrist as Beak gave a smirk.

"How much did they do it for?" I asked, wanting to know everything.

"Ten big ones."

"Why didn't you tell me?"

"What is this clown doing here?" Beak sighed, looking down on me, frustrated.

"Beak…" Sean warned.

"Because outside of this room we are all rivals," Beak explained. "I don't care if something bad happens to you."

"Touche," I replied, looking down at my bloodied fists, hands opening and closing, giving my anger away.

"I don't give a shit about your dad and if someone decides to kill you, they will fucking kill you."

"Beak…" Migsy repeated in a sterner tone.

"You sound as stupid as Kooky," I sneered, disappointed at the quality of criminal on display.

"Maybe I'll take up that contract," he shrugged, determined to have the last word. "Small change, but life's not all about money, is it?"

"Come on gentlemen, remember where you are," Sean interceded again, this time hitting the table with a gavel, making me jump. *'Where the fuck did he get that from?'* Peter protested, awoken.

"So, what's all this about The Temple?" Migsy asked, steering us away from each other.

"A load of shite is what it is," a voice popped up, one I'd never heard before. Pins apparently.

"Agreed," travelled around the table.

"So the press made it up?"

"No, there's a bigger play, we just don't know what it is."

"If profits are being affected then I am sure we can come to some sort of arrangement," Migsy suggested, fishing, "deal with it in a civilised manner."

"You don't allow drugs and they still take them. They've still got to buy them from somewhere, so we're fine."

The club was having a minor effect at most. It would have been a different conversation ten years ago, but most of them didn't own clubs anymore, investing in property and assets along with the standard sunbed and nail bars as they were the first to notice the downward curve.

"So, a contract went out last night and the media have lined it up," Migsy said, cutting through the chatter, trying to get the discussion back on track. I sat silent, hoping someone would give me the answer I needed, but they were back along a tangent, talking about the state of business whilst reminiscing about the good old days. Despite their rivalries it appeared they actually enjoyed each other's company, the conversations free and full of laughter as they spoke to perhaps the only people that fully understood them. There was fear behind the bravado, however. Instead of expanding, each was hunkering down, building a defensive wall to protect what they had from outsiders backed by faceless money, changing the dynamic of the drugs trade. Pins placed punt and cunt in the same sentence as he became agitated, arms flailing as he explained his unseen world. Whilst they had been investing in legal assets it appeared that legal money was coming the other way, seeking out the profits of their sphere via the usual parasitic middlemen, solicitors, accountants and enablers, seeking access to their lucrative trade.

"It's no different than you lot is it?" I said, acting provocative, "You don't get your hands dirty. Just brokers, leaving it to the kids to kill each other."

"There's blood all over the hands in this room, sunshine. It's a long apprenticeship."

Beak just tutted, muttering obscenities under his breath.

"So, the price on me?"

"What about it?"

"Well, what do I do?"

"Be careful."

"We've all got contracts on us."

"Yes, but I'm not you. I'm a fucking priest."

"Really?" Sean said, glancing at my hands and arching an eyebrow.

"How do we find out? How do you get paid?"

"It's completely anonymous, dark web," Sean repeated.

"Can I have word that none of your organisations, or affiliates, will take up the contract?" Migsy asked the table.

A series of 'aye's' travelled around, returning to medieval language as each of them focused on me.

"Cheers," I mumbled as the ground shifted beneath me, their faces pixelating into solid blocks of pink, giving the anonymity they craved as I struggled to hold on to reality.

'No such thing as reality,' Peter whispered.

"That doesn't mean you're off the hook," Sean warned. "You've heard the conversations tonight."

"A mysterious out-of-towner?"

"Yes, though of course, there is the other option."

"Which is?"

"He's back…"

"Who?"

"The Nightman."

We were asked to leave as they went onto other business. Migsy remained quiet, driving through silent streets as dawn was breaking, finding distraction in a couple making their way home, staggering, then vomiting on the pavement. We exchanged a glance and a smirk, "Fucking reprobates."

"What now?" I asked as we pulled up outside my front door, relieved to find no police cars present.

"Things are in motion," he replied with a shrug. "Get showered, then I'll take you back to the club."

"The Nightman…" I began.

"The fucking Nightman," Migsy repeated, arching an eyebrow, staring at nothing through the windscreen.

"He might not…" I offered optimistically.

"Or he might," he answered with a shrug. "Maybe we're next on his list. We've got to find him before he finds us."

I'd felt no regret as the blood washed from me, tinging the water red as it swirled down the plug hole, spinning away until it ran clear.

'Goes anti-clockwise in the Southern Hemisphere,' Peter informed randomly, making small talk, as I wondered what was wrong with me, feeling barren, remorseless as I thought of my father, closing my eyes to see the photograph flash before me, allowing it to run free, forgive, forgive, as I waited for a floodgate to open, a tidal wave to wash over me so I could crumple under its weight.

I was familiar with mourning and the reactions people go through: the anger, denial, non-acceptance as they stared into space. Everyone was different in the strength of response, that initial shock, disbelief, then screaming, shaking, insomnia, loss of appetite, followed by exhaustion, leaving them dazed and numb, lamenting over regrets and fears.

I'd seen them hitting walls, smashing windows, self-flagellation leaving them covered in blood, crying uncontrollably, inconsolable; that is what I wanted to be, normal. I tried to put my emptiness down to shock, a coping mechanism, a temporary denial to avoid pain and when the shock wears off, I could start grieving, because I needed to feel that pain.

'You'll feel nothing,' Peter revealed as memories of my father were being locked away with the rest of the dead.

I knew he was right. I was one of those that bottled it up, frustrating, wanting to shake their emotions out as I now stood, wondering if this is how they felt, a nothing that no amount of shaking would change, just an empty void, a shell, standing, dripping, cold and unmoved, Peter.

'You can't mourn until he's dead.'

"Who?" I asked my reflection in the cracked mirror, watching my face as it contorted down one side.

'Kooky, you need to kill him.'

There was a controlled and controlling hate that coloured everything. Instead of Dad, images of last night filled my mind as I repeated the violence, muscles twitching, their memories fresh as it played over. Fact mixed with fiction as I imagined scenarios of Kooky, kicks and blows beautifully delivered before toying with him, slowing things down for that moment when he'd realise. Memories from The Pit joined the party, sending my heart racing, the veins throbbing in my temples as my thoughts wove a violent and bloody fabric, my lips drawing back, baring teeth like a dog before I dropped to my knees and prayed, asking for forgiveness, understanding, the words empty as they left my lips in a whisper. My mind was elsewhere, wondering where my father was now, amongst the stars perhaps, a dark energy expanding.

"Do you want a cup of tea love?" The voice called from the hallway.

"Yes please Ginny, I'll be down in a minute."

Time was fluid, fluctuating, on fast-forward, events changing rapidly as if decisions had been made behind closed doors, in those secret rooms. I didn't remember getting dressed, the cup of tea, the journey as I arrived on the cobbles and turned the corner to The Temple. I was no longer in control, an observer looking through my own eyes, my movements mechanical, detached from everything, giving the soldiers a murmured hello as I approached the barricade whilst flicking a wave towards Degsy sitting on his perch, his pale stomach bulging out below his sweatshirt as he raised a hand and spat out crumbs from his petrol station scotch egg.

My emptiness vanished as I entered the club, a hollow corpse now overflowing with one emotion, regret as I faced the cavernous space, feeling like I didn't belong. I'd changed since yesterday, completely. I was now impure, corrupted, my true self, driven by rage and revenge, those most un-Christian of qualities. I wanted to run as familiar faces approached, fearing they'd notice the change, my red eyes, forked tongue, horns piercing my scarred head. I was feeling like a stranger, unrecognisable as they embraced me, pulling me in tight as my body recoiled but remained limp, letting them paw me, molest me.

'This is how it feels,' Peter whispered, dripping with condescension, *'with your banal utterances about an end to suffering, being in a better place.'*

It was role reversal. Their words and voices loaded with emotion, demanding some in return, wanting me to lean into them, to need them. I muttered the obligatory thank yous before reaching Gabe who planted his palm on my forehead as I stood still, feeling obliged to let him do his thing whist Libby hugged me from behind, her beer fumes wafting around us as I tried not to breath. Next came Molly who'd stepped out from the Red Square, handing me a cappuccino in a Styrofoam cup with a bite mark. She washed them. Sustainability.

"You can have that half-price love, sorry about your Dad."

"Thanks."

It seemed to take an hour to wade through their sickly sweet sympathy, like treacle as they demanded a reaction, a breakdown as they piled on wave after wave of pity and compassion. I considered shedding crocodile tears to satisfy them, pay my debt and hopefully get past, but that could have encouraged them, driven them into a frenzy, so I had to take my time, looking solemn whilst remaining cheerful as their faces blurred then dissolved, personalities disappearing as the faceless ones kept coming. I didn't know them. Migsy was in the office waiting with his feet on the desk as he let out a huge yawn, the night before catching up with him.

"She's gone," were his first words.

"Who?" I replied in panic. I hadn't seen Judy for what felt like days. So caught up in myself, I'd not even asked Ginny about her.

"Mary."

"What? Why? How do you know?"

"Because she had to," he said, pointing towards my desk. The computer screen was on.
"But she was doing so well."
"She had to," he repeated.
"Why? What is it?"
"Misguided," he suggested with a tut. "She's left you a gift."
There was an envelope with my name scrawled upon it, a note inside, written in barely legible handwriting,
I told you I'd give them to you, knew them bodycams would come in handy! It's my parting gift, time to leave, the bodies are piling up.
"What does she mean by that?"
"It means she's got a sixth sense."
"Eh?"
"Clarkey, The Reporter, your Dad, she's got a point," Migsy said, echoing Peter's words. "The Nightman's knocking on your front door; oh, wait, that got shot as well."
I watched the video on the screen, Kooky and The Rip caught on body camera, groping and abusing, snorting drugs, far too relaxed in their surroundings. They'd let their guard down, their egos getting the better of them talking openly about business, drug deals, territory, beatings and killings. Clarkey's name woke the rage from its temporary reprieve, my default emotion, as they sat in a circle laughing, re-enacting his murder followed by clips of youths brought in and beaten for fun, passed around and battered until unconscious or a blade flashed, then beaten more, disfigured or urinated on if they'd become bored. Then there were the girls, some of them barely conscious, passed around, forced into sexual acts, given another line if they weren't feeling compliant whilst others revelled in it: the violence, the debauchery, doing the rounds, fellating Kooky as he stood overlooking it all, like Caesar.
I recognised most of them, some from last night. They'd look different this morning, the abusers, smashed up and full of doubt.
'You did right,' Peter whispered. *'What use is prayer in this place?'*
It was hard to disagree.
"What do we do with it?" I asked, breaking from my inner dialogue, looking up at Migsy.
"It's already done," he said with a hint of disdain. "She's sent it to the police."
"So, they're after him as well?"

"I'd assume so. He'll go to ground, too many eyes."
"So tonight?"
"Not worth it, he'll be gone. Missed our moment, I'm afraid."
There was disappointment and relief. It was a pause, a chance to come back, to the real world, to Judy, to Ginny, to the club which had tolerance and forgiveness built into it, hoping it would give me another chance. But Peter was right, there were some things religion wasn't shaped for, at least my version; perhaps I was impatient, to see justice now instead of the next life.
I was relieved to see The Succubus arrive at lunch time, holding me in an embrace, allowing myself to sink into this one as she stayed quiet, not trying to saturate me with words, her hold enough.
"You okay?" was as deep as she went, my nodded response sufficient.
"Building Fort Knox?" she asked.
"Migsy's asked them to make the barrier a bit stronger. Mary went to the police with some rather controversial footage, so not sure what's going to happen."
"There's a bit stronger, then there's that," she laughed as I realised how much I needed her, loved her, loathed her, my anger dissipating as I stepped back and looked at the bulge, my future in the real world, all that mattered.
"What do you mean?"
"You don't know?" she asked, offering her hand, guiding me, allowing me to conceal feelings as she led me past the disabled Dodgeball team, through the daylight of the door to be faced with a line of arses poking out of jeans as their owners slapped in mortar and tapped blocks into place whilst whistling tuneless tunes.
"What are you doing?" I asked the arses.
"I was getting tired sitting on the barricade," Degsy replied with a groan, as he stood up, his hand going to his lower back.
"So you're building a wall?"
"Yes, Migsy told me to."
I glanced across to Migsy, who shrugged. "I just asked them to make it a bit stronger."
"Why?"
"You know why," he replied.
"It's illegal, you can't," I said, turning back to Degsy. "We'd need planning permission or something."

"Planning permission? Seriously? Like you need planning permission to burn down a building or board up our park?" A snort came from one of the builders as they continued working their way along, one course at a time.

"It's okay anyway. We're putting a door in," Degsy offered.

"Oh, well that's fine then."

I glanced over at the soldiers who were looking on bemused, their words falling upon deaf ears as the bricklayers continued regardless, cracking jokes and telling them to fuck off when they could be bothered. The military were a permanent presence outside the barrier, placing us under surveillance, a welcoming party, watching who comes in and out as people started to arrive, responding to encrypted messages flying through the air, as if this was the last chance to enter. They could sense something, smell trouble in the air; perhaps something remarkable was happening, though I could only see a breezeblock wall as I turned back towards the club, laughing quietly as I spotted Degsy's car parked down the side before stopping as a sudden urge to be alone crept over me, a cold shudder travelling through me as Peter demanded I move quickly, to have a meeting with myself. I needed to suffer.

I wondered if I'd taken my tablets, knowing my thoughts were erratic, my grasp on reality slipping as I clanged up the stairs, reaching into my pocket and swallowing a couple more as I recoiled from the noise which seemed louder than usual.

The office was perfect, empty as I closed the door and clicked the lock, leaving the lights off, buckling as anger overwhelmed me. I was raging again, though this time at myself, for smiling, for laughing, a day after my father was murdered as the surgeon watched from the corner, his hand stroking quickly as I ran across and threw a punch, my fist flailing through empty space. The bodies were piling up Mary said, and she was right, I could hear them, squirming in the darkness.

'It's your fault,' was Peter's first malignant whisper, the first salvo of a brutal onslaught which left me drenched with sweat, whimpering under my desk as I tried to stay silent, still, to ride through it, but I had to move, pacing around the room erratically, crashing into things in the darkness, finding no escape from myself.

Peter roared as I clawed at skin and tugged at my hair, grappling with myself as I smashed my face into the desk before slamming the letter opener through my left hand.

'Not enough,' he screamed, laughing, demanding more as I slowly banged staples into my arm before I swayed and it all went white, the walls, the ceiling, I'm trembling, I can't move.

It felt different, like reality was changing as I lay, focusing on my arm stretched out before me, illuminated by the strip of light coming under the door. I didn't recognise it, the pale exposed skin, the faint web of white lines running up from the wrist, hairs standing on end as dark veins came to the surface like liquid filled balloons. I wished it would crumble away, like a vampire in the sunlight, into a pile of atoms, a heap of stardust blown in different directions, never to meet again as my soul became liberated before remembering God as I pulled myself back to my knees, feeling my crotch, relieved it was dry before praying, grateful that the words would actually come as my mind was muted and blurry. Weeping, I begged for salvation, before my thoughts drifted to the spotty teenager, pleading for him to end the game.

Two shadows interrupted the strip of light as the game continued, the rapist, the succubus gently tapping on the door.

"Are you okay?"

I remained silent, afraid of further punishment if I spoke with her.

"Peter, come on, answer. I know you're there."

"Yes," I replied quietly.

"Can you let me in?"

"Yes," I repeated, unable to say no as I lifted myself from the floor and stood, my head spinning, the room swaying as I switched on the light, blinking rapidly as my eyes adjusted, feeling like I'd just woken up from something.

"Christ, you look like shit," she said, stepping towards me, her hand going to her mouth as her eyes glowed red.

"You're covered in blood. Who did this to you?"

"God."

"Let me get some help."

"No…"

"What do you mean? You're covered in blood."

"Just water," I mumbled, "Please."

"Your Dad?"

"Yes."

She pulled me close, I could feel the bump pressing but I was wary of her now, her touch cold, reptilian.

'A *reptile baby*,' Peter whispered, as she murmured the usual reassurances before disappearing, retuning with a cleaners bucket full of water, gently washing me before taking my hand and leading me down the stairs, not so loud now as she jabbered away in front of me.

"You shouldn't be alone."

She was right, my spirits rising as we entered the hall, seeing familiar faces, absorbing strength from them as they kept me from myself.

Then we were outside, the wall before us complete, with a row of people standing on chairs and bins looking over it as screaming came from the other side.

"What's that?"

"Think it's Degsy," Judy replied.

"What are they doing to him?" I asked, as the wails continued. "Doesn't sound human."

"Dunno."

"What's he shouting?"

"Timotei or something," she replied, standing still, listening intently.

"Isn't that shampoo?"

"He's doing the Hakka," Stan announced as we got to the wall.

"What?"

"The Hakka," he repeated, slightly annoyed that I'd asked again.

"Why?"

"Because he's finished the wall."

"I didn't realise he was a Kiwi."

"He's not, he just likes it."

They shuffled along, allowing me space on a chair to glance over, watching three of them performing independent routines, like body-poppers randomly sticking out their tongues in a wide legged stance. The soldiers before them looked genuinely concerned, not for their own welfare but for Degsy, wondering what traumas he had gone through to end up like this as they finished with a scream, eyes bulging, drawing a finger across the throat as the spectators behind the wall broke out into a frenzy of cheers and applause.

The soldiers looked bewildered as they turned their backs and they came through the doorway, victorious, tears streaming down

Degsy's face, overcome with emotion.

"Cries at the word Hakka," Big Jim murmured from the crowd.

"Cries at The Fox and the Hound," Elvis replied as pats on the back and hugs were coming thick and fast, his tears becoming wails, drawing more people to him into a self-perpetuating cycle.

I remained outside, milling around, talking to others or to myself, afraid to go back in, frightened of the club as the Hare Krishna's were doing their rounds. It felt like a normal evening, the good old days which were not that old as tables and chairs filled the streets and shop windows lit up.

"What are you going to do, it's nearly curfew?" I was asking.

"All night bender," or "We'll kip here," their defiant replies as if sensing an ending or new beginning.

"They're not gonna come here, are they? With our wall?" they rationalised as a big cheer went up then chants of 'Degsy' as he lapped up the adulation, two pints away from pissing himself.

Whatever was happening was beyond my control. I was outside of it now, an exile as it functioned without me, a sealed little world, an island as I switched the lights on for probably the last time, sending bright colours spinning across the elevations in defiance.

From that point I just observed, watching colours reflecting in the windows, necking a quart of rum quickly, determined not to enjoy it, sitting sour in my stomach as a drone flew over the wall before crashing to the ground, shot down with an air rifle, Kemosabe running out to recover his prize before re-assuming his position, waiting for the next one to hover over.

"Pull," he shouted with a giggle, an inner city pheasant shoot.

Music was pulsing from the doors, the revelry steadily growing as alcohol was consumed, though I couldn't allow myself to join in as I stepped into the drugs clinic, finding the consumption room empty as I became degenerate, searching through the bins in a minesweep that even Libby would find deplorable as I pushed in the dirty syringes, one after the other, drawing out blood then pumping it back in again, hoping for some residue to take me away from myself.

'Have you considered the long term implications?' Peter giggled.

"There is no long term," I muttered.

Then I was back, standing on the edge, slightly numb, pretending I was invisible, dead, observing friends enjoying each other's company, all the faces there as I took comfort in my melancholy. Most of them sought me out, treading on eggs as they spoke in serious and sombre tones befitting of the occasion, understanding my reluctance to join in, probably glad as they did their bit before returning to laughter until Judy came to rescue me, cutting through them, taking me to one side.

"You okay?"

"Yep," I replied. The needles had numbed me, taken the edge off.

"Migsy wants you in the office."

"Why can't he come here? I'm in mourning."

"Because it's important."

"Come on then, let's see what he wants," I replied, clinging to her like a child scared of the dark.

"Just you. I don't want any part of it."

"Of what?"

"He's found Kooky," she whispered.

She hadn't finished her sentence as Peter kicked in, all aggression and purpose as he pushed past, entering The Temple and striding across the dancefloor towards the stairs. I jumped them in twos as they boomed in the space, my mind racing with pleasure, about what I would do, about closure, about justice, an eye for an eye, Old Testament style as my heart was beating, my temples throbbing. I turned the handle and strode in.

"Where is he?" leaving my lips as I looked around.

"Here," came the reply as the door closed behind me.

Time stopped as I froze mid-stride, turning quickly to see the silver barrel pointing at me, anger, confusion then relief washing over me. I felt like a child again, powerless as I waited for it to ring out but it never came, it was his mouth that made the first sound.

"Alright?"

"She said Migsy..."

"Migsy, Kooky, were all the same."

I could sense the fear in his voice, trembling slightly at the high points. I admired him in a way, the lengths he would go to, beyond that of a normal person.

"You know why I've got to do it?" he asked, "after last night."

"I had no choice, you killed my father."

"That's not true, but I doubt you'll believe me."

"I don't..."

"And you'll kill me?" he asked, seeking justification.

"In a heartbeat," I replied, giving it to him.

"Then you understand."

"I do," I nodded, opening my arms wide, the fear and anger leaving me as I realised this was it, my nightmare nearly over as Peter screamed with rage.

"You don't seem bothered."

"I'm not."

All I could think of was Dad.

"You're a hard cunt, I'll give you that," he said as he raised the barrel towards me, seeming to take for ever as it trembled in his grip before a huge blast sent me flying to the ground, my vision going white, eardrums burst and head exploding in fireworks of pain.

There was nothing to look at, nothing to hear, just white as I lay there, my thoughts clear as I felt no discomfort, no emotion, just contentment, peace for the first time as sounds slowly swirled before beginning to permeate, drifting in from the outside world, the door opening then slamming shut.

"Fucking Hell," made me smile as I slowly opened my eyes, expecting to look down onto the scene, at my body, empty and lifeless. Instead, I was looking up at Willo's face, looking down at me, panicking.

"What the fuck happened?"

I remained silent, doubting he could hear me from the afterlife.

"Peter, get up, come on, we can't fuck about."

The world came rushing back as I sat up with a jerk, taking a deep breath as I started feeling my body again, glancing across to see Kooky slumped against the wall, a deep red stain spread across his chest as he stared back at me, eyes wide and glazed, an eternal look of surprise set in his features.

"You shot him?"

"No," I replied, shaking my head.

"Did he shoot himself?"

"No," I replied. "There must be somebody else here," as I shakily got to my feet, looking around frantically behind desks, not understanding.

"There's nobody here," Willo shouted, grabbing me by both arms, his voice barely perceptible through the whistling in my ears.

"There must be…"
"We've got to go," he said, running out of the door before reappearing and locking it behind him.
"They're here."
"Who?"
"The army, the police, all of the bastards. They drove through the wall."
"What for?"
"It's a raid, they're arresting everybody."
"Fuck."
"If they see this, you're fucked."
"But I didn't…"
"They don't give a shit, you'll go to jail."
"We're trapped…" I stammered,
"There," he said, pointing up at a grille in the wall.
"The aircon duct?"
"That's it," he shouted, pushing my desk screeching across the room, drowning out the first sounds of battle as he eased a knife into the slot and started unscrewing whilst I stood numb, unable to take it all in, watching as he climbed up, scrambling in, his legs kicking as he tried to gain purchase on the smooth surface.
"Peter," he shouted, jolting me from my stasis, rousing me to follow, moving against the drag of lethargy as I clambered up and pulled the grill closed behind me, twisting like a contortionist in the smooth narrow space, the smell of cordite overwhelming.
"This is the place," I said, sliding behind Willo until he reached a larger vertical duct.
"Thank fuck for that, there's a ladder," he grinned before swivelling around onto his belly and lowering himself onto its rungs. I looked back at the grille, the scorch marks between two slats giving a clear view into the office before clambering down until landing on a smooth, horizontal surface. I followed as he crawled before me, hitting a dead end, huddling behind another grille, fresh air wafting in from outside.
"Someone's been in here, can you smell it?"
"Certainly can, but who?" he replied.
"Dunno…"
"Migsy?"
"Why would he hide in a ventilation duct?"

"Fat bastard wouldn't fit anyway. It's like a priest hole, isn't it."
"What?"
"This, like how they used to escape from the old castles and stuff."
I placed a finger to my lips as the metallic clattering of the grille above filled the tube, the air vibrating with sound waves and tension as we paused like frozen statues, wondering if it had just fallen off until voices, then sounds of movement started echoing around us. The muffled thud of a body clambering into the narrow space reverberated along the duct, joined by the visible, a beam of light filling the void above, as we glanced at each other and I closed my eyes, sensing the bodies writhing around me. I tried to move, unable to in this confined space as the metal walls were pressing in, condensing the fear and rage.
'Fight,' Peter screamed, pulling me back from an attack, *'Fight!'*
Silence was no longer an option as I started kicking, trying to move the grille to the outside but it kept bouncing back as the shuffling above came closer, a radio blurring into life, echoing around the chamber, confirming their identity as I started to panic, lashing out at the grate before Willo clambered over me.
"Wait," he whispered, grabbing hold of the slatted metal and gently twisting. It moved, squealing to the right, pivoting on one screw, creating a narrow opening through which I gratefully slid, the feeling of claustrophobia replaced by one of freedom, the analogy not lost on me.
"The ladder, get the ladder," I hissed as Willo leant back in, pulling as a hand had grasped the other end, the sound and light becoming physical in a tug of war between anonymous opponents as I clambered in next to him, joining in the contest until they let go before being dragged into the void as we yanked the ladder out, sending it clattering onto the ground as Willo, the more composed of us, took a second to push a rusty nail into the empty bolt hole, banging it in with a rock, the grille now locked.
We fled across the wasteland, almost laughing as adrenaline surged, giving no thought to long term implications. We were in the moment, now, giving in to primal instinct before turning to see the silhouette of The Temple surrounded by throbbing blue lights captured in emerging smoke and the first sounds of combat.
"Come," Willo whispered as I followed obediently, my mind still numb, sedated by drink, drugs and trauma as we made our way

through back alleys, scraping along walls and tripping on cracked flags, cursing silently as my hand was filled with splinters off an old boarded up entrance, before entering the house through the back door, giving me a moment to pause, to breathe, the flash of happiness overwhelmed by pain, then anger, at the cruelty of life as I realised home was no longer home. It had been taken from me.

"Alright love," Ginny greeted with a wave as we walked through.

"They're coming Gran."

"Who?"

"The police, can you hold them up for us?"

"Course I can love, I'll just act stupid."

We ran upstairs and started throwing things into a bag, Willo shouting down the phone as sirens were approaching until the flashing blue light filled the room. My heart leapt with a thumping on the front door then a long pause as we could hear Ginny shuffling about shouting, "Alright, aright," as she slowly made her way down the hallway.

"Fuck," I whispered as fear crept in with thoughts of Dad and prison.

Willo ran across the room, opening the wardrobe then climbing in, hide and seek as the doors closed behind him.

"This is no time for fucking around, they'll find you," I hissed, chasing after him, wondering if he was abandoning me, if it was his turn to be overwhelmed as I yanked open the doors to find a bright white room behind a row of shirts, hanging on a rail.

"What?"

"Come, we haven't got long," he beckoned from the other side.

My feet were rooted, I couldn't move.

"It's a fake wall," he shouted, his voice spurring me into action as I heard Ginny talking to the police below.

"Oooh no love, who is it you want again?"

"What is this? Narnia?" I whispered.

'Mr Ben,' Peter shouted as I threw my bag then clambered through, looking around in awe at the surrounding clinical white surfaces of a parallel universe.

"It's my lab," he replied, his manner changing, becoming professional as he hurried me across the sterile room.

Despite the urgency, I was dragging my feet, unable to speak as I tried to absorb it, grabbing a handful of pills and blotting paper off a steel tray then stuffing them in my bag. He pulled me into the decrepit hallway, half-indoors, half-out as I looked up at the night sky, flashing a rhythmic, electric blue through a gaping crack in the walls and hole in the roof. Ivy cascaded down the peeling damp wallpaper in this subsequent parallel universe, where the pandemic had succeeded, wiping humans from the face of the Earth.

"If only he hadn't eaten pangolin in the fish market," I murmured.

"What?" Willo replied, his face crumpled in confusion. I'd stopped, gazing at the crack.

"Might have been a bat," I continued.

'It's like the fucking Faraway Tree,' Peter whispered.

Urgency replacing wonder as I returned to this world. We now had to move slowly, fighting instinct, stepping carefully down the rotten timber treads until I slipped on the algae coated wood and bounced down the bottom two, landing on the grime coated tiles of the hallway.

"Minton," I said, admiring their quality beneath the grime, putting my hand to my mouth as he reproached me with a glance. He peered through the perforations of the canned up window before pointing silently towards the back door as we continued to slowly creep.

I could hear their voices, Judy amongst them, shouting on the other side as Willo slid a key into the corrugated panel, a makeshift door, before sneaking out into the overgrown jungle, the next abstract world to stop at the top of the tree as I gently placed it back without making a sound. My eyes were adjusted but I still couldn't make sense of the dense tangle of green before me as I followed the shape of Willo, creeping silently through the undergrowth until a "pssssst," and we froze, Willo beckoning me forward behind a crumbling wall, finding One Ball sat astride a quad bike, giving a flash of teeth and a cheerful wave.

'Expected Moonface,' Peter giggled.

My instincts said no as I hesitated, The Cornerman looking at me, confused, before a hand grabbed me by the arm and dragged me forward, climbing pillion onto the back.

Noises were emerging from inside the house as they'd discovered Narnia, a loud crack of splintering wood followed by a scream revealing they'd reached the hallway as the stairs slowed their pursuit. They were now proceeding more cautiously, their beams of light sweeping past the openings, joining those coming around the sides from body armoured silhouettes, unable to stop the ground from crunching beneath their boots as they crept, oblivious to our presence as we sat in the dense copse.

The chance of a silent escape disappeared as One Ball switched on the engine, his lights immediately illuminating the black clad police who recoiled in shock as he let out a squeal of joy before sending the quad bike lurching forward, straight towards them, their graphite clad forms diving out of the way as others ran towards us, shouting, radios blaring, attracted to the commotion as he slid the quad around the corner, accelerating quickly for the road. I was hanging on by my fingerprints, sure I couldn't last much longer as he slalomed from left to right, emerging into the street light, swerving between police cars and soldiers as he cackled manically. I bolted upright, hearing Judy scream my name, almost slipping off as we sped into oncoming traffic, head lights flashing, horns blaring as they swerved to avoid us. One Ball accelerated, bouncing onto the pavement, giving us a chance to see the scale of the operation, blue flashing lights everywhere, like multiple strobes from multiple sources, illuminating a column of throbbing blue smoke rising above the club as the battle progressed.

I clung on as he swerved through the park gates, avoiding the road block that was rapidly approaching. Then we were into the trees, trunks flashing as we rebounded off the uneven ground, expertly swerving around obstacles before bursting out onto the colonnaded terrace, a remnant of The Piggeries, giving a grand panorama of the battles below.

It gave us a moment to pause, to catch our breath and comprehend what was happening. Looking down onto the club a mass of bodies were moving, waves travelling through them, like a concert, as they fought an almost medieval battle, all violence along a front line, truncheons meeting fists. A Molotov cocktail illuminated the scene briefly, exploding against one of the army trucks as Lurkers attacked from behind, removing any organisation from the military ranks as they broke formation and it descended into a free-for-all, as guerrilla tactics gained the upper hand. Reinforcements were arriving as spots of light cut diagonally across the black of the park, scramblers and quad bikes like fireflies, supply lines to the skirmishes delivering troops and ammunition, bottles to be ignited.

Above, there was similar chaos. A strata of smoke hung, capturing
pulsing blue light, as a line of police formed a halo at the top of the
hill, attempting to control the estate whilst a helicopter hovered
overhead. Its light descended like a tractor beam, malevolent,
illuminating an unknown front of the battle before becoming
agitated, moving more than it should, as if alive, feeling pain from
the hundreds of laser pointers directed back at it, until it rose,
climbing out of range, focusing its all-seeing eye onto another scene.
"What's happening?"
"A big fuck-off raid is my guess," Willo replied. "They've been
wanting to do this for years."
I thought back to Kooky, the timing. "You don't think they were in
on it, do you?"
"Wouldn't put it past them……Go," he shouted, then, "Go, go, go,"
as he started bucking up and down, pointing into the black as a
shadow broke from the trees and came running towards us.
"What?" I panicked.
"Nightman…"
"Fuck," One Ball shouted, as the quad took a millisecond to
accelerate from nothing, long enough for a hand to grab my collar
and wrench me off as the bike lurched forward. I instinctively
lashed out as I hit the ground, kicking and punching fresh air, a
ghost, as I flailed at nothing.
"Hello sweetheart," were the first words I heard from The
Nightman as he stood looking over me, fear keeping me immobile,
paralysed by fables and rumours. It struck me how normal his voice
sounded. I'd expected gravelly and coarse, evil dripping off every
syllable as his hand moved down towards me, my limbs remaining
motionless before time moved from slow motion to fast forward
and he was gone, the huge frame of Smiler ramming into him,
knocking him sideways to the ground before a spray of gravel filled
the air.
A hand grabbed my backpack and dragged me along, choking me
as I thrashed around, trying to grasp hold with both hands until we
came to a stop, allowing me to scramble up. I turned to find the
silhouette of a figure, standing, watching Smiler just about maintain
his balance as he fled down the hill. The bright light of the
helicopter swept past, illuminating The Nightman for a moment as
he dusted himself off and turned back towards me. I couldn't help

but stare at this enigma, a giant, built by urban folklore, standing before us in human form. Our eyes remained locked as we accelerated into the void, the blackness between battles, watching him disappear into darkness as the helicopter's beam continued its journey, its light passing by, seeking something, someone.

We stopped in the deeper darkness under the trees, all panting with exertion as Willo was hissing frantically into his phone, "The tower? Fuck, The Old Cellar? Shit…"

"What's up?" I asked, as he placed the phone into his pocket.

"They're closing in," he replied, moving urgently, looking out nervously from our darkness.

"Who?"

"Snatch squads. It's not just The Nightman chasing you."

"Why would snatch squads be after me?"

"Because you're a murderer."

"I'm not."

"To them, you are."

We looked across the fields to see a barely perceptible band of darkness tightening, a kettle in slow motion, as rapidly moving lights inside jerked frantically, pinging around like atoms, like fish sensing the net.

"Phone," Willo said, holding out his hand.

I looked at him perplexed.

"Give me your phone," he repeated, as I realised what he was asking, handing it over as he stuffed it into his inside pocket.

"We're splitting up."

"Where are you going?"

"The estate," he said, pointing up the hill. "They'll never get in, it's safe in there."

"Well, where am I going?"

"He'll take you to Migsy." came the reply.

The helicopter's beam was swaying left to right as it searched within the confines of the net. One Ball switched off the lights and drove steadily in large arced curves, like the doodles of a child, avoiding the sweeping beam from above before it stopped and moved in a straight line to the terrace, where we had just been. Silhouettes in black arrived like ants moments later, scurrying around, frustrated, waiting for instruction in this grown-up game of manhunt.

I raised my arms, feeling branches whip across my face as he drove through shrubbery before coming to a halt behind undergrowth, the ground clear and musty smelling, where daylight could not reach. He was whispering quietly into his phone. I still didn't trust him, wondering if he'd heard about Kooky.

'*Slip away,*' Peter whispered, as if One Ball might hear.

I felt exposed as he occasionally turned and glanced at me, before re-joining his conversation, leaving me wondering if this is where it would happen, vengeance, revenge. Options were limited, it was with him in here, or out there with The Nightman, as I sat and patiently waited, my fist clenching and unclenching, wondering how to ride a quad bike as I silently moved to the edge, ready to run, until the moment was lost as a scrambler approached, headlights off.

'*Take him now,*' Peter hissed.

"Best night ever kidda," the rider announced, overflowing with joy as he climbed off to embrace his associate.

'*There's two, fast and hard,*' Peter counselled, as I remained on the cusp of fight or flee.

"It's not finished yet," One Ball grinned, "they've bought all their toys with them."

"What do you want?"

"I need to get him up to the subby."

The hoodie looked past him, the faceless hole pausing on me.

"Alright Father," he greeted.

"Alright," I replied, glancing at his raised fist, realising it was Love Knuckles.

"Joining the party?"

"Wouldn't miss it for the world," I grinned, trying to put on a brave front.

"The subby?" Love Knuckles continued, turning back to One Ball.

"That's where they've set up camp."

"Willo said. It's the only place left, apparently," One Ball replied with a shrug. "Can you do it?"

"We'll get you in, mate," Love Knuckles confirmed, turning to me. "They're fucked up there."

I glanced across to find they'd turned into wolves, slathering, saliva dripping from their open jaws filled with pointed teeth, circling as I wondered if I could control dogs with my mind. I was calm, deliberating if this was drugs or psychosis, probably a bit of both, it didn't matter, it was a suitable metaphor, they were dangerous, whichever form they took. It was their pack instinct that was keeping me safe however, as he went on to explain that government had shuffled police forces and they were battling South Yorkshire on the ridge. It was a cruel touch, ill-conceived and certain to backfire as the us-and-them mentality rose above local issues, Kooky and The Rip relegated for the time being as differences were put to one side and tribal instinct brought us together, under one banner. It was a paradox that never made sense to me, how they could unite on one level, yet still mete out such cruelty to each other on another.

Love Knuckles explained how South Yorkshire's finest were in disarray as all communications had been blocked. All fronts were isolated, acting independently of each other, creating chaos as they didn't know the lay of the land.

"Hacked they reckon. Whenever they switch their radios on they just hear '*Ye-Ma.*'"

"Be Hacker Packer that, mate."

"Ano, clever bastard."

They went on to formulate a plan, sending messages like executives on their Blackberry's as the eye in the sky was mobile again, like a malevolent God, our Sauron, its beam of light searching as I jumped at every sound, hyper-sensitive, expecting The Nightman to come rushing from the darkness.

"We're gonna make a diversion," Love Knuckles announced proudly after a few minutes. "You need to sit-off by the sub-station until you see Migsy."

"And what? Is he going to drive up and collect me?" I asked sarcastically.

"No idea," One Ball replied. "Just following orders."

"Swap clothes," Love Knuckles instructed as he started undoing his jacket, pulling down his trousers, leaving them gathered around his ankles.

"What?"

"Swap, they're looking for you. I'll make sure they follow me," he replied, now in underpants and socks.

"But…"

"Just fucking do it," One Ball demanded, glancing out, stress levels rising as I capitulated and started stripping off.

We were clumsy as we tried to exchange clothes quickly, grunting, falling over as we were trying to observe our surroundings, tripping over as I tried to pull my trousers over my shoes.

"You sound like you're fucking cottaging," One Ball hissed, as grunts became groans became giggles as we lurched around.

"I'm not ugly enough," Love Knuckles complained as he stood minutes later, dressed as a priest.

"Do I have to walk like an ape?" I retaliated, receiving a grin for my efforts. I could see little difference, just the white collar as I faced him, dressed head to toe in black Lowe Alpine, complete with a cap. There was more talking as they made final arrangements, then fist bumps before the newly ordained Love Knuckles quietly moved off. One Ball was busy covering the bike in branches, in case the helicopter picked us out apparently.

"Did you know, the stealth bomber shows up on radar the size of a pigeon?" he declared, piling on sticks as I watched bemused.

"A pigeon that travels at 500 miles an hour?"

"If they shine a light on us, we look like a bush, same concept," he suggested, teeth flashing in the darkness as he revealed the hidden genius of his idea, continually whispering 'stealth' to himself, between giggles, as he continued applying branches.

"Speeding pigeon, speeding bush. I understand your logic," I murmured as our mobile shrubbery quietly made its way to its agreed destination, sat in a dip behind the boxy form of the old brick sub-station. We'd climbed off and silently pushed for the last twenty metres, concealed behind the foliage, watching the road before us swarming with police.

"What now?" I asked, as we lay in the dip. It was wet and muddy at the bottom, though completely dark, as the hill and fence before it deflected any light.

"Dunno," he replied. "Just wait, I suppose."

"Just sit here?"

"Dunno…"

I felt like Saddam, sitting in his drain, looking at One Ball, wanting to shout but at the same time cling to him, he was all I had. At this moment in time he wasn't going to kill me, which allowed me to stop looking inward and consider the remarkable scenes happening around me, finding it difficult not to fall into childish fantasies of

snipers or special forces. It felt like we were stalking prey as we
watched the back of the police, focused on the entrance to the estate
in front of them where the battle was fierce. Matchday flares of red
and blue smoke filled the air, whilst explosions of fire washed
around shields as black shapes crouched behind them. I kept
glancing backwards, where the real danger lay, purple and orange
spots swirling around my vision as they adjusted from the
pyrotechnics to the pitch black, my eyes tricking me, considering
shapes that looked darker black, perceiving movement, fully
expecting him to emerge.
"Fuck," One Ball whispered as a giant flaming leopard rushed
towards them from the estate. A body jumped out of the front seat
as it crashed into the shields, knocking them spinning like skittles,
some screaming in pain as they could not escape its trajectory.
I smirked, wondering if it was Stretch before another bright light
illuminated their helmets and shields, causing them to pause and
turn to their right, re-focus, as the sound of motorbikes, broken
glass and the whoosh of ignited liquid filled the air as another front
opened up prompting the police to re-arrange frantically.
"That's it, get ready," One Ball whispered.
"That's what?"
"The distraction, get ready…"
The police had now split into two fronts as instinct conquered
training and they fragmented, half shuffling towards the unseen
attackers, whist others remained untangling themselves from the
wreckage of the burning leopard. Another wave of bottles exploded
around them, the heat and light flashing over, revealing us, though
their attention was focused in a different direction as we remained
unseen. They slowly shuffled forward, disappearing from view,
One Ball getting twitchy, peering up, his head swivelling, like a
periscope.
"He's supposed to be here," he hissed, desperation shading his
thick accent, making him sound like the child he was.
"How is he supposed to get here?" I hissed back, his desperation
contagious.
'What the fuck are we doing here?' Peter cursed.
He yelped, pulling me back into the dip as the helicopter appeared
almost directly overhead, hovering, descending towards us as I put
my hands to my ears. It felt like I was in a tornado, about to be

lifted, flipped through the air by the updraft as the grass was rhythmically beaten flat around us as we lay in its blind spot. I was there but not there, a cyclone of thoughts, my mind hurtling at a thousand miles an hour, images flashing, a flight of ideas matching the beat of the rotors, moving from one thought to another: the riots, a police car, Kooky, blood, The Pit, a cage, a key, a lock…
"Stay still," One Ball hissed, holding me down as I attempted to stand and chase the thoughts as they disappeared into the darkness. I couldn't stay still as I tried to reply, explain, but I was jabbering, struggling to string a sentence together, looking up to see it's light moving quickly, searching the darkness, penetrating shadows. There was something hypnotic about it, like a pendulum swaying towards us, getting a little closer each time before moving along the road as chaotic communications sent it elsewhere, seeking something or someone else.
Onc Ball was on his knees, ready to run as the light started its next sweep towards us.
"We've got to go," he shouted this time, a look of panic painting his face as it flickered orange. "It's going to see us."
I knelt up to see it coming closer, caught in two minds, wanting to run, wanting to lie down and cover my eyes as One Ball's instincts took over and he fled into the darkness towards the quad bike.
The Mayor had appeared on the edge of the dip, naked and masturbating, trying to give away my presence as I stood up and stuttered, frozen to the spot as the edge of the beam touched the edge of the dip. Smoke canisters erupted before us, Everton this time, turning the air blue, revealing the precise lines of lasers emerging from the estate, irritating the machine as it continued its search.
"Take me," I shouted, opening my arms wide, closing my eyes, waiting to be bathed in its light, my body hanging limp as I surrendered, too weak to run anymore as I waited for the brightness that would take everything away. I could explain it to them, I reasoned to myself, I didn't kill him.
My vision was growing lighter, red veins becoming visible, like rivers in a delta against a pink background, before abruptly returning to darkness. I opened one eye apprehensively, then the other, watching the light sweep away from me, capturing the rapid motion of a Quad Bike bursting from the undergrowth and

skidding onto the road, the silhouettes of bodies just about hanging on as it flew through the air, slaloming through the debris. They took the police by surprise, crashing through the back of their line just as they'd reassembled, sending Perspex flying through the air as they fell into disarray, swarming like angry ants, pursuing their attackers as they sped towards the alleyway under the arching trajectories of Flaming Cocktails. For a second I thought it was One Ball, perhaps Love Knuckles, buying me a second, but it was the shape of Willo caught in the glare, his features glistening, smeared with blood, as they careered towards the estate.

"Macca…"

"Macca…" Migsy called, his head appearing around the corner of the sub-station.

"Migsy?" I replied, wondering if he was a hallucination as he materialised from nowhere, in the middle of a riot. "How…?"

"Come on," he hissed from the other side of the railings as I ran towards him, looking apprehensively at the metal spikes, like skewers on top.

"But, how…?"

"Squeeze through," he urged, turning left and right, exposed as he pushed himself into the wall. There was still chaos behind him as the beam from the helicopter now pointed down into the estate.

"I can't get through there…"

"Come on, we haven't got time," he growled as I pushed myself into the gap between the railings and the building, the rough brick scraping along my back and face as I turned my head sideways, looking backwards, getting halfway through, pushing forward before getting stuck tight.

"I can't fit," I grunted as Migsy started tugging on my arm, "Molly's donuts, I've got to go back."

It felt like an age as we stood on opposite sides of the fence, glancing up at the spikes, considering options before his eyes flicked past me, panic contorting his features. I turned already knowing what it was, finding the darkness coming towards me, a human shape materialising from the black, there but not there, definitely there.

"Fuck, get me through," I shouted, launching myself forward, panic rising as I watched the shape solidify, becoming more certain. All I could think of were next days' newspapers and twitter feeds, buzzing with the image of my bloodied body hanging between the railings, eyes and mouth open in a permanent scream.

'*Not like this,*' Peter screeched, wanting me to go back, fight, as I was being pulled the other way, my eyes bulging as Migsy started yanking harder.

My shoulder crunched, the sound of fibres stretching then splitting, threatening to dislocate as my chest tightened until my lungs emptied, my ribcage threatening to fracture, then collapse. Skin was scraping off the side of my face, sending vibrations through my skull as a tooth ground against the unforgiving stone until I was stuck fast, my feet in the air, arms and legs flailing, a crucifixion without nails as I surrendered, waiting for the blade to slip between my ribs. Migsy screamed in one last effort, my body stretching, snapping, hung, drawn and quartered, then I was through, dropping onto the pavement as rivulets of scarlet ran down my face.

I gasped, my lungs filling with air, my first words, "My ear, I've lost my ear," as I staggered to my feet.

"Your ear's still there," Migsy shouted, pulling me by the shoulder but I wouldn't move. Despite the battles exploding around us, I remained, staring at the gap, wondering how I fitted through, a miracle Jesus would be proud of. Hands grabbed the railings from the other side as, despite Migsy's protests, I stayed, wanting to see him at last. His hands were massive and bloody, eyes wet and glinting in the darkness, panting with exertion as the flash of an explosion illuminated the rest of the dark shape.

"Smiler?"

"Don't go with him," Smiler shouted, shaking the bars like a gorilla in a cage.

"What's wrong?"

"Don't go with him," he repeated as Migsy's arm came around my neck and lifted me off my feet, pulling me around the corner and in through a metal door which he closed with a clang behind us, before setting the bolts.

He let go as we stood in darkness, the sounds outside muted, our breathing heavy.

"What's he saying that for?" I demanded.

"We need to move."

"No," I said, digging my heels in, pushing him away. "What's he saying that for?"

"He's been turned, they've got to him."

"He can't have, he's..."

"He hates what you're doing down there, in case you haven't noticed. He's cut a deal, he's set you up now he's trying to cash you in."

"He shot Kookie?"

"Yes."

"Fuck," I shouted, before pausing. "But, he couldn't have, he's a fat cunt."

"I dunno, covered himself in butter or something. I don't want to believe it myself, now come on..."

"Where?" I asked, as the tiny flashlight of his phone illuminated the room. "We're stuck in a sub-station. He'll just tell them we're in here."

"He didn't see us come in and he doesn't know about it. Nobody knows about it."

"It's in the park next to the main road, everybody knows about it."

"But nobody notices it," he replied walking behind the buzzing machinery. "It's hidden in plain sight," he continued as I heard him grunting, stone grating upon stone.

"What are you doing?" I asked, following him around the machine to find a gaping hole in the ground, his face looking up at me from the darkness.

"It's our way out."

"Down there?"

"It's a tunnel, there's loads of tunnels."

"I'm not going down there."

"So, what are you going to do, stay here?"

"No, well..." I stammered.

"They want you for murder."

"But I didn't..."

"We both know that, but they've got you all sewn up. It's what they do."

"But..."

"Murder. Life in prison. Could you go to prison?"

"No" we both knew the answer,

"Then get down that hole."

And so I descended, six feet underground, into Hell, though I didn't realise it immediately as the stone grated then clunked closed with a thud, sealing us into the darkest darkness. There was a feeling of disorientation, weightlessness, only the sensation of feet touching the ground telling me which way was up. There wasn't a sound, not even a whisper, despite the battles raging overhead, just a deathly silence.

It was the smell that did it, its tendrils creeping into my nostrils, that familiar scent of damp and decay rushing back, dragging memories with it, reaching in, emptying the recesses of my subconscious, my truth laid bare. I had achieved the impossible, travelled through time, I was a child again and in this darkness my demons dwelt.

I inhaled and paused before letting out a scream that seemed never ending as my chest ached recalling the railings above, a thousand years ago. My mind had gone as my lungs refilled and my mouth opened wide, its widest, as another scream left my body. It was animalistic, bestial, a sound I could not recognise as I felt myself strain then explode into atoms, disappearing, bouncing off surfaces as I travelled along in waves, into the darkness, before my emptied lungs inhaled, pulling whatever remained back together again, the shattered fragments of a person.

I paused, wondering if I was dead, if I'd walked into my tomb, until a hand touch my arm.

"Azrael?" I screamed, jerking. "Azrael?"

"It's Migsy," the darkness replied, all around me.

'Maybe he's dead as well,' Peter shouted, the panic contagious. 'How long have I been dead?

"Macca?"

His voice sounded unsure.

"Not here, not here," was all I could say, my teeth chattering, words distorted, slurred. "Noooot herrre, n-n-not hhhhere…"

"It's okay Macca, we're not there," he replied as realisation hit.

"Nooot here, not heeeere…"

"You're okay Macca. You're okay. It's not that. It's not that."

"Why did you do this? Why did you do this to me?" I pleaded to the darkness, now just a soul, floating in space.

"It's the only way out," he said, his voice sounding stronger as his hands grabbed me, pulling me back into my body. "You've got to trust me."

"Trust…"

"Trust me," he repeated, "It's not The Pit."

"They're going to make us fight."

"They're not here. It's just me, Migsy. You're alright."

I flicked like a switch and Peter was back. I was tensing up, tugging at my buttons to take off my torn shirt. I was calm, cold and calm, ready to fight as I started loosening my arms and legs, opening and closing my hands and shuffling my feet, body twitching as I practiced moves in my mind.

"Macca?" Migsy asked, sensing a change in temperament.

"Who is it tonight? One of the Welsh lot?" I asked. My voice sounded different, a child's voice.

"Macca, it's not….."

"Lead me in, lead me in," I replied, reaching forward with both hands, finding his shoulders then turning him around and jogging on the spot. "Fast in, fast out, fast in, fast out…"

"We're not there. This is different."

"My hands aren't taped. It's going to be messy."

Migsy started walking forwards, the light off his phone identical to the small flashlight they used to give us. It looked different though, the same dirt floor and roughly hewn sandstone walls but the familiar landmarks, the stones and grooves were not there.

"Is it a dark one do you think? Turn the lights on, see what's left?"

"No."

"Might be glass, don't mind the glass…"

"No."

"Hope they don't throw a dog in. Take its eyes, shin behind the neck and pull, wait for the crunch."

"No."

We passed a dark opening then another, my pulse raising slightly with each one as my ears strained, listening for the crowd but Migsy continued walking forwards.

"Remember Foden?"

"Don't talk about that…"

"The best there'd ever been they said, mentally deranged, can't stop…"

"Stop it."

"You were carrying his head," I giggled, seeing his bulging eyes and blue tongue lolling out to the side, through a hole torn in his cheek, his thick blood dribbling a trail onto the dirt floor below. "Stop it," he shouted, spinning and grabbing me by the throat, too slow as his fingers slipped and my fist arched over landing square on his nose. He staggered back as I giggled, "Where are they? I'm ready."

He shone the phone down another dark opening, illuminating the worn stone and nothing else.

"It's down there," he said, reluctantly, as a hand slowly emerged from the darkness, a curling finger beckoning me before its owner stepped into the light, the Schoolmaster with his tight trousers and knitted tank top. He was smiling though his mouth looked cavernous, empty, as he whispered soundless words, his other hand travelling to his crotch, gently squeezing.

"It's still there," Migsy continued, "but we're going this way. It was twenty years ago. They're not there. It's finished."

"Nobody there?" I asked, staring at the finger, curling like a worm on a hook.

"Just you and me."

"Am I fighting you?"

"No."

"They'll do it, make us fight."

"They won't, it's finished."

"I'll win," I goaded, thinking of attacking again.

'Get the first hit, make it a good one and the battle's won,' Peter advised, repeating the mantra.

He didn't reply, just continued forwards, my eyes following the tiny light as the path started descending.

'The throat?' Peter suggested.

"Do you remember Wingnut, collected ears?" I called after him, following the spot bobbing like a firefly. "Don't know why he collected them when his own were fucking huge."

The light continued, bobbing away.

"Should have collected noses, his was all over the place," I persisted, breaking into a jog, catching up.

"Remember that lad in Wales, returned the favour?" I giggled. "Looked weird without ears."

I felt a gradual change as with distance, Peter's influence eased off. There was no clear line where I switched from one to the other, a storming off because he did not get his fight, it was a gradual process, where doubt started creeping in, a coming down, as ancient memories became less pervasive, thoughts more rational as the past returned to the past and memories of today gained access, also tarnished with violence and murder; the new me is the old me.

"Where are we going?" I asked the creases to the back of Migsy's neck.

"Somewhere safe," he replied, stopping and turning to face me. "You okay?"

"Yes," I tried to reply calmly, though we both heard the tremor. It felt like my body was shaking all over.

"You're back?"

"I'm back," I answered, trying to grin, but it wouldn't stay on my face.

"Where are we?"

"Under the park."

"No, I mean where are we? What is this place?"

"These tunnels have been here for hundreds of years, the city's riddled with them. It's like a honeycomb below ground. Over time they've been forgotten, extremely useful to the likes of us."

"Where do they lead?"

"Everywhere," he replied, shining the torch along the glistening walls, tree roots cascading down, filling the gaps between rock.

"You know the big oak in the middle of the main field?"

"That's it?" I asked. "The Tree of Life?"

"That's it," he nodded, grabbing one of the enormous roots sucking moisture from the ground.

"Some of the tunnels have collapsed, others are concealed. There's probably a whole network below us."

"So they'll lead us out of here?"

"Nah, we can't get that far, they've blocked all the roads. I'm just going to take you somewhere safe to hole up."

"The club?"

"It's a warzone there, they're fighting like absolute bastards. They're blaming that place for a lot of the instability in the country, believe it or not. Now they've got you as a murderer and cult leader rolled into one, armed and dangerous. Gives them a good reason to kill you on the spot."

"So where?"

"Down here," he replied, before turning his light and continuing through the darkness.

It felt like it was raining as drips seeped through the roof and fell onto us, soaking us to the skin. Drip, drip, drip, was the only audible sound, Chinese water torture as we walked through, hunched over until the water started splashing around our feet before rising up to our calves, then knees.

"What's this?"

"A river," he answered as I took off my backpack and threw it up the bank, my mind filled with images of rapids.

"How do we get across?"

"Just gotta walk…"

"Is it deep?"

"Yes, goes right down to the bottom," he mumbled, breathing heavy, sending waves into the darkness, his light becoming many as it reflected in ripples, getting smaller with distance before pausing.

"Macca?"

"Yes."

"What are you doing? Why are you naked?" he asked, illuminating my pale body in a circle of light.

"Because of the river."

"It's not deep," he sighed. "I was joking. Get your fucking clothes on."

"Have you got Charon's number?"

"Who the fuck is Sharon?"

"Doesn't matter," I replied as I put my shirt back on, throwing my trousers over my shoulder to cross the water, feeling discomfort as we continued, the wet, the dirt, the chaffing.

"What's that?" I asked as a huge wall of concrete emerged from the darkness, a monolith from another world. Only parts of it were smooth, the rest looked deformed, like a fatberg where the wet mix had burst out of its shuttering, drying in a bulging, tumorous mass.

"That's where we're going," he replied as he bent over, sending clanging metal echoing around the chamber as he pulled a ladder out of the shadows and leant it onto the concrete foundation.

"You first," he instructed as I looked up the ladder, disappearing into darkness at the top.

"Where is it?"

"You first," he repeated as I started clambering up its thin rungs, glad to be somewhere at least as I reached the top, shuffling along a

tapered ledge, my back scraping along concrete until it became
wide enough to stand free. He climbed up behind me, grunting
with his phone in his mouth, the spot of light rising, returning the
tunnel below to darkness as a feeling of vertigo sucked me towards
the edge. It looked like I could fall for ever.

Migsy could hardly fit onto the space as he opened his arms wide
and tip-toed along like a ballet dancing hippo, dragging his face
along the wall, taking tiny side steps until he reached the door
where he started fishing around inside his pocket for keys. It
opened with a squeal, metal on rusted metal as he leant into it,
starting gentle then forcing it open with his full weight to get away
from the ledge as I followed him through, relieved to be on firm
ground, looking around another room full of machines.

"A sub-station?"

"No, a lift pit," he replied, looking up into the darkness. "It hasn't
been used for years, so we put the door in."

"Where are we?"

"The flats."

"What flats?"

"The Syrians," he replied with a flick of the eyebrows. "They're
expecting us."

He climbed up a short ladder then prised open the lift doors to the
shaft, turning back with a grin before beckoning me forward with a
wave of the hand as we entered the communal space. It looked like
a prison, magnolia and Georgian wired glass as I followed him,
peeking through the lobby doors at the small group standing by the
front entrance, looking out onto the streets through the vertical slot
in the slightly opened door. This world filled the air again, the
sound of sirens, the smell of fire, as Migsy knocked on the window,
grinning as they jumped and spun around in shock as Said strode
towards us.

"I don't know what to ask first," he said, stopping short, thinking
twice about embracing me. "How you got in here or how you ended
up in this state? You look like you came out of the sewer," he
continued. "Covered in shit and piss…"

"Alright, alright," Migsy said with a grin.

"I don't understand," I said. "We are still in the middle of it. How is
this safe?"

"They ignore us. It's as if we don't exist. The only people who come to us are dodgy motherfuckers like this one," he said, pointing at Migsy. "Trying to arrange a smuggling route through the Middle East. They won't come here."

They led me upstairs to one of the flats where there was an empty bedroom waiting. I felt like I could collapse with exhaustion as we reached the tenth floor and tumbled into the shower, washing away the dirt and grime before finding a bowl of soup and hot bread waiting for me alongside a white kaftan laying neatly folded on the bed. Migsy walked in wearing a pair of jeans that were too tight and a shirt that he couldn't fasten.

"Surely I should wear that and you should wear this," I complained, though he wouldn't accept it.

"I've got to go back out, and if I'm caught wearing that thing, they'll come straight here."

"And what am I supposed to do?"

"Keep your head down."

"Of course I'll keep my head down, wouldn't be seen dead in this," I replied, nodding at the kaftan. "It's not even La Coste."

"We need all this to settle down."

"You need to tell them I'm innocent."

"They know you're innocent but that's irrelevant."

"So what? I just stay here until they find me?"

"You stay here until stars align. Things are changing rapidly. It might be completely different tomorrow."

"Or they might not…"

"They might not," he agreed.

"I haven't got a phone. How do I get in touch with Judy?"

"You don't. I'll get something sorted."

"I feel like a prisoner."

"Feel free to walk out of the door any time," he grinned. "But then you will be a prisoner."

"I need a drink."

"It's dry."

"No, I need a drink," I repeated aggressively, feeling cramps in my body, it had been too long.

"Not in here you don't," he replied solemnly. "You need to dry out, get back in the game."

"I can't, I…."

"Take these," he said, handing over a bag of pills, "something to

make it easier."
"What are they?"
"Help, to get you through it. You're alcoholic."
"But...."
"I'll call in when I can, see how you're getting on."
He was right, the whole building was dry, even the Pepsi was diet,
though there were other things to take the edge off, controlling my
sickness. Doors were open and people moved freely between each
other's flats, where they would sit and talk, sometimes for hours.
They were sparsely furnished: no belongings, decoration,
distraction or televisions, just chairs, set around the perimeter of
rooms, a contrast to this world they had entered, where people
stared at screens.
It allowed me to move freely, accepting invitations for lunch then
talking about deep and meaningful subjects, their lives, my life and
God. It seemed like an age that I had spoken like this, serious
conversation which could descend into argument, but intellectual
argument, where my beliefs were challenged, as were theirs. In
between the mental sparring I would excuse myself, eagerly
anticipating their bathrooms and drawers, home to a cornucopia of
chemicals designed to alleviate the traumas and stresses, memories
and experiences that were now shaping their futures. It was
something I identified with, lives defined by the barbarity of others
as my hand reached in and my heart raced with glee; no medication
could erase memories but they could stop the feeling, numb the
mind as I filled my pockets with some familiar faces, popping one
into my mouth along the way: Tramadol, Diazepam, Paroxetine,
Temazepan, Xanax, Ritalin, Fentanyl to name a few, plus other more
exotic names which I threw into the mix, like Jamie.
They were calming, a temporary crutch during this period of
transition, allowing me to function in my new life as a fugitive.
It was the youngsters that had screens, laptops for schoolwork,
behind which they sat studiously until my name or picture
appeared on the newsfeed. Then they'd run and seek me out,
shouting uncle instead of father, and pointing at the same story
again and again, usually my head covered in scars, then Kooky,
looking like a choir boy, murdered in cold blood. They'd then focus
on the riots, a siege, as they tried to take my last stronghold,
defended by brainwashed extremists, to give justice to this young

innocent, the battle complete with special effects and pyrotechnics as helicopters hovered overhead, their film cameras pointing down onto the multi-coloured scene below. It became most vivid at night, a Kristalnacht for The Lurk as we stood on the roof like generals, watching a panorama of different battles on different fronts. Meanwhile Peter was raging, pacing around in my head, screaming in frustration as we remained locked up in our tower, watching the violence unfurl before us.

It was a battle that went down in history, The Temple The Alamo: tear gas, water cannons, then rubber bullets raining down on them as the assailants became more desperate. It was three days of solid fighting before the defences fell, and, though defeated, the defenders were bathed in glory as the battle was taken onto different fronts, played out on screens around the world as live streaming countered the corrupted media.

It took on a life of its own, spreading through the virtual world, one million views, two million, three million, four, showing the reality of battle in all its glory, creating anti-heroes as they clicked on Big Jim, swinging like a berserker, or Mekon Don, like a relentless machine, his teeth white, grinning through the blood as the blows rained down onto his unguarded head. Then there were the ladies with their body cams, fighting like alley cats, guerrilla warfare as the carbon coated attackers had to enter the buildings. They were predictable thus vulnerable as a flash grenade would go off before they came running in and were pelted with whatever was there. Unofficial footage showed them stretchered out in pink or turquoise, multi-coloured from the art studios, or covered in flour, like ghosts, already dead.

'The Temple has Fallen' the newsbar declared proudly as all of the children came running out of their rooms at once, unsure whether to act out grief, looking for my reaction. I had no reaction to give, my eyes were empty, pupils large and dilated as the tablets worked their magic. I wiped my arm slowly across my mouth to make sure I wasn't drooling.

They'd arrested and detained over a hundred, mostly on Disrespecting Government legislation as my face flashed up and a random Baroness, in navy with a brooch, confirmed that they'd been indoctrinated with extremist views and were a threat to the public. She carried a smug demeanour but their successes were short lived, intelligence, wit and humour the weapon as a wave of memes followed, questioning where our version of Guantanamo may be, Runcorn the favourite, before being judged too cruel and probably against the Geneva Convention.

Memes revealed that the real battleground was far away from here. It was information, the internet, destroying any moral high ground as Britain's finest were mocked, reduced to comedy figures as they stood before bloodied and bruised pensioners, their prized catches from The Temple.

More familiar faces started to appear on the mainstream news bulletins, smirking as they sat in custody, flanked by officers before a logo filled backdrop as real identities were laid bare, their pseudonyms revealed, before switching to Westminster where a greying man praised the forces, explaining how it was the cumulation of over three years of undercover work.

"Smiler," I mumbled to Said who was sat next to me.

"Knew he was a motherfucker the moment I set eyes on him," he agreed.

I knew the purpose of the broadcasts as I watched, *this is your fault, only you can stop this*, their message loud and clear as they paraded friends one after the other. But they were defiant. Elvis appeared to have lost his tooth but was still smiling a big gummy grin as he tipped a wink to the camera, whilst the highest profile arrest, Margaret, whom they'd equated with Pablo Escobar, looked particularly sweet in Lavender. Their guilt did not matter, it was all about the spectacle, the establishment too slow and ponderous to have any chance of competing with the kids and their new toys in the thick of the action.

Migsy returned after a few days wearing clothes that fitted and a new wardrobe for me. Said took him to one side, whispering urgently into his ear as Migsy's eyes flicked over occasionally, his mouth curving into a grimace. I didn't care, I'd been withdrawing into myself more and more as the reality of my situation was bearing down on me, taking a pill to kill the thoughts before they could grow. Peter was gone, I was empty, there wasn't a single voice, whilst conversation with others had become less frequent as I'd turned inwards, running out of words, spending most of my time laying down, just breathing, eating and shitting, though even that had stopped.

"Y'all right?"
"Suppose…"
"Struggling without the booze."
"Yes," I replied with a lazy nod, waiting for him to mention the drugs but he remained silent, leaving it hanging.
"Have you seen Judy?"
"She's gone…"
"Gone? What do you mean, gone?"
"Gone, vanished, disappeared, poof," he said, clicking his fingers.
"Have the police taken her? She's pregnant."
"No, they haven't got her."
"Ginny?"
"Arrested, they've even taken her husband into custody."
"He's been dead for years."
"I know, but it was assault and battery with his urn."
"Does Ginny know where Judy has gone?"
"No, she's up and left. All her things are still in the house, just vanished."
"Fuck, she's pregnant." I could see images of her lying unconscious at the bottom of the stairs in the house next door.
"We're looking, but nothing is coming up. She's not taking money out of her account, nothing."
"They must have her."
"We don't know that. Maybe she has family somewhere?"
I realised that I knew nothing about her, just the backstory Migsy had told me.
"I have to hand myself in. I've caused enough damage."
"You've done nothing, remember that. You're starting to doubt your own story."
"But, if I hadn't…."
"Stop," he shouted. "You know the truth, you know what's real."
"But, what they are saying may as well be real, they all believe it, they…"
It took them a week to reach The Lurk where they ground to a halt, meeting barricades and entrenched positions, a Paschendal, a Hill 60, as they fought for days without gaining an inch. It was a battle they could not win, fighting house by house, street by street of the two surrounding estates before even reaching its edge, their resistance becoming legend as stories started to emerge from the

blue and red cloud of smoke that never moved, despite the wind that blew across the city. Helicopters were lowered in to disperse it, disappearing in a barrage of explosions as fireworks emitted flashes of light, as if a storm had settled on top of the hill.

There were the inevitable casualties, the physical wounded but also a high level of mental trauma as people broke down, their debriefings turning into tall tales of witchcraft and sorcery, inexplicable occurrences that defied belief. They were mocked at first but as tales were repeated, fear started to spread through the ranks as they whispered rumours of a hallucinogenic within the smoke. For some reason gas masks did not work, perhaps it was Russian, probably Chinese, absorbed by the skin as the stories continued, of statues that came alive, pentagrams and witchcraft, Romans, superheroes, pirates, Spice Girls, Zorro, Flintstones, vampires, Toy Story characters, then a giant snake and a man eating crocodile, as all the La Coste badges came together.

The national press ridiculed as further external forces were brought in to replace locals and South Yorkshire Police, who were probably corrupt and whose morale had collapsed.

"If the unidentified hallucinogens are having this effect on us, then why doesn't it effect the people in there?" some wonk proclaimed, whilst a Gammon blabbered on about bravery and his time in The TA. But, the new assailants soon fell down with the same maladies as they tried to explain the inexplicable, missing the obvious, as Lurkers ran around in Moat's fancy dress outfits.

Amongst the confusion, the authorities were cumbersome, ineffective as the slow progress then halt was unexpected. Reporters waited outside their vans, night after night, fretting over viewing figures as they had the same conversations with the same politicians as the expectations of the 24 hour news cycle were not being met. In the meantime, real time scenes were being broadcast from within The Lurk showing battles and their aftermath, making heroes out of everyday people. They understood propaganda, spectacle and comedy, as a drone dropped a bag of soiled nappies onto a BBC reporter, becoming one of the most viewed files in the history of the internet as millions were now tuning in, waiting for the next instalment, another front opening as they tried to take down the broadcasts whilst subversive forces brought them back online. Political pressure was building as they ran out of things to talk about, rumours started spreading, whispers of storming The Lurk with live ammunition. Nobody knew where they originated, but such was the need to fill the news that the latest Spartans and Grand Wizards were given oxygen as they rationalised that the extremists within were armed to the teeth. They were probably right, but the outside world was outraged as the media wheeled out further old men to support their viewpoint, repeating phrases like brainwashed, cult, terrorist and martyr, words that had lost all meaning as every power base in the world now used them to justify unjustifiable actions.

A line was about to be crossed, one that peaceful protesters were not willing to accept as they started to move from the city centre towards the slopes of the park, where they were met by an outer ring of police. There were skirmishes as the crowds at the bottom of the hill were becoming agitated, then violent, as rumours spread of a delivery of live ammunition. St. George's Plateau was now empty with all focus on the hill as groups started breaking through the line and the park became inhabited again, as the small dark masses started making their way towards the cloud, attacking the assailants, a siege upon a siege.

Lucky started appearing on social media, demanding a cease to hostilities and release of all detainees. His charisma, lank hair and sweat band created an instant icon, complete with a noble cause. He was instantly adopted by #underclass, projected as a Che of our times, perhaps Fidel, or Madiba, remaining focused and calm as explosions and smoke erupted around him. He was uniquely disaffected, innocent even, certainly untouched by fashion as he delivered his sermons from the war zone in possibly the most exciting broadcasts of our time.

Banners started to appear at protests around the country, FREE THE LURKERS, SUPPORT THE LURKERS, emblazing placards and t-shirts as they became the cause celebre, unifying the disparate protesters. As one side started printing posters and t-shirts, the other started to dig up his past, searching for dirt, but all they uncovered was heroism. The fact that he'd never alluded to this past made him even more miraculous in his follower's eyes, as he became the latest face of the protest, a leader, a messiah, a dangerous zealot.

He had them in a bind. He was the past they were trying to sell, that understated myth of Britishness with its bravery and stoicism, gentlemanly honour; but the more they tried to pull him down the more they lifted him up, and the more vociferously they defended him.

"HE WAS SUNK, FIVE TIMES, FOR HIS COUNTRY…" they shouted aggressively, "AND HE STILL GOT ON THAT NEXT FUCKING SHIP."

We crowded around the screen as a pause in battle was announced, cameras pointing as a delegation came from the alleyway headed by a bedraggled but smiling Lucky who was all too pleased to speak with any reporter willing to listen. He was defiant, listing the demands that the government had made before immediately refusing them. I was top of the list, they thought I was in there, as Lucky passionately refuted the allegations.

"He's not an extremist and he's not a murderer. He's been set up. Framed. A distraction from what is really happening in this country."

I wanted to thank him, hug him, be part of them as I lay in my stupor, wondering if I should just walk out of the door. But I did nothing, just lay, taking a tablet whenever a thought began to form as time started to stretch and I just slept, maybe for hours, days or weeks, consciousness now coming in flashes, eating, shitting, taking a pill, feeling degraded and humiliated, teeth furry and stinking like an old dog living its last days.

Migsy would appear, fuzzy then sharp, topping up my little bags of pills then moving me out of my pit with the help of a little blue one which filled me with energy, bringing my mind out of the fog where it would shoot off, racing again as I became reacquainted with lights and colours which appeared brighter, filled with joy.

"Where are we going?" I asked, following him down the tunnel, walking behind his wall of torch light, past roughly hewn sandstone walls and the dark openings of passageways veering off to the left and right. We paused, before turning off down one, then another, a couple of symbols marked on the wall the only indication of a street name. They looked ancient, another language. Occasionally we would walk past small boxes containing a torch and water, "Just in case," Migsy said, as we continued zig-zagging through the underworld.

I couldn't stop talking, as was often the case after the blue pill, jabbering, making up for all the lost words I'd not said over the previous week. Migsy usually continued striding silently ahead but occasionally responded once I piqued his interest.

"They've been here since the city has been here," he replied, after my incessant questions. "That one was a store for Prince Rupert," he continued, shining his light into a stone lined room with an arched vaulted ceiling.

"Where are we?" I asked as we started approaching ornate red brick walls. The ground was still dirt, rising up as we stooped beneath a massive arch before entering a cavernous space filled with an electric blue glow. I lifted my arms as we walked between the cannabis plants which had grown to shoulder height, continuing as far as the eye could see. A Cornerman stood and nodded towards us before disappearing beneath the foliage, a grafter looking after his grow.

"Where are we?" I repeated, as we slipped through plastic sheeting into another arched space.

"Williamson's Tunnels," he replied, "parts they haven't uncovered yet. You're going to make an appearance."

"Is it another Secret Service night?" I asked excitedly.

"Yes."

"Wind them up," I said, eager, like a child. "Show the bastards they can't beat us."

"Chinese whispers," he agreed. "There'll be rumours of you all over the country soon."

"But mainly for The Lurk, let them know I'm kicking and screaming."

"Still making trouble," he grinned.

I was fidgeting with excitement, scanning the damp brick walls for any sign of life but there was none. It was beautiful, an arch intersecting an arch, "What is this place?"

"Strangely appropriate," he replied, rummaging through his rucksack. "Williamson was a tobacco tycoon, gave soldiers returning from the Napoleonic Wars jobs building tunnels."

"To where? What for?"

"They reckon he was part of a religious cult, preparing for the Armageddon and all that. Here…" he said, passing me my quality street outfit.

"Where's the rave? There's nobody here…"

"Patience," he grinned as I pulled the surplice over my head, bouncing on my toes, "you'll love this."

He switched off his torch and led me through the darkness until his hand reached forward, creating a gap in the curtain through which flashing bright light poured in, filling the space with colour. There was a light humming sound but was otherwise silent as I glanced across to Migsy, "Are we early?"

"No," he grinned, "Have a look."

I pulled the curtain further to one side to reveal a huge cavernous chamber, the banquet hall, its brick curved ceiling arching above a sea of heads bobbing and arms raised, packed, a writhing mass of bodies dancing, as if somebody had pressed the mute button. "Silent disco?"

He replied with a smile as I looked back at the joyous scene before me, The Temple in miniature. They were spectacular, fairies with wings and faces of glitter, feathers and headdresses; superheroes finishing their shift, letting off steam; Daddy's Little Monster, gyrating alone on a podium as I walked out next to the DJ who handed me a microphone, all movement stopping as heads spun around to see me in the spotlight. There was the odd shout then a continual murmur as I gave a sermon, my voice echoing around the silent chamber. It was short and sweet, probably a rehash of an old one before the music started and I watched the mythical beings, gods and goddesses worship me before sinking back into the music blaring through their headphones, dancing in the colours, in joyous sounds, until I'd wake up the next day in tangled sheets, my body aching and I'd reach for my medication.

I was drifting then, waking as they manhandled me, splashing water, shouting my name, slapping my face as they zoomed in and out of focus. *I am weak, just let me go…* waking as a needle pierced my arm and I was rigged up to a drip, hanging off a nail in the wall as I glanced around at the naked lightbulb, stained mattress and peeling wallpaper. The room was filled with noise, foreign voices as they shouted at the same time, incoherent, the sound only stopping as I slipped away into unconsciousness, the new normal as I became desperate for Migsy's arrival.

When he wasn't there, I needed to drink, twitching nervously and swallowing whatever medication I could find to satisfy the thirst, it never did. I'd stopped talking, turning my back on my hosts as they left meals by the door, small talk ignored as I lay there, mute, leaving their questions unanswered. Consciousness was difficult to distinguish, waking up incoherent, seeing a figure sat at the end of the bed, watching as I tried to say words, words I couldn't find. My body was drenched with sweat though I was freezing cold, trembling as every muscle ached and mucus run down my face. I reached for the pills but was just given water before being gently but persuasively pushed back onto the bed. They had somebody watching me, the panic overwhelming, walls closing in, I wanted to run but had nowhere to run to. I couldn't remember where I was, the sound of explosions in the distance my only reference, telling me I'm in Syria.

Then Migsy was there, my hopes rising, but they were arguing, pointing at me before Migsy slapped Said, knocking him to the ground. He gave me green pills this time which sharpened everything as he led me through the now familiar tunnels, before taking a new turn. I knew what this was, giggling in anticipation as I listened to the gentle sound of voices echoing off the walls, getting louder as we got closer. Reassuring memories washed over me as Peter rose within, roaring silently as I allowed him to take over possession, my thoughts becoming savage, my body animal. I was young again.

I didn't need Migsy anymore, remembering the way as I walked with urgency, his hand shaking my shoulder as I strode past.

"You own this fucking place, Macca," he said like we used to, his voice loaded with excitement as I walked through the metal gate, giving that familiar clang, as it locked behind me.

I glanced up to see faces looking back down through the bars, the sound of excited voices and smell of alcohol filling the air. There were film cameras this time, they'd never had them before, as I scanned the audience for familiar faces; there was Yoda, as Migsy took his place next to him. Others were recognisable, older, though I couldn't put names to them.

The gate opened before me and a man strode into The Pit, scratching his feet in the sand and strutting like a rooster. I'd never seen him before but it didn't matter. He was muscular, covered in tattoos, swastikas that went nicely with his shaven head as he looked down on me, giving a smirk before looking up at the baying audience above who were passing money to the bookmakers shouting out odds. He raised his arms and started turning, as if victory was his. I assumed he'd misunderstood the rituals of this place, perhaps waiting for an announcement, the ringing of a bell but there was none and I was upon him, headbutting the temple, following with knees then fists as he landed sprawling on the ground. I didn't stop when he ceased struggling, giving the audience what they wanted, what they came here for, blood, as I kept pummelling away before leaning down and sinking my teeth into him, tasting then swallowing as the cheers echoed around the chamber. "Send in the Kraken," I screamed, before collapsing with laughter.

I gasped as my stomach was cramping, my body contorting, convulsing as electricity ran through my mind then into every frayed nerve, twisting as my body stammered, stuttered, crashed, leaving a taste of blood. My body was angular, rigid, writhing on the bed but thoughts were liquid, quicksilver, flowing dreamlike, trying to grab them as they slipped through. My eyes were flickering open seeing a crowd in the room, faces I recognised but couldn't remember, coming in and out of focus. They were talking at me, their mouths moving but mute, then I was falling again as the edges of my vision started to drip inwards, purple ink blocking everything out until there was nothing, just white.

"I'm sorry, I'm sorry," were the first words I heard, before realising it was me who was saying them, still deep as I struggled to catch my breath.

"You'll get better now," a calm voice replied. "You're tapering off." I was unsure if it was real as I looked around my dark void for a source, but the voice seemed to be coming from everywhere. God. "What happened?"

"Grand mal, a fit, a seizure. Whatever you want to call it."

"Who are you?"

"A doctor, or used to be."

"Am I in hospital?"

"No."

"I need one of my tablets. Can I have a tablet?"

"No."

"Just one," I pleaded, reaching out a shaking hand.

"No," came the stern reply, as a cold cloth was dabbed onto my forehead.

"I might die," I whimpered, a running tear bringing sensation back to my face. I believed it.

"No," repeated the cruel voice, as I begged; I couldn't say enough pleases.

'Perhaps this is Hell,' Peter giggled, *'for eternity.'*

"It's the tablets that put you here and the shit that Migsy's been feeding you. Did you think nobody would notice?"

I did.

God was right. The next time I awoke, my thoughts were more coherent. I knew immediately where I was, though the nausea rose and overwhelmed me as I grabbed the nearby bucket and vomited, my body twisting as it ejected the poison. I lay down again, letting my head clear before sitting up slowly, waiting to see what would happen.

"Welcome back," God greeted.

"Thank you," I replied as my feet touched the ground, testing them as I pressed down. I was weak, trembling slightly as I stood up.

"What's happening? Outside?"

"It's a bit of an impasse at the moment, both sides unwilling to admit defeat. The fighting has stopped and people can move freely, but they've still got checks in place."

"Are they still looking for me?"

"Yes, but they still think you're in The Lurk so there's a ring around there then a wider ring around the district."

"So we're still trapped?"

"Yes," he nodded. "We can move around pretty freely, but you…"

"I'm going to hand myself in. I can't allow this to continue, too many people are suffering."

"They've let them all out," he replied. "Lucky sorted it during negotiations. They've all got tags on but Motherfucker is having fun with those."

"Hacker Packer?"

"Yes, that's what I said, motherfucker."

"How long have I been…?"

"A week"

"I'm so sorry."

"We've seen it all before, addiction, overdose, we're experts."

"But still, I should be better than that."

"You won't be our problem much longer," he said, handing me a clean white neatly folded kaftan. "Migsy is going to move you today."

An hour later I was led to a room, finding Migsy and Yoda, the single light making their faces look drawn as features cast deep shadows; they looked like they'd aged years in a month. A surge of joy rushed through me as I took a step towards them but stopped after one stride, feeling the joy was not reciprocated. Their faces were cold and serious as I glanced from one to the other, Yoda little more than skin clinging to a skull, his cheeks cavernous, just wet, red rimmed eyes indicating life as they studied me intently, trembling left to right.

"I didn't kill him."

"Well somebody did, that poor child," Yoda replied, finishing with a tut and a head shake.

"Tell him," I said, imploring Migsy who remained silent and expressionless beside him.

"He was a scum bag," Yoda said without any further prompting. "I wouldn't have minded if you had."

"Judy?"

"What about her?"

"I need to see Judy," I said, shifting my gaze to Migsy. "Is she okay?"

"Judy was the snitch," he sneered.

"Undercover officer," Yoda corrected.

"What?"

"Yes," Yoda replied, calmly. "She'd been there for years, watching Jacko. They were about to withdraw her but then you appeared out of the blue, a person of interest, so they decided to move her on to you, see how things might pan out."

"Me, a person of interest?"

"She's cut the city's crime rates in half overnight. All of those supposed friends you have, that spread their misery throughout society."

"She grassed them up?"

"She did her job."

"And I was part of the job?"

"Yes, you don't even know her real name."

"But, we're having a child together."

"She aborted it," he replied without flinching.

"She was too far gone," I protested. "They can't..."
"Special dispensation," he shrugged nonchalantly.
"You don't seem bothered."
"I'm not, and if you look deep into your soul, you'll find that you are not."
"How could you know how I feel?"
"Because I know you better than you know yourself. There are no feelings in there. You're incapable of love."
"You don't know that," I stammered.
"Your only emotions are anger and rage. You try to mimic love, happiness, sadness, empathy and you've become good at it to the untrained eye. But, to me you are barren, a desert, where only the harshest of feelings survive."
We stood in silence as I absorbed his words, unable to deny any of them. He was right. I felt anger about Judy, anger about my aborted child, but nothing else. I could crumple to my knees and turn on the taps at the drop of a hat, mimic the full agony of it all, but inside I was calm, concentrated, making sure I'd learnt my lines and was acting the script accurately.
"I know things have been a bit tense between us lately, but that's harsh, even for you. I just feel anger coming from you," I said, attempting to redirect the psychoanalysis.
"There's no anger, there's nothing; we're similar in many ways."
"Why didn't you just stop all of this before? You set me on this path, 'create your own church,' you said. You even joined in."
"Because you went too far, with your magazines and webcams, sending your spiky little messages. You became high profile and people are listening."
"What does that mean?"
"If you'd have just stepped back when I asked you to, fucked off to The Isle of Wight. You delivered, put us in the perfect place, justified your existence, but then you continued, unchecked, you wouldn't stop, so we had to create a narrative."
"The newspaper articles? Gangsters, getting angry?" I asked, glancing at Migsy, who remained unmoving.
"We have to create a frame, paint a picture, though you're a slippery little snake, I'll give you that."
"Kooky? Judy sent me to the office…"
"You made it very difficult for us…"

"Kooky was supposed to kill me?"

"Yes, but somehow you killed him."

"I didn't kill him!" I shouted.

"It matters not, the trap was set, and though you are alive, there is no way out for you."

"But…why?"

"You're a liability, a problem that needs to be dealt with."

"I'm just a Priest."

"You're out of control, you are an extremist…"

"By bringing people together? By helping people?"

"By surrounding yourself with sinners then assimilating them, like you always do, changing colour like a chameleon."

"They are good people."

"They are scum, thieving and playing the system. They could win Oscars for their performances. 'Do not participate in the unfruitful deeds of darkness, but instead even expose them.'"

"Sounds like you should listen to your own advice."

"My actions are for the greater good of The Church, unlike yours, which seek to undermine."

"By welcoming others?"

"By denigrating our religion," he shouted as anger flashed in his eyes. "By placing the others on an equal footing, as if they are fit to clean our feet. 'There is but one God', do you remember that?"

"I'm trying to pull people together, to heal divisions."

"You're elevating humans above the divine," he spat. "We're not supposed to come together. 'No one comes to the Father except through me.'"

"You're too narrow minded…"

"Enter through the narrow gate, for wide is the gate and broad the way that leads to destruction."

"So that's it? Close the doors and bring up the walls? Back to the dogma?"

"The world is changing and we need to make alliances; The Church has chosen to stay loyal with its traditional allies."

"By going back to the dark ages? Are you going witch hunting after this?"

"Why, do you know any?"

"The people will never allow it, they're on the streets…"

"Two sides, one shouting envy, the other greed and they are both right. All that needs to be confirmed are what concessions need to be given. At the end of the day, those in power will still be in power."

"Not this time, they've gone too far…"

"Revolutions come and revolutions go," he shrugged. "We just need to ensure that we are on top when the wheel has finished its turn."

"We're here to spread the word of God."

"Wrong, we're here to retain influence and power. The word of God is our product."

"We help the needy, the poor."

"And we will," he laughed. "But The Church needs more of them. It's where we are at our best, giving an illusion of hope, distraction from a shit life, like a narcotic, like those tablets that you keep taking or the whisky you keep pouring down your neck to escape."

"And you call me an extremist."

"Life won't improve for them whoever is in power, they all take, it's human nature. We've lost our place to the side of power, big business has taken it, the banks, the money, but now they are the enemy, always wanting more, as is their nature, now we want it back."

"Royals, religion, a holy trinity, you sound like an old Etonian."

"Our traditional allies."

"But they are not the future," I shouted, "and they know it, so they keep trying to drag us back to some Dickensian past."

"Give them some credit. They do, at least, have an allegiance to the idea of a country."

"And why not when it has served them well for generations with all those titles, pomp and ceremony, giving meaning to their lives."

"Giving meaning to everybody's lives."

"Unachievable for the majority. What about meritocracy as opposed to the historical stitch up the country has been mired in for centuries? Isn't that what these protests are all about?"

"What has been will be again, what has been done will be done again, there is nothing new under the sun."

"We won't allow it, they won't allow it, their time has been."

"Some say the same of The Church. Is that what you want? For us to disappear?"

"No, but we are reforming, the club…"

"That's just bread and circuses as Juvenal would say. We're reforming aggressively, down a more well-trodden path, shaping the government thus the people."

"It can never work."

"Have you not heard of The Welsh Revival? The Awakening?

"The Awakening? Seriously? It sounds like some teenage vampire shite."

"We do the same but roll it out on a national scale, then we go further. Theocracy is the future of The Church and the future of our nation. The Muslims have stolen the march on us in that respect."

"It already is a theocracy."

"But people don't realise it because we don't make full use of it. We need countries to declare their religion with The Church involved in every decision a nation makes."

"You can't change the future by looking to the past."

"Of course we can, we just use modern tools to achieve it. Social media, pushing into the old fault lines, issues they thought had gone away, racism, nationalism, homophobia all coming back. Nuclear war is back on the table for fucks sake," he giggled. "There are no depths that politicians will not sink to."

"Politicians?"

"I told you, we are unified. The government goes to church every morning now before Parliament. The Crown, The Church and the government, different branches of a single entity, a single ideology. The people are ripe and ideologies are such wonderful things, like contagious epidemics that travel around the world, creating fanaticism."

"Fanaticism? Can you even hear yourself? You sound like a Nazi. Maybe you two have something in common after all," I said, flicking my eyes towards Migsy.

"A fine example that explains their power. People succumb to them and carry out the most atrocious things, history if full of them..."

"Atrocities?"

"Mao's Cultural Revolution and his Little Red Book was a good one, reverberating around the world. The Shining Path in Peru, Nazi Fascism, Communism, Democracy, Capitalism, all wonderful examples of ideologies. Anyway, we digress, as tends to be the case when you are involved," he said almost affectionately. "I will miss our conversations, but..."

"You can't be allowed to change The Church," we both said at the same time before the room fell into another endless silence.

"So why are you here?" I asked, changing the subject, looking at Migsy who shuffled uncomfortably. "Why are you still walking around freely?"

"Because we've cut a deal, Migsy and I," Yoda replied, glancing over at his new buddy. "He keeps his freedom as long as he is useful."

"You two?" I blurted out. "But you hate his guts."

"It goes beyond us two," Yoda replied. "There are much greater games afoot, things too big for your drug addled little mind."

"A drug dealer and The Church?"

"You would be surprised," Yoda said with a giggle. "Whilst separate organisations may be opponents on one level, once you get higher, they tend to converge on similar people with the same simple aims, particularly where big money is involved."

"Your holy trinity is dealing now?"

"The British government were the biggest dealers on the planet, the Opium Wars?"

"Ancient history."

"Have you seen how much power pharmaceutical companies hold over the government?"

"Stop deviating," I said, looking back at Migsy whose face was void of expression, a blank page.

"How long has this been going on? Did you know about Kooky?"

"He's a survivor," Yoda intervened. "He's like you, like Peter, doing anything to survive, renouncing three times…"

"Did you know about Kooky?" I repeated forcefully.

"No, he didn't know about Kooky," Yoda said. "We tell him what he needs to know. He does what he needs to do."

"Are you his solicitor or something? He doesn't even say no comment, cat got your tongue?" I asked, turning back to Migsy.

"No," he mumbled after a minutes hesitation.

"Smiler knew, didn't he?"

"He figured it out."

"He was warning me."

"You didn't want to listen."

"So why have you been keeping me here?"

"You're my bargaining tool, they want you and I have you. They were going to come knocking on my door someday. I had to have a way out."

"You were sold to the highest bidder, which was us," Yoda laughed gleefully.

"So you drugged me up and showed me off, your merchandise?"

"I didn't know you were self-medicating as well."

"Was it real? The Secret Service? The Pit?"

"Don't know what you're on about," Migsy replied, as a smirk touched his lips.

"I don't know who to be more surprised about, Judy, him or you," I said, pointing to them in turn.

"Oh, save us the 'Et tu Brutus' act," Yoda groaned.

"I think it's warranted. No matter what you think of those people out there, at least they have some loyalty."

"Honour amongst thieves."

"We were only together for a few years, to be fair," Migsy declared, clearing his throat, receiving a glare from Yoda.

"But what a few years, eh?!" I replied sarcastically.

"Oh change the fucking record," Yoda moaned with a sigh.

"Kooky's not the only person killed through your actions."

"You killed Smiler?"

"No, he's too smart, faster than he looks."

"Then who?"

"Your reporter, going around with your conspiracy theories and unfounded allegations."

"What?"

"That was Migsy's first job."

"You killed him?"

Migsy shrugged his shoulder, "Didn't take much persuading, couldn't stand him."

I was focused now, like I'd swallowed a little blue pill as I started to fear for my life for the first time. Yoda didn't notice but Migsy's eyes were instantly on me, sensing the change.

"He was an innocent man, investigating what they did to us. Them bastards in the folder..."

"What folder?" Migsy asked.

"The folder, with each of them in there, in the home..."

He gave a nonchalant shrug, "Don't know what you're on about."

Peter wanted to lunge forward as the rage mounted.

"It never happened Peter, none of it's real," Yoda poked, sensing my anger.
"What?"
"It never happened, the abuse, in the home. It's just a mental construct of yours that we've had to play along with, all these years."
I stared at him open mouthed, at the point realisation hit me, that everything I'd believed in had been a lie. Not the home, or the abuse that they were now denying, but Yoda, Migsy and the stories they had woven tightly around me. I couldn't speak as I stared at him in disbelief.
"Migsy?" I whispered.
"He's right, it never happened," he repeated.
"And The Pit? I suppose that never happened?"
He just shook his head this time before looking at his feet as I stood dumbfounded, feeling foolish that they'd sucked me in, serpents whispering words I wanted to hear. Again, it wasn't mourning, but anger, that I'd opened myself up to them, lapping up their smoke and mirrors. This reality was a lie.
"It's not your fault," Yoda said, smiling for the first time. "Your brain doesn't work like a normal persons. It never has."
"I saw psychiatrists about my issues. I dealt with it."
"Oh, it went away did it?"
"I deal with it."
"But you don't, do you? You're supposed to be a well-balanced cocktail of medication, but you're completely off kilter. I should have kept a closer eye on those people, working for the others, I think."
"Others? What are you talking about? Conspiracy theories?"
"Stuff you don't understand."
"What about those inconvenient others who named the same people? It happened to them at the same time, in the same places. What is that? Some sort of mass hallucination?"
"You've jumped onto their bandwagon," Yoda replied with a shrug. "Taken somebody else's cause as your own, as people with your condition are wont to do. You completely believe in the fiction, allowing it to take over and define your life."
"I remember every detail," I hissed. "Every touch, every smell, the taste, the pain…"

"Pure fabrication," Yoda dismissed with a waft of his hand.
I glanced at Migsy, who stood silent, saying nothing.
"So, you didn't share these experiences? You had a blissful childhood in the home?"
"Can't complain," he mumbled. "Custard was a bit lumpy."
"I'm not sure what game you are both playing here, but let's stop it now. We all know it's bullshit. Did you expect me to just nod and say okay?"
"Not at all," Yoda grinned, enjoying himself. "But, there is good reason for that. Medically speaking, you have just left the prodrome."
"Oh, fuck off with your Mel Gibson fantasies."
"You have hallucinations, don't you?" he continued with a grin. "You see people, don't you?"
I stood silent, looking at him then the floor, as he toyed with me, a cat with a mouse.
"Can you see any of them now?" he mocked.
"No" I lied, the caretaker was standing naked in the corner. "How did you...?"
"Your head twitches, your face goes white, eyes flicking across the room, etcetera."
"I see the people that abused me," I replied, feeling the blood rise in my face as I revealed my embarrassing secret. "I see them every day. I deal with it."
"You've now evolved into full blown psychosis. You used to know that they were not real, but now you're convinced that they are," he continued. "Your bizarre delusions have changed as you have become unhinged. Your brain has changed physically and a lot of the time that can't be fixed."
"I'm no worse than I've ever been."
"You're losing your mind. You have no contact with reality."
"That's not true."
"You hallucinate, see things that aren't actually there. You're delusional, believing in things that are not real."
"They are real; It happened." I shouted, glaring at Migsy.
"They are persecutory delusions, we can't argue against it, whatever we say, you will never believe. Most minds are shaped to block out bad memories, but yours appears to create them."
"You're lying…"

"Each time we recall a memory it is a re-rendering, like a Chinese whisper, gradually deforming, becoming something else. Your mind is your real enemy. That is the only thing that's been abusing you."

"So, what now? It appears you're not here to help me and Said tells me I'm moving today."

"We have options," Yoda said, leaning back.

"You're going to kill me as well?" I asked Migsy. "It seems to be something you're getting good at."

"Not yet," Yoda replied. "We are actually here to help you."

"If you hand me into the police, I'll tell them everything."

"See, there you go again, with that stupid mouth of yours. It's going to get you killed."

"So, what?"

"They are waiting outside."

"Who?"

"You will be sectioned, under The Mental Health Act."

"No…"

"This will help you avoid the law and give you the help you need…"

"I can't, I'm not…"

"…in a secure and caring environment," he finished.

"No."

"You'll end up there anyway; you're fucking insane," he shouted.

"None of what you are saying is real," I shouted back. "Just lies, both of you."

"Look at this," he demanded, holding forward his phone. I squinted at the tiny screen, it was fuzzy, pixelated until a figure began to emerge, a silhouette, stamping down on a body on the ground."

"It wasn't Muslims," I sighed, tired of repeating myself.

"I know it's not, it's you," he replied as I refocused on the screen, feeling nauseous as my foot stamped down on The Leatherman, again and again.

"This is you. This is your Church. How are you any better than those that did the same to you?"

"It was a mistake," I stammered, "I thought it was…"

"This is what you've become. Come with us, your life will be comfortable, nothing else to worry about. Imagine that."

All I could think of was the garden centre in the village, with its permanent underlying tension.

"I'm not going."

"You're going," Migsy countered as I looked up into the barrel of a gun.

"I'll tell them everything about you," I threatened, the words struggling to come out such was the anger behind them. I was allowing it to run free, course through my veins as Migsy sensed it and held the gun firm.

"He's completely reformed. Works with The Church, runs the club, a fine community institution," Yoda mocked, piling on the sarcasm, "They won't believe a word that you say."

"I can't..."

"You can. Grow a backbone for fuck's sake, see how it goes. If you don't like it then you can kill yourself. What have you got to lose?"

I turned towards the door as Migsy closed the space between us, shoving the gun into my lower back. I felt empty as the door opened before me, like I'd lost my freedom, my movements and thoughts somebody else's.

"Where am I going?"

"Back door," Yoda said, walking in front of us into the deserted hallway as I shuffled forwards, unaware that Peter was going to do anything until the fire extinguisher was in my hand, the door it had been holding open, probably for decades, squealing as it started closing for the first time in years and I was spinning, the sharp edge of the extinguisher connecting with something, Migsy's chin, as my body turned full circle and the sound of the gunshot filled the space. He was going down, extinguished, beads of blood appearing in a curve along the side of his face as I came fully around, catching up and bringing the extinguisher down again, lopping the top off his ear as he continued his descent before crashing into the ground, head lolling, hitting the floor as his massive bulk bounced before settling, still this time.

Peter laughed as Yoda pounded on the wired glass of the door, rage filling his eyes as Migsy's bulk was keeping it closed. He was furious, kicking the door forwards, banging it into the back of Migsy's head with each grunt.

The door behind him opened and two, then four, identically dressed clones entered the hallway, attracted by the furore as panic rose within me with the appearance of others. It was no longer personal, institutions were pushing in, taking over, as I spun on my feet and ran towards the other exit, screeching to a halt as I heard steps on the stairs.

"They're out there as well," Said shouted, standing on the flight above, out of sight. I considered the front door before turning back, glancing up at him.

"Thank you, and sorry for bringing this to your door," I said, before barging into the creaking door below the stairs which held firm for a second before screaming open in protest.

"May God protect you," I heard him reply before fleeing into the darkness.

I paused, feeling my way around whilst my eyes adjusted, waiting for the outline of the door I knew was there to become visible.

'It's not there,' Peter giggled.

It slowly appeared, as if by magic, as I felt its shape, feeling for a handle, hoping it would open. It did, providing access into the lift shaft, memory taking over as I dangled a foot into the darkness, attempting to slow my breathing whilst my heart was doing the opposite, trying to break through my ribs, thump out of my chest and bounce along the floor. I sunk lower, vertigo kicking in as I looked into the black, before finding metal.

The tinkling of breaking glass then shouting voices came from above as they continued battering the glazing, the wire delaying them, staying true. Climbing down tentatively, I stumbled as the ground came a step early leaving me sprawling on the floor, their voices now closer as I felt around for the last door.

'What if it's fucking locked?' Peter shouted as I nearly fell through, grasping onto the frame as my body swung around and hit the wall on the other side, knocking the wind out of my lungs, finding we'd left it open. I hesitated, trying to orientate myself as my feet remained behind me, leaving me hanging over the void. Shuffling one forward, I felt for the edge which seemed perilously close once my toes moved from something to nothing.

A grunt behind me told me someone was near, my hands grasping out as my back scraped along the concrete. Migsy came through the doorway, pausing then shuffling along after me, but he was slow, his bulk threatening to tip him into the darkness as he kept pausing, panting.

"Macca? Macca? You're not well."

I heard a clang as my foot found the metal ladder resting against the ledge. I reached out and grasped with my hands, eventually finding it in the darkness before hearing a metallic click. I'd paused too long, he was on me, pointing the gun into the black as I held my breath, the only sound my heart beating.

"Just stay still. We need to talk. I'm trying to help you, for fuck's sake."

It sounded like he was right next to me, whispering into my ear as I stood, frozen, before placing my foot onto the top rung and silently launching myself into the darkness, infinity, as I floated to the equilibrium, weightless and liberated, the only sound the passing of air before gravity exerted its influence and I started accelerating towards the ground, which still felt like it could be hours away, if it even existed at all.

Everything was illuminated for a split second as the muzzle flashed, lighting up the space I'd occupied a second before. Sound quickly followed light, deafening as the bullet ricocheted off the ceiling and Migsy gave a roar of frustration, barely audible behind the reverberating gun shot. I could see the floor as I jumped off, landing on the ground with a thud then scrabbling forward as the sound of the clattering ladder was lost in the noise. I remembered the dark opening of the passageway, burnt into my eyelids by the flash of the gun and headed in its general direction, my hands scraping along the wall until they found a void, into which I disappeared.

"Did you get him?" I heard Yoda asking, his voice almost next to me, bouncing off the hard stone walls.

"No."

"What?"

"No," Migsy repeated apologetically.

"Well, get down there after him."

"We can't, he flipped the ladder."

I could hear the anguish in his voice as the words left his mouth, wanting to call back to him, mock him, but there was fear there, he was afraid of Yoda. It felt better to disappear as my hand fell into another opening, taking a turn into the unknown.

I eventually paused and sat, dissipating into the black, thinking of the past instead of the future, there was no future. They'd stripped away everything: the club, the church, my current incarnation, but it didn't matter, God gave me strength. I could live with the

nightmares, but there was pain in their denial, their attempts to delete my history, for it defined me, the rest was meaningless.
I let their words swirl around me in the darkness, sounds becoming ghosts, alternative facts, appropriate for the age but nothing new to me. From a child I had been told my truth was not real.
Migsy and Yoda were no different than the people who did those things, the ones we looked up to, formed relationships with, adults who then manipulated, telling you that you were wrong, instilling doubt, creating the framework of a new normal where you end up not believing yourself, blaming yourself, the Gaslight Effect in full effect, but, deep inside I was resilient, there was a core that I could retreat into which was full of hate, a burning rage, forged in childhood within which I now sat.
"False prophet," I heard bounce off the walls around me, unaware that the words had left my lips as I felt my old life slipping away behind an event horizon as I clambered back to my feet and worked my way along the passageway, trying to re-orientate myself in this new, abstract world.
The only way was forwards, placing one foot before the other until my hand found nothing, an intersection turning right, away from Migsy, deeper underground towards the gentle sound of running water until I was splashing then ankle deep in it's cold embrace. I took comfort in its memory, kneeling down and swilling some around my face, washing away the grime of my old life before scooping a handful to my mouth, hoping it wasn't sewage.
There was something about the cold that gave clarity, a survival instinct that washed away muddied thoughts, allowing me to think rationally for a moment. I paused before striding across, knee deep through a barely discernible current until the bottom shelved gently upwards and I was stood on the other side, sensing the uphill slope climbing through the park before me. Instead of moving forward, I sidestepped along the water's edge until I felt the wall, dropping to my knees then crawling in the dusty gravel until my hand touched fabric, giving a rare flicker of happiness. My hand fumbled for the zip then slipped inside feeling the comforting touch of hastily packed clothes, dry and familiar, all bundled up with a toothbrush. There was a flicker inside as I remembered Willo, disappearing through the wardrobe of my previous existence as thoughts continued to the rest of them. I was usually good at walking away

but I was pining to be with them in the real world, amongst their anarchy and chaos.

I stood still, listening, before moving back towards the wall, each step more of a shuffle, sliding along the rough floor, the stones rolling noisily underfoot, echoing loudly in the silence. I realised that I didn't have a plan nor any idea of a route out of this darkness. Up the hill was the sub-station and behind were the flats, both of which were probably being watched, with side alleys disappearing off into different directions to God only knows where.

I remembered the boxes, trying to recall which side alley Prince Rupert lay.

'The right,' Peter whispered, keeping his voice low, in case Migsy should hear, *'It's on the right.'*

My pace picked up, still feeling empty but not so aimless anymore as my hand returned to the rough stone walls until they'd vanish and I'd stumble before righting myself. I was holding my hands outwards, like a blind man, gently flailing as I searched for the other side of the opening, the slope my compass, it's subtle gradient orientating me as I continued on my way, feeling for the third passageway on the right, fighting the despondency, a property of the darkness bearing down on me as I doubted Peter and the authenticity of my memory, any memories.

"Wouldn't it be easier if Yoda was right?" I whispered. "That I'm mentally ill? That none of it's real? Then I could be healed, it could go away."

"Whose side are you on?" Peter admonished aggressively before thoughts returned to Yoda.

"False prophet," I shouted again, "he's a liar."

But part of me yearned for it to be true. I didn't want him to leave, despite his betrayal. Maybe it wasn't betrayal? Perhaps I was collapsing slowly, a slow burn.

'There was no love there, just hate,' Peter countered, trying to turn my line of thought back to anger.

"It does make sense though, I might be mad."

'You were naïve, eating up their lies, their empty words. You should have left years ago.'

"But sometimes you have to trust people," I argued rationally.

'After what they've done to you?'

"But did they…?"

'There is only me,' he hissed. *'The path to God is through me.'*
I sat, listening to the discourse in the permanent night, where thoughts were amplified, the silence deafening. I didn't want to feel anymore but knew the pain was necessary, to help me move on, to bury the past as Peter stamped down on any attempt to forgive or frame Yoda's words in a good light as he walked the path to resentment. I pulled myself up as the words continued, trying to distract myself as I dragged my hand along the rough stone, mumbling occasionally, trying to get a seconds respite from his admonishments.

"The darkest hour is just before dawn," I kept mumbling, trying to distract myself, but it was relentless, increasing in volume as I tried to smother his voice.

"Shut up," I shouted, my arm waving into emptiness as I followed the wall around the corner, feeling chisel marks in the sandstone as my path levelled off then dipped slightly, causing my teeth to clatter as my mouth slammed shut, a muscle memory, triggering a bolt of fear, that dip…

'The dip,' Peter screamed.

"The Pit," I shouted through the roar of freed memories, the sound reverberating as I put my hand to my mouth before taking it off again, not quiet, rhythmically mumbling, "not going, not going," as I dropped to the ground again, shattering into a million bits, or bytes.

"I'm losing myself," a voice whispered.

Plato was right all along, it was a simulation and my character was finished, game over. There was no artificial world being rendered around me anymore, this was my truth, darkness, an infinite limbo, purgatory, into which characters disappear when they are chopped in two, blown up, shot by a sniper or simply disappear down a hole, as I had.

It was death, an eternal nothing.

"I'm in space," I shouted as an alternative struck me, fragments of memories of the astronomy class as I looked around for distant points of light amongst the darkness.

"I am space. Dark matter. I'm expanding the universe," I giggled. But, I was still a breathing, panting, living organism, touching my hands to see if they were still there, then feeling the walls to see if our atoms could merge, become stone, a petrified Golem devoid of all feeling as opposed to this pathetic Gollum I had become.

'How fragile they've made you,' Peter mocked, as I went through the act of crying, remembering the countless experiences of grief I had observed, screwing my face into a grimace, turning my bottom lip out and upwards, hands twisting whilst my body buckled and slumped to the ground in slow motion. I introduced sound with a whimper, trying to withhold emotion before arriving at that moment, when the dam wall breaks and I am overwhelmed, getting louder, trembling slightly as the tears flow beautifully along the deep crevices in my face.

I stopped halfway, critiquing the performance, the tears almost pausing on my cheek, lacking authenticity.

"Try self-pity," I mumbled, recalling the expressions of guilt and loss I'd seen, usually in men as they realised they had lost everything, the result of a gamble or a fling that walked away. It always happened when they had been caught, exposed and cornered, with no other exit. Then they'd became magnanimous, accepting their guilt and amplifying it, as if it comes as a complete surprise, completely out of character.

I crumpled again and started gurning, the tears flowing as I started shaking my head, putting my fingers to the bridge of my nose.

"Why did I do it?" I mumbled, "What have I done?" My body heaved, racked with guilt, letting out a loud wail as I was overcome. It sounded good as it echoed from the walls, travelling for eternity, taking little pieces of me with it, but it still wasn't right. Perhaps victims….

'Stop crying,' Peter demanded, breaking my focus.

"Will you just fuck off" I shouted aggressively as I came out of character, the anger rising within me at his impertinence.

'You've gone soft, you're losing focus,' he continued.

"I'm losing my mind."

'The box,' he whispered, reminding me, offering a sliver of hope.

"What use is it?" I spun around and screamed. "I'm still stuck down here."

'We're nearly there,' Peter protested. *'We're near the end.'*

"If we get out, we're going to jail," I groaned as panic settled in, before running straight into the wall ahead of me, feeling my nose explode against the rock then the copper in my mouth. My vision flashed white, white ceiling, white floors before returning to black.

'We'll die first,' Peter replied, reassuringly. *'We can never go to jail.'* His words provided comfort as I thought of my father lying dead in his cell, snatching my hands back from the wall as I felt the bloody letters streaming down, FORGIVE, my tongue crossing my palm, confirming the taste.

"Walls of flesh," I whimpered before continuing slowly, edging away from the words, the voices becoming quiet as we all concentrated, my body tense, straining with each step as it searched for the ground, only relaxing when my foot made contact before going through it all again, terrified of the next dip and what it might do to my fragile mind.

'Stop!' Peter whispered. I followed his instruction, reaching out my foot until it touched something solid, the box giving a hollow knock, a small flicker of happiness as I lifted the lid then reached in for the torch, scrabbling, almost dropping it before the button clicked and the space filled with light.

I'd covered my eyes with my hand, blinking rapidly as they filled with water and floating colours, peering around at the stone corridors disappearing into the black, all that they'd bothered to render, before looking at the arched stone doorway before me. A face emerged, smiling, the caretaker's son naked, his penis erect before he disappeared again into the black. I instinctively followed, ducking under the low entrance and entering the empty room, something, somewhere at least as I lowered myself into the corner, comforted by the feel of the manmade walls, pausing before turning the light off as I knew what came next, the fear, catching me, covering me, wrapping me in its darkness as I lay prone, foetal, dead, thinking of Judy as I trembled in terror, alone.

I was conscious or unconscious as my hand walked towards the bag as if dismembered, Thing, independent of its owner. It felt around as I kept my distance, battling the currents in my mind until it found what it was searching for, the dead limb taking the small, hard ball between its fingers before drawing it out past layers of dry clothes. It presented the tablet to my trembling lips, holding it there as my mind approached and inspected it, a distraction at least as it considered the implications. Chemicals were still in my blood, demanding company, drawing me in with promises of escape only they could provide, for this place was hopeless, my position was hopeless.

"Murderer," I shouted, listening to the echo, knowing Death was close by, listening in as my options had run out.

"Not going to prison," I mumbled after an unknowable amount of time, surrendering, swallowing Willo's pill before placing my face to the dirt, waiting for what comes next. It can't be worse than this, my only consolation.

CHAPTER 4

CRUCIFICT-

I was awoken by sound, a noise emitting from the walls, the floor, the ceiling, louder than any possible noise, remaining constant until gradually tapering off, making the ensuing silence more intense, by which time I realised that despite my breathing, I was dead. It was so loud it couldn't exist in the normal world. It was a figment of this new reality, this parallel layer, end level, or whatever it was. I lay still, unsure if my eyes were open or closed as my hand travelled across the dirt, the fragile scabs peeling open again, stinging as grit rolled into the exposed flesh until they grasped the torch.
My eyes took a moment to adapt to the light before surveying the ancient stone of the room, with its crude and massive blocks forming solid, damp walls, and arches at regular intervals supporting the ceiling, their curvature shallow, almost flat, carved with antiquated graffiti which had long lost its meaning. I reached out to it and trailed my finger down its lines, losing myself for a brief moment as light glinted from them, glowing like Dwarfish runes before disappearing as I stepped back trying to take in the whole. Miriam was right, there was magic here, how did you not see it? It all made sense, everything for a reason.
"Miriiiiam?" I shouted, wondering if she could hear me and somehow materialise as I looked around, waiting for her to pop into view or a doorway to come grinding out of the rock.
'Does she even exist?' Peter asked, as the walls remained firm. 'They said Jesus was a sorcerer.'
"There's no magic here," I mumbled, as hope drained away.
'But it will make a fine tomb,' Peter consoled as a contentment washed over me. I sat back down and turned off the light, laying down, wondering how long it would take to die.
'What did Jesus do?' Peter asked, playing a game, unwilling to let me die peacefully.
'In the tomb?'

'For three days?'
"Spoke to God," I replied, before shouting "Gooood?"
No answer came.
I had too much energy to stay there, sitting up and flicking on the torch, the bright white of a plastic bag causing me to stop and return the sweep of light to the doorway where it sat, clean and bright, like something from the future. A rat was sniffing as I observed it from the past, wondering how it got there and who was the benefactor.
"Who put that there?" I asked the rat who just looked at me before scuttling off.
"Who put it there?" I shouted to the wider audience. I could hear them, squirming out of sight, but there was no reply, apart from my own voice bouncing back, the question returning unanswered. It contained food and water, enough for a few days as I knelt down and started eating, ravenous, becoming rodent as my body took over thought, satisfying its need for fuel, converting it to energy that seemed to coarse through me as I walked out into the passageway.
"Migsy?" I whispered, looking side to side before shouting, "Migsy?" Waiting for a response that never came, placing him in the same category as Miriam and God.
'Said?' Peter offered.
"Saiiiid?" I cried, again to no reply, just a pair of red spots appearing, twinkling in the distance, eyes disappearing, reappearing as they looked back at me before playfully vanishing into the black.
I took two steps before stopping, running back to collect my bag then picking up a rock to mark my route. My mind was racing, there was somebody down here with me, something, a minotaur, prowling the labyrinth, half-man, half-bull, nostrils flaring, red eyes blazing as he sensed human flesh.
"Theseus here, now fuck off," I shouted cheerfully, tilting my head back and laughing a deep, booming laugh before walking in the direction of the spots, marking the turns with rough crosses, covering indecipherable symbols, Migsy's secret language scraped into the rock.
"Ariadne?" I shouted, confused, then, "Anubis?" as I followed, watching them pause just long enough for me to see where they

were going, tempting me, luring me in.

"Persephone? Hades?" I whispered, before realising it was Lucifer, playing his games, until he got bored then he would undoubtably come to me. It could be nobody else down here, in the black as the spots floated, disembodied, like fireflies leading me to a special something. It was this that kept me moving, the something, better than nothing, even if it did mean my death, as death couldn't be worse than this nothingness, buried alive or floating through space. The markings were rendered useless as the torchlight flickered, then disappeared, coloured floaters filling my vision before fading, returning me to the darkness. I was now lost, with only two red spots to guide me as he allowed me to get closer.

My senses were heightened, becoming creative as I could feel bodies moving, masses of them, squirming over each other like maggots, hearing their whispers as they remained just out of reach, surrounding me, eluding me as I waited for them to collapse in on me any second. I'd listen intently as we continued through the forever changing labyrinth, sometimes hearing the low rumble of traffic, rats or the quieter cockroaches, scurrying over the permanent white noise of bodies caught in limbo, or the outer edges of Hell.

Occasionally light would shine down from an opening above, a wormhole to another universe where I sometimes heard voices or the birds singing. A translucent stalagmite orientated me, colours and textures locked into its glistening skin, its smell signalling Poison Pete, who had been pouring his chip fat down the hole in the ground for the last twenty-five years. Then it was back to the maze, with its subtle tapestry of smells and sounds replacing sight as the dominant sense.

I bundled around corners, scraping against walls as my skin became moist again, old cuts joined by new ones as I waved my arms ahead of me, picking up loose objects, sticks, clubs, no, femurs and fibulas. The ground was uneven as I was now walking on them, hearing them splinter beneath my feet, stumbling, feeling the unmistakable semi-circle of teeth set within a skull. My body was on the edge, repulsed, wanting to scream in terror; it felt like some animals lair, human bones the discarded remnants of hunted prey, chased blind and screaming down the passageways until succumbing. But I was not afraid, this was the end game, he had bought me here to instil terror, show his magnificence within a stage set Dante would have admired.

I looked up and there they were, still, directly in front of me. I could hear his breathing as the spots had joined a body, imperceptible in the darkness, but a mass that was definitely there. I recoiled impulsively, grabbing a skull as I fell onto my back, the bones scattering around me, giving an almost wooden sound.

"Stand, don't run," came the voice, almost a whisper in the silence and I froze, the hairs rising on the back of my neck. I was a child again, the forgotten child, from the time before I was defined, tarnished, my mind filled with lost memories, of streetlight curfews and Sunday baths, football and kerby.

"You recognise me, don't you?" the voice asked.

"You're tricking me. I'm not playing your games," I replied, full of insolence as I stood again.

"Who I am or who I was?"

"Is there a difference?" I asked.

"Oh yes," came the frank reply from the two points of light.

"You're pretending to be Canty."

"Haven't heard that name for a very long time," he replied.

"Have you changed it?"

"They did."

"You were Iblis, Shaitan…"

"No."

"Now Satan, Lucifer…"

"Dracula, Loki, Yaotzin?" he interrupted with a giggle. "Any more mythical names you would like to add to the list?"

"So what's your new name?"

"A fiction much more vernacular, The Nightman."

"You? Canty?" I replied, mocking. "No chance. You were a little angel."

"Angels fall," he replied as I looked up, my body frozen, instincts alert as I stared at the lights pointing at me. He'd moved a step closer. My heart was pounding, the instinct to flee strong but all directions looked the same and the red spots were hypnotic, continuing to move slowly towards me, reptilian almost.

"Are you going to kill me?"

"I've thought about it, believe me," he chuckled, stopping at what felt like touching distance. "But no."

"Why not?" I asked. "You've been trying for months."
"I've been trying to reach you, but not to kill you," he replied with a tilt of the head. "But, they kept close tabs on you, which made me interested. It saved you from me, if that makes any sense."
"Doesn't matter, you're too late. I'm dead anyway."
He let out a laugh, unexpected, just normal.
"I've always struggled with punctuality."
"You shot my front door."
Another smirk, "It's all that I could do, they were watching if you remember."
"But why would you shoot a door?"
"To frighten you away."
"From who?"
"The myth of me, from them, The Church."
"You burnt the church down."
"No, they burnt down their own church. They didn't want you to do Jacko's funeral, and besides, they didn't need it anymore. They probably sold it."
"The funeral, you tried to shoot me."
"If I'd wanted to shoot you, I would have. I saw you, in the cemetery, down the gravestones with Smiler. I was trying to get to you but they still didn't fuck off."
"Why didn't you just do what normal people do? Phone, email if you've got something to say? You've got a mobile haven't you?"
"Because they're controlling all of it."
"Fuck," I shouted as I looked up.
I hadn't realised I'd been looking down, the spots now stood two metres away from me.
"It doesn't make any sense. Why would you try to help me?"
"Because of what they did to us."
"Us? We were kids together, that's it, you wasn't in the home, you didn't go through it."
"That's a story for another day."
"We've got eternity."
"Your Dad. Why did he go to prison?" he asked, catching me off balance.
"He murdered somebody. An accident, a one punch thing."
"But he didn't."
"What?"

"He didn't. Your real Dad was the victim, he was murdered."
"No…"
"Yes," he replied. "The man you've been going to visit wasn't your real father."
"Don't be ridiculous."
"My father had an affair with your mother," he explained calmly, "and you are the result."
"No, that's bullshit, you're fucking with me. My mother died during birth and my father raised…."
"Your so-called father looked after you for a while, a living reminder of his wife's infidelity. Then, one night, the inevitable happened. They were in the Flat Iron, words were said, a punch was thrown and hey presto, your fake Dad killed our real Dad."
"So that's why you want to kill me? A your dad killed my dad thing?"
"I don't want to kill you," he sighed. "I wouldn't have bothered with the long chat if I was going to kill you."
"So you keep saying."
"I did, for a long time, but then he's not your biological father."
"So you're my brother?"
The lights moved to an angle as he cocked his head.
"You're saying The Nightman in my brother?" I giggled, until the laughter took over, unexpected considering the circumstances, welling up then overflowing as tears started rolling down my face.
"Half-brother," The Nightman corrected, ignoring my hysterics. "So he did the same to both of us. Killed our real father and caused everything that followed."
"That's bullshit." I replied once the laughter abated. "I used to go and see him. He would have said something."
"When he realised he was going to prison, he sold you to them."
"Oh fuck off…"
"To a syndicate," he continued, "centred on the home."
"No, he would've…"
"He hated you but he had to play the part, for a cushy life in prison."
"Why would he?"
"He was controlled. He was one of their representatives inside, there is a network. He was also responsible for you. If you went too far off the tracks, then he would be punished."

"That's why he sent me to Yoda?"
"Who?"
"Yoda, the Bishop, when I was thinking of moving on, from The Church."
"Probably."
"But, that doesn't make sense. They killed him in prison."
"When they'd lost control of you."
"But they wouldn't let me see him. He was in solitary, then sectioned, how could he…?"
"Maybe they had already decided that you had both served your purpose."
"So I killed him?"
"Yes."
I sat silent as my mind rifled through memories, looking for clues. They were all over the desk, through the glass, our entire relationship through a screen with an actor playing a role.
"No," I replied, finding something to clutch on to. "He wrote forgive on the wall while he was dying, his last words."
"I've seen the picture."
"Then why would he….?"
"He's not telling you to forgive."
"He wrote it, there on the wall," I replied, anger rising.
"Was he dyslexic?" he asked sarcastically.
"No," I shouted, wondering if this was all part of the game, calming myself before continuing.
"He was intelligent. He wrote reports, studies of…"
I felt a hand grasp my arm and flinched. It was warm, not cold. Dry, not slimy. Looking up, he was right there, the two red lights, little circles of LED's, six of them, red swirls coming from each, lines of light forming intricate patterns, flowers in the darkness, they were beautiful. His breath was audible, I could feel it, smell it, as the slight outline of his figure became visible, becoming physical as the red light bounced back off me. My head was filled with noise, Peter screaming attack but I ignored him, remaining calm, the drugs lowering his volume somehow, dulling his influence. His voice cut through the noise, I'd almost forgotten what we were talking about.
"He was telling you who killed him."
"Frog? Fucking Kermit?"
"Father O'Given."

I shiver ran through me as I saw the writing on the wall, FROGIVE, in bloody streaming finger marks running to the ground. I'd never known him at the rank of Father, he'd always been above that, a Bishop, but then what?
'What the fuck is he?' Peter asked as I remembered Yoda going berserk at the police for leaving the folder on the desk.
'Coincidence,' Peter whispered dismissively. *'Fake news.'*
"Why do you think he was there for so long? Life sentence after life sentence?" he asked. "He wasn't a bad man."
"Just the wrong place at…"
"Oh, come on."
"They attacked him," I protested.
"Why? Just before parole?"
"Because that's when they were most vulnerable, they…"
"With that rational, nobody would ever get out. They invented IPP sentences for people like him, Imprisonment for Public Protection, meaning their sentence could be indefinite, a life license. Even if they let him out, they could bring him back in at any time."
I stood silent, wondering if this was how it happened at the end, truths told, the great lies that shaped each life revealed, confirming it was all pointless, a cheap trick, my existence a joke for somebody to laugh at. The red spots remained fixed on me, the hand still clasping my arm as it pondered my reaction, waiting me to break down, or fight, something, but there was nothing, dark matter, an electromagnetic field.
"So, if you're not going to kill me, what now?"
"You need to stay somewhere else."
"How can I trust you?"
"You can't, but what choice do you have?"
"None. How can you trust me?"
"Because you have no other choice."
"Desperate men do desperate things."
"I watched you, picking up the bone then laying it down again, picking up the skull then putting it down again. You've had plenty of opportunity to attack."
"I'm dead anyway, no point," I replied with a shrug.
"It's not over for you. I don't know what the answer is yet, but there will be one. Anyway we've got to move, Migsy will be looking for you,"

"Migsy the Minotaur," I grinned, surprising myself.

"He's already started, your little alarm call earlier."

"That was you?"

"I fired a shot, he ran away, but next time he'll come better prepared. He thought he was the only one that knew about this place."

"So are you going to get me out of here?"

"There's nowhere to go," he replied. "Your face is everywhere, you won't last a day."

"I can't go into custody."

"I know, because they'll kill you there too. Here," he beckoned, handing over something, nudging my arm. I reached down, feeling the shape, straps and solid, familiar but unfamiliar.

"Put it on," he instructed.

'A head set, Elvis's VR head set,' Peter mumbled, suspicious, wary.

I placed it over my head and the room was revealed in a pale green light. The Nightman was standing before me, surrounded by a macabre scene of bones, broken skeletons strewn around the chamber.

"You haven't changed a bit," I said sarcastically, remembering Canty, watching a smile form on his lips, the only feature visible below the mask. He flicked off the red lights, dropping them onto the floor where they fell amongst fragments of bone.

"The lights?"

"Had to get you to follow me," he replied. "Don't need them."

"Very theatrical," I murmured.

"And this place?" I asked looking around the catacomb then down at the hollow eye sockets of a skull staring back at me.

"It's the Non-Conformists Burial Ground."

"Fuck," I replied, remembering the flat featureless park above with its single solitary path. "And what? You brought me here to scare me? More theatre?"

"No, I brought you here to show you I know."

"You know what?"

"About you, your history."

"I don't get it, they're ancient bodies," I said, looking around the room, "plague victims, their souls have long since departed."

"In most chambers you're right, but not this one."

"I don't get what you mean," I replied, wondering what I was

missing, searching for clues amongst the rib cages and vertebrae.
"This is where they put the bodies."
"I can see that…"
"From The Pit."
I felt myself swaying as I looked around frantically, sea sick and
nauseous as the ground was moving beneath me. Minute noises
signalled things happening just out of sight, click, click, clicking
before they started standing, walking towards me, their bodies
naked and broken, covered in blood.
They were faces I hadn't seen for years, erased by trauma as they
came from all directions, stepping into the pale green light. Michael,
Gibbo, Hassett, Taylor, Monkey, China, Chaddy, Blind Billy, The
Blue Hulk, Matty, Chief; there were hundreds as I spun around,
tears running down my cheeks. How had I forgotten them? They
were the bodies in the darkness, writhing, always there, out of sight
but now made visible. It made sense, that this should be the place.
Canty wasn't going to kill me, he was just a messenger. I was
supposed to be here, with them, as I dropped to my knees, waiting
to be engulfed, feeling the first hand grabbing my arm, dragging me
up with some strength as I waited for the others to reach me and
pull me apart, scattering me around the room.
"Peter."
My eyes were wide, looking up in ecstasy, waiting for release.
"Peter," he shouted as I glanced at him, startled, before looking
around the empty space, bones still bones, their only animation the
slow pace of decay.
"There's something else I need to show you."
"What," I stammered as he hooked his arm around mine. "This not
enough?"
"It's important," he replied, leading me through a series of arches,
recesses packed with bones before stopping and pointing at a
writhing mass as he walked forward, pushing his hands into the
heap and scooping living shapes away, the rats baring teeth in
defiance before turning into starlings, fleeing in unison, leaving
behind a shredded bin liner with a skull and finger bones poking
out, gnawed clean by the rodents.
I retched, bending over, gagging, then vomiting as he leant forward
and tugged at the plastic, a putrid smell filling the air as he
continued searching until he found what he was looking for,

beckoning me over before peeling a section back, revealing marbled blue flesh.

"What?" I asked.

"There…"

"What?"

"That," he said, pointing.

Then I saw it, an edge of colour, the remains of a tattoo, a long curved beak, a flower.

"Mary," I stammered, "Mary?"

"They killed her," he replied coldly, strangely unperturbed by death, by meat.

"Who?"

"Migsy."

"Why Migsy?"

"Because there are only two of us that know this place."

"But, it doesn't make sense, why would he kill her?"

"Because she fucked up their plan. She gave you the home movie."

"No, he hated Kooky as much as I did."

"Kooky was only there because Migsy wanted it. Do you think he just stopped? One of the most powerful criminals in the country becoming a nightclub assistant?"

I stood in silence, embarrassed by my naivety.

"Migsy had him in the palm of his hand, doing his bidding. Clarkey didn't die because Kooky was pissed off with him. That was Migsy, playing with you."

"It was Kooky," I replied, a belief so fixed that I was unable to consider anything different.

"Did you not see his hand shaking, when he pointed that gun at you?"

"Yes, but…"

"He was a glorified drug dealer, soft as shite. Get a good fight out of him, did you?"

"No, knocked him out."

"Exactly, he's not a fighter…"

"Wait," I interrupted. "How did you know?"

"About?"

"The shaking. How did you know?"

"Because I shot him, from the duct," he replied, as if stating the obvious, "and what about your reporter?"

"Migsy," I mumbled quietly before turning, pointing.
"But you…the reporter. That's it, you disappeared, the kids who were in the home."
"I disappeared because there was a price on me. I've never been popular but the money being offered was high and they were willing to take risks. I almost considered killing myself…"
"You were killing them, making it look like accidents. You were working for someone."
"Migsy was working for someone. I only kill people who deserve to die."
"So it was Migsy?"
"Yes."
"Then why would he show me the cuttings, the list?"
"To create a story about me. To recruit you, maybe?"
"No…"
"Yes."
"You're lying."
"Why would I lie? I tax dealers and criminals, that's it."
"Proper Robin Hood,"
"No. I know what I am, fucking horrible, but I have to eat. You're not the only one with a shitty story."
"So why did you come back all of a sudden? Chasing me through the park?"
"Because I had to break cover. They'd put a price on you. You're worth more than me you bastard. The years I've put into this then you fly-by-nights turn up….."
"Why didn't he just do it himself? He had the means."
"Stop," he hissed, placing his hand on my chest.
"What?" I whispered, as he put his finger to his lips. Then there it was again, the almost imperceptible crunch of gravel, of footsteps slowly treading, then stopping.
Canty waved me forward, keeping his finger to his lips as I followed along passageways carved out of sandstone bedrock, tip-toeing then pausing, listening for footsteps following; they were there. We continued, turning left then right, right then left until we reached a dead end, a pile of rubble suggesting a collapsed tunnel. Panic started setting in, a claustrophobia as I turned, looking back down the passageway, expecting an approaching Migsy to emerge; Instead, it was the Judge stood there, looking at me, a glistening line

of saliva dripping down from his mouth onto his already wet, saggy body.

A grating made me turn as Canty was bent over, pushing a flat stone to one side, revealing a dark opening below. He beckoned me forward as he sat on the edge, placing his hands on either side before lowering himself into the black until I heard the ground crunch beneath him. I followed, trusting the floor would be there as I dropped the final yard onto the top of a small flight of steps before stooping below the low ceiling. This was different, modern, a perfect cylinder of rusted iron, completely dry as I descended down the crudely built concrete block steps before standing on the curved floor. Every tiny sound was amplified as he lowered the panel back into place behind me, a grinding of stone on stone then click, sealing us into this next level as I stood in silence waiting for him.

"He doesn't know about this," he whispered as he eased past. I was surprised at how quickly I'd become relaxed in his proximity as I followed behind.

'You could kill him now,' Peter hissed.

"Is this the second circle?"

"What?"

"Lust? I knew I wouldn't stay in Limbo for long, Christ exists."

"What the fuck are you on about?"

"I won't be here for long here either," I continued. "How many levels are there?"

"I've found two in this area; they've found three in the Williamson Tunnels."

"Gluttons. I'm probably going to seven, eight or nine. Is there a lift?"

"Will you shut up?"

"Do you think he heard us?"

"Definitely, the same way we heard him, despite his trying to stay quiet."

"Then he might be right behind us."

"No, sound travels far and fast in here. It's one thing hearing it but something else entirely finding it."

"But he'll know, that we were talking."

"Only if he was very close, which he wasn't. It gets broken up, blurry. He'll just think it's you howling at yourself again, though at least he'll be cautious, he thinks you've got a gun."

"Where does this lead?" I asked, my internal compass malfunctioning, leaving me completely lost.

"Up there," came the reply as the rungs of a ladder appeared in the distance, ascending through a dark ellipse in the ceiling.

We rose up through a manhole in the ground of a cylindrical room, the clattering of the cast iron disk echoing around the stone drum as I looked around at the dramatic volume of an industrial space without windows. Victorian machinery hung down from its centre, heavily greased cogs, pipes and pistons, a steam punk chandelier with a single bare bulb dangling below alongside other ambiguous collections of cogs and flywheels, pipes and cylinders, positioned around the room with furniture scattered in between.

It looked comfortable, secure, strangely domestic as he closed his front door in the floor behind us, taking off our masks before turning on the light, blinking in the brightness, glad to see vibrant colours again, exploding in my vision like Catherine Wheels.

"Sorry about the mess, don't get many visitors," he said sarcastically.

"Where do Splinter and the Turtles sleep?"

"More like Beauty and the Beast," he grinned. "Remember that program? You used to come around to ours and watch it?"

"Did I?"

"Yes, after minding cars. Get chippy then count the money on a Saturday night?"

I tried desperately, digging through memories, looking for a glimpse of him, his father, my father, but there was nothing.

"Don't remember," I answered, leading to an uncomfortable pause as we studied each other, his eyes quick with features set deep, a cruel mouth.

"Where are we?" I asked, breaking the silence. I was trembling again, freezing as my body called out for nutrients.

"You'll be surprised," he replied before walking towards the only door, taking a key off the metal shelf of a generic machine, bottle green, bolted to the ground so giants couldn't steal it, before taking us through a corridor and up a clanging decorative cast iron spiral before opening a wooden hatch to the sky.

It was night, my body welcoming a reference to time and space as I took a deep breath of the cool air, my atoms expanding in all directions into openness, an uncontained freedom dispersing in the breeze for the last time. I opened my eyes and was still there, on a terrace between two massive sandstone buttresses, glimpsing the flickering lights of the city through the chicken wire full of dirty pigeon feathers.

"Rats with wings," I mumbled.

There was no way to avoid their filth so I stepped on it, Canty placing a hand on my shoulder to stop me moving any further.

"Not too close, you can't let them see you."

"It's the water tower," I said, stating the obvious, admiring his brazenness as I recalled the tiny figure railing against the storm; a scene from a rain spattered bus window a lifetime ago. I wondered if I'd known all along.

"Yep, bought it in the auctions," he replied with a hint of pride as he removed his hand from my shoulder, the play of forces flipping, restraint replaced by the gravitational pull of the drop, one that would end everything, but it was inside that I was falling, dragged over the edge by the weight of mourning and the realisation of the life I'd lost right in front of me, taunting me from the other side of the chicken wire.

'Taken from you,' Peter whispered, reminding me he was still there, *'by the whims of politics and power.'*

I could make out landmarks, the church, the pubs and the swirling streets of the estates where they lived, friends, eccentrics whose company I missed as I looked at windows, trying to catch a glimpse of normality, maybe somebody familiar, though even now it was obvious that things were not normal as the site of police blocks became apparent.

Everything was rose tinted, happy memories flooding through as I put people to places: The Knowalls, the drinking, Ginny, The Temple, oh, The Temple, as I searched the horizon for its light, the sightline blocked by the crest of the hill. I slumped down onto my knees, into the shit as hopelessness returned, covering me again. It was too powerful, a tsunami, too big to fight alone as I looked away, up at the stars and realised why people didn't look up anymore, showing how insignificant their lives are in time and space, their personalities, problems and achievements nothing against the vast beauty of God's creation. I tried to lie down before his hand pulled me up and led me back to the stairs, allowing myself to be guided, noticing little, just doors welded closed from the inside.

'*You're still in prison,*' Peter whispered, '*just a different jailer.*'

∞

He'd left through the hatch, his key clicking the lock in place, sealing me into my new cell. I'd been laying on a sofa, pretending to be asleep as the panic hollowed me out, stripping me from the inside, the water and food making no difference, my body wanting more as I searched through the bare fridge and shelves, knowing the answer lay in the battered, dirty bag, slumped in the corner. I placed my hand inside, feeling how many were left, there were sixteen meaning I'd taken twelve though could only consciously recall taking one as I swallowed then lay down, waiting for the peace it would bring, silencing the voices and fears that filled me. The problem was hope, I'd decided.
I'd been happy to die and had found a sense of peace with that decision. Now I suspected I was still alive along with the despondency and fear that came with it, as with life, Peter also continued, the devil on my shoulder.
I could feel my thoughts quietening, the edges of my vision flickering as the chemicals took hold. It was beautiful, illogical, as my body relaxed and my heartbeat accelerated, my thoughts going beyond the confines of my mind and the evil that dwelt there, beyond the walls of the cell then I'm in a Black hole and everything is stretching, shapes becoming lines as they travelled forever, converging on a single point, this is my new reality.
We talked a lot over the next few days as we travelled through the passageways, a city in its own right below the parallel universe above. He'd announce his arrival with the key in the lock then the manhole moving to one side, then we'd eat, saying little, before entering the passageway together as he became tour guide, showing its various sights. It reminded me of the area above in many ways, the first impressions of a barren and bleak place misguided, obscuring a richness that existed when stones were literally overturned.
"When Dad was murdered I was also sent to a home," he revealed after an hour of silence, walking down passages, ducts and roughly hewn stone.
"My mother couldn't handle Dad's death and started drinking. I

went off the rails and ended up in care."

I wasn't sure if he was waiting for an answer as I followed behind. "Go on," I urged when I could bare it no longer, but we turned into a new place and remained silent, floating like ghosts through interlinked cellars of ancient buildings, their stone floors and brick walls thick with cob webs and algae, sealed off from the floors above. It was a forgotten world as we passed workstations with tools and apparatus on desks covered in a deep layer of dust, a Marie Celeste as we would pause, listening to the drone of televisions or conversations coming through the floorboards above, light shining through the gaps, illuminating dust motes in the air, pipes rattling as water passed through them.

When we returned to the darkness he told a familiar story of life in youth detention, a much different experience than my own, but no less traumatic as our lives had travelled on parallel trajectories originating from the same point, a single punch in a pub involving people we could not quite remember.

"I was sent to youth detention where you had to fight, there was no option. They said I was delinquent, unintelligent and beyond reform, but really I was just lashing out. I had no idea what was going on in my mind."

He'd known he was different from the others, a loner by choice, watching and absorbing the environment around him. It was the violence of youths, locked in rooms then expected to change, some trying whilst others became stuck in destructive cycles, going round and round, their frustrations overwhelming them, leading to extended sentences ad nauseum.

"They were raw emotion, slaves to thoughts and feelings that they couldn't understand, but I could control the rage, switch it on or off which was my key to getting out of there. I wasn't a bad person when I went in, but I definitely was when I got out."

He was released at sixteen, the magic number it seems and with nowhere to go moved into a hostel which was the same but with grown-ups and more self-destructive vices to numb the pain. It didn't take long until he started committing crime, but it was the world around him that made him despondent, how the predators circle the weak whilst snake oil salesmen offered drugs to erase the pain of their lives for just a few quid.

The more he saw, the angrier he became, with taxing dealers the predictable conclusion.

"It'd be different now, there must be some sort of safety net but there was nothing for me."

"The Church picked me up," I mumbled, telling him something he already knew.

"I was determined not to hurt innocents," he continued.

"Oh fuck off, you sound like Batman."

"It's true," he protested. "I could justify the dealers but ripping off good people just makes me one of them."

"So you're a good guy?"

"No, I'm horrible, but I've seen far worse than me; the dealers, the pimps, the traffickers…"

"But, you don't get rid of them, you tax them."

"I get rid of some that really offend me, otherwise," he shrugged, "I've got to make a living. It was the surrogates got to me. Kept for breeding, like pigs in a pen, trafficked then trapped by lies and debt then farmed out as prostitutes once they'd popped a few out."

"So you?" I prompted, stretching the vowels, wanting to know the ending.

"Ensured their freedom. Was a decent revenue stream but I found the whole thing a bit distasteful."

"So you took it upon yourself, to kill their keepers?"

"Yes," he answered with a shrug. "We are a disgusting species. Getting rid of a few bad ones isn't such a bad thing, is it? What does your God think of that?"

"Judgement is for him and him alone."

"And you?"

"I'm a bit more flexible," I grinned.

It stuck me how similar he was to Jacko, how they manufactured fictions about themselves, framing their stories and deeds with honour, a noble cause, allowing them to sleep at night.

"They only get replaced anyway," he muttered. "You get rid of one and someone else is there the next day. It's a good business model."

Reality was abnormal here as boundaries blurred between journeys, consciousness and the vivid dreams of sleep. They infected each other, bleeding over borders as reality was filled with fantasy and dreams permeated reality, making it difficult to know what was real and what was make believe. My reality was upside-down, inside-out, entwined with hallucinations. They couldn't both be real.

"How do I know which reality is reality?" I whispered, the drugs in full effect as I watched the shapes moving around me, as if in a kaleidoscope. But visions were real, not material, but real. It was how God communicated, sending messages, waking dreams showing fantastical things.

'Peter had visions,' my Peter reminded me, giving his stamp of approval. *'Animals in a sheet! Kill the animals! They are unclean!'*

Then there was the matter of time, imperceptible after days enclosed behind walls with no reference to day and night, the sun's trajectory across the sky. Time curved, becoming flexible, changing speeds, sometimes fast, still, or excruciatingly slow but it was now just a feeling, guesswork, there was no real way of knowing. The drugs allowed me to ponder deeply on the matter, meditating for seconds or years, realising how random we were, humans, naked apes attuned to this planet, the speed of its spinning, the strength of its gravity, its celestial circle around the sun.

A memory flashed through that may or may not have been real, sat on Yoda's sofa, trying to sound intellectual, fawning to The ABC, 'A day on Venus takes one hundred and sixteen Earth days.'

"What if a day lasted a week?" I giggled. "What might we look like? What would God have placed into the Garden of Eden?" I asked the ceiling, returning to now. Abstract creatures appeared in my vision, a giant foot with a single eye as I let my imagination run, inventing new species, a collage of existing creatures, continually morphing before me.

Time warped further with each journey, travelling through different decades, centuries, as lost memories of the city were revealed; time capsules of previous era, sealed up and buried, preserved by forgetfulness. The main route we'd been using was the Everton Tunnel.

"Goes down to the docks by the Pier Head," Canty explained, walking before me.

"Prince Rupert excavated it in King Charles I reign to hide gold from Parliamentarians, ingots made from melted down rings apparently."

"You haven't found them yet?"

"Nah, still looking."

It felt that anything was possible under here, building and the opposite of building, taking away, excavating to create space, but it

was more than mere materials, it was curved space time, the earth
continuous and never ending, a fabric of loops and strings,
pathways where the past is permanently there alongside the
present, acted out for eternity. The maze of passageways acted as
wormholes as a door would appear and we'd travel into the
Eighteenth Century, through old basement dwellings, "where the
poor would have lived without light or air," linked by cobbled
pathways following the pattern of old streets above. Another door
and a full underground street appeared like a movie set just missing
its cast, former slums with their shops and alleyways, rooms with
barred windows set in dirty brickwork in front of wooden frames
with no glass.
Through another wormhole and we were in the Twelfth century,
passing tiny stone cells, dungeons and store rooms and the long
straight escape tunnel from the old castle, cut by hand as I placed
my fingers in the marks of ancient chisels, the blood sweat and tears
of labour that ate through the bedrock.
"James Street," Canty murmured.
Then came the Industrial Revolution and the long straight tunnels
of coal and steam, disused train lines with their semi-circular black
stained brick walls, steel tracks and gas lights still in place, arching
overhead at regular intervals.
"The Old Victoria Waterloo," he explained, his voice echoing in
both directions as I waited for the sound of a steam locomotive to
appear, its wooden carriages shunting behind.
"Did you know, Waterloo Sunset was actually about Liverpool?" he
continued, his small talk pointless, irritating.
"What are we doing?" I asked as it appeared the ghost train was
late, a question I asked with every journey,
"What do you mean?"
"The history lessons. Are we just filling time? What?"
"Just be patient," he replied. "I'm working on something,"
"What?"
"These are our motorways," he continued, ignoring my question.
"Our fast track across the city, the warrens are for when we need to
disappear."
We disappeared again, into the claustrophobic darkness and the
sound of writhing bodies.
The abstract world crept into the underworld via radio and

newspapers, their issues seemingly trivial now that I was no longer
a player. It struck me how a metre or two of earth created such
distance between me and them, now and then. It was a different
state, like the dead watching the living, caring little for their
problems and causes, understanding how flimsy it all was, thin and
fragile, those virtual beliefs. The sticks they beat religion with were
true of all aspects of society, but none of them could see it; the rules
by which they lived just fantasy, make believe, keeping their lives
shit whilst they obeyed.
They started to disgust me. I'd get angry, reading how things were
so bad.
"Just believe in something else," I shouted. "It's easy, a new fiction
to replace the old."
I was seething until a headband caught my eye and I smiled, seeing
Lucky's face beaming from the front of The Echo, bringing their
reality back again, my heart leaping as his voice came from the
radio, emerging from the white noise and lifting me from my
comatose state.
I requested more newspapers which were duly supplied and
consumed, rifling through the pages finding Lucky or his
supporters wearing Lucky headbands, some with built in lank hair.
The club was now his headquarters, an image of the building
teasing another smile as a massive headband was illuminated on
the screens, next to a picture of Discharge, looking wistfully into the
distance with 'Come Together' written huge behind him. I giggled,
the sound echoing around the chamber as I wondered how they had
managed to pull it off before realising that images of protesters
were from different cities around the country, the headband now a
unifying symbol.
Newspaper articles were disparaging, columnists framing him as 'a
primitive bandit' or other historic references for the current malaise.
"It's a mafia…"
"An urban mob…"
"A mass movement organised around this sect."
"Peasant rebellion!" I cried.
The radio carried much less bias than the printed word, particularly
away from the national channels playing their limited music, as if
nothing was happening. But it was; Lucky had pulled the disparate
parts together to create a formidable force, an identity for the

disenfranchised, particularly the young. I looked forward to listening to him in my vacuum, filling in the gaps when Canty disappeared and I'd take a tablet to keep the dissenting voices away and travel down a tangent, looking for God's word. I was attentive, energised, pacing around the room at the excitement of what I was hearing as the voices bounced off the walls.

I danced as I heard a professor drone, pinching my nose and copying his voice.

"Traditionally, these protests are relatively unstable and will usually dissolve, but here we have the beginnings of an organisation, with leadership…"

"So, you're saying you're happy about them burning down shops? Bringing business to their knees? Plunging…"

"They can only go on for so long, maintaining profits whilst keeping everybody content. It overpowered democracy with the banking crisis, forcing governments to support corporations instead of people. We're a welfare state, but only for the rich. Money has won and the fabric of society is unravelling, decomposing…"

"I'm unravelling," I hollered in agreement, "I am the world and the world is me."

I turned the dial, becoming sound waves, travelling through the static until Lucky's voice filled the room again, sounding calm and educated. He was everywhere, on almost every channel. I could hear him in songs, his voice in the background, almost imperceptible.

"Can I have internet?" I asked as soon the hatch opened, scraping across the floor.

"No," came a brusque reply as he lifted himself up, taking off his goggles and placing them on the floor, before throwing a bag of petrol station supplies towards me.

"Am I a prisoner then?"

"No," he repeated calmly.

"Then why can't I have internet?" I demanded, like an insistent child.

"Because you might contact somebody, and that puts me in danger. Come this way," he instructed, putting his goggles back on as I followed him down the rabbit hole and through the winding tunnels, down new routes until a flight of stairs appeared before us. He reached up, opening a grating stone hatch which led into another reality, a tiny room, like a fairy tale containing a well-worn wooden bench and sooty black fireplace at one end.

"Where are we?" I asked, expecting the three bears as everything started rumbling, a low vibration at first, becoming louder until sound was coming from everywhere, its waves inside me, through me, the walls shaking, the door bouncing on its hinges as they threatened to collapse in on me, crush me in this tiny space. I didn't know if the sensations were real or inside my head as I glanced across at Canty who seemed unperturbed. I was obviously being punished, tortured for an indiscretion as I put my hands to my ears and the sound continued on its upward trajectory, the vibrations intensifying towards an unknowable crescendo where my eardrums would tear, blood run down my cheeks.

But it peaked, easing down until I could hear my own scream, giving a brief flicker of hope before it began to rise again. I glanced around, looking for knobs or buttons, a volume control as I closed my eyes and covered my ears, curling into a shell, defenceless against the sensory attack.

"I'll stop asking, I'll stop asking," I whimpered, wondering what I had to say to stop the assault, my submission working as it gradually quietened down, returning back to silence, the sound of a bird singing in the distance, real or imaginary, causing me to open my eyes to find him opening the door, a crack at first as he peeked out before opening it fully. We were on the surface after all, the daylight blurry in my tear filled eyes.

"Come on, quick," he said, beckoning me forward, out of the door and into a canyon, a cutting with silver lines snaking off into the distance, the ferns a painful, brilliant green, poking out of the walls in the moist cracks between brick and sandstone where they'd gained a foothold. I felt like running, following the ribbons as they gradually came together and flowed around the corner, but a more powerful fear overcame me, that of returning to this world, of facing people as recognition came through the haze of my mind.

"Lime Street?" I asked, looking back at the little black house with its door ajar, a vague memory, a carriage full of football fans many lives ago.

"There you are, freedom, you can go..."

I looked down the tracks, shining as they reflected daylight; it was bright for this time of year.

'You can't, you're not ready,' Peter urged.

"I don't want to," I replied in agreement, turning back, worried the door was going to close.

"I like it there." I just wanted to get back to my cell, to listen.

"Then come back before you're seen and stop all this shite about being a prisoner."

Then I was back, listening to Lucky, or things about Lucky, thinking how clever he'd been, giving the movements a political direction as he harped on about Democratic Socialism and the Scandinavians who seemed to get everything right before a caller came with the usual response.

"Them Scandinavians have the highest suicide rates in the world."

"Let's not do anything then!" I shouted to my audience, for I was no longer alone.

I spoke to them whenever Canty wasn't there as they were all in the room with me now, standing around the perimeter, two to three deep, each one twitchy, anticipating sexual gratification as I lay in the middle of the chamber. They were liquid, moving as I walked through them, closing in around me though silent, never touching, all stuck in that moment of anticipation.

"He said you didn't happen," I giggled but they were oblivious, their expressions impassive as Lucky filled the room.

"He's the next evolution of #underclass," I explained to the charity worker, trying to illuminate before lunging forward, throwing a punch at the Barrister, connecting with nothing but air as I'd stagger and fall down before getting back up, lurching like the #underclass towards populist opportunists, preaching like firebrands, selling a utopia over the horizon.

"It could never work," I stammered intellectually to the crowd arching over me, gesticulating wildly, talking with my hands as I explained how they had inevitably failed. "They scream 'tear it down' but have no concept of a new society, making their impact short lived, a bright burst of energy ultimately wasted, easily pickings for seasoned politicians. Their arguments are flimsy," I continued, as if being interviewed by the TV presenter who was slowly stroking himself, "based on pure emotion with no idea of a new world. Just a rejection of the present and a romanticised longing for another."

But they were just interested in sex as I sat in the middle of the

room and rocked backwards and forwards, backwards and forwards, listening, listening.
Lucky was different in that he was not calling for a complete revolution but a reformation which could be absorbed into the current system. Everything he spoke appeared irritatingly reasonable as he looked to improve the existing structure, fix what was broken through a filter of equality.
"They'll fuck you too," I whispered in warning. "Make promises they'll never keep."
They attacked him and those around him as they always do, through the platform of mass media, but he understood the game, having to become saintly, better than everybody else, like me, like Jesus, leading through morals and values, being virtuous as they attacked him, deflecting with wit and humour. He was the new messiah of The Temple, champion of the people.
"You clever bastard," I grinned as the radio delivered its sermon. It was the young who'd embraced him, full of admiration for his history and broadcasts from The Lurk. He connected with them, talking of shit jobs on shit pay, a life in poverty whilst living in one of the richest countries in the world.
He'd ignored the mud-slinging and sent their passive-aggressiveness back in the form of peaceful protest, mobilising hundreds of thousands on a whim, creating panic as he announced a general strike. Within minutes they were donning headbands and gilets jaunes then walking out of their low paid jobs in unity, leaving businesses empty, deliveries undelivered, call centres deserted in scenes repeated from city to city, their success self-perpetuating, contagious amongst protesters, creating an aura of invincibility.
I wished I was there with them, part of the movement as I careered around the room, swinging combinations at my past. They were energised, politicised, coming together, forming alliances, far removed from stuffy old political parties or trade unions.
MASS DELINQUENTS a unified media declared solemnly, as if an entire demographic were infected by a new virus, or an alternative Chinese ruse, pointing to the Red Guard Groups of Mao Tse-Tung. But, despite provocation, they behaved impeccably as the strikes were repeated randomly, sending businesses spinning, hands out to the government as turnover plummeted and looters found

opportunity as the low-paid security deserted their posts.

"Deserters must be shot!" I shouted.

There was an uncomfortable pause, a Mexican Standoff on a national scale as they tried to weigh him up. I could feel the tension in my cell.

"Take our country back," was whispered in halls of power, "bring in cheap immigrants to do their jobs."

But fear was spreading with the deeper realisation that they had lost control. Public order was now maintained by Lucky and #underclass.

Lucky continued with the theme of being irritably reasonable by proposing a temporary pause on the destruction of assets by The Little People. They stopped immediately, on the premise that the revelation of offenders would continue, banked for future action. In truth, many of the activists needed a night off as, though laudable, their work often required long journeys in unsociable hours.

"Don't go," I shouted in alarm as the voice confirmed that they wished to open up a dialogue, inviting Lucky for talks without recognising #underclass as an official movement. Fortunately my voice was heard, realising he had no obligation towards the government or its fancy dress politics and refused their request.

"They're devils, corrupting, thieving devils," I whispered to the visions stood around me in their various states of arousal. "They're trying to draw him out, away from his people so they can negotiate a price, make him offers, power, a comfortable life as a cat's paw."

I started scratching his words into the stone floor as he spoke of rebalance, a status quo acceptable to both parties:

           Ban tax havens

State created money

               Sustainability

                   Virtuous circles

I realised that I had heard them all before, in the magazine; I could almost hear the Economics Professor whispering into Lucky's ear as I continued scratching:

      Free education

             Democratic Socialism

Co-operative capitalism
Fair distribution of wealth

I looked up as I heard the iron circle lift in the floor, the watching crowd disappearing as they always did, switching off the radio on the way as he clambered up with his usual bag of supplies. He turned around slowly, finding Lucky's soundbites covering the floor and the walls.

"What's all this then? Ten Commandments?"

"Lucky," I replied, stating the obvious.

"Lucky what? Lucky me? Do you do this to every house you kip in?"

"On the radio, he's fixing the country."

"You haven't got a radio," he replied with a frown. "They don't use stone tablets these days, got iPads."

"You won't let me have one."

"You didn't use your own shit I suppose, that's something."

He was no longer taking me through the tunnels to educate me, but to get me out of my cell.

"You're going mental," was his expert opinion on why I needed to move. But, he didn't understand, he couldn't see them, he couldn't hear their voices as it became apparent that he was just a messenger, ignoring me for the most part as I rambled on behind him.

"He's not promising riches for all, he doesn't mind the rich, which is genius. It deflects everything they're throwing at him, and in a reformed system they still have a place…"

"Right," he sighed.

"He's got to navigate a fine line, taking from the rich in the guise of fairness. If he takes from the poor, he's fucked. He'd lose their support, and them bastards know that."

"There's someone I want you to meet," he announced, taking me by surprise, stringing more than one word together as we sat in an old subway tunnel between roller shuttered shops. It was closer to my time, probably seventies looking at the tiles and signage, John Player Special in gold, dominating the peeling advertising hoarding opposite.

I took a deep breath, regretting it immediately as the smell of piss still lingered, tainting the air after all this time.

"Who?" I asked, fear the first emotion following the revulsion of the piss.

"A client," he replied. "Somebody who can explain some things to you. Fill in the gaps."

"Can they help?"

"I can't promise anything."

"Who?" I asked again.

"Somebody who knows you."

"So I know them?"

"Yes and no," came the reply.

"Why is it always fucking cryptic with you?"

"It's the only fun I get."

"Can't I just live down here? Quite like it."

"No, can't stand crowds," came the reply as he turned his back, walking away as the fear crept up on me, movements were afoot. The solitude had turned my look inwards. I was isolated, it was dangerous, I wasn't sure of how to relate to others, how to face the world as I reached over and removed another pill from the bag, settling almost immediately as my body embraced the peace it would bring.

CHAPTER 5

REVELAT-

He was striding with purpose as we headed towards the docks, on the fast track as I walked behind him, jabbering away.

"We see it around us, inequality, insecurity, the forced selling of the commons, and once they have consumed themselves they will seek to consume others, war, where the poor will fight and die, millions…"

"The old Tate and Lyle," he mumbled as he continued forward, taking me a slightly different route through white, sparkling, sugar coated caverns, straight out of children's fantasy.

The air felt cool where we stopped, there was a stillness with the barely perceptible sound of vehicles passing overhead. I stood staring at a stone circle in the wall opposite, a whole line of them disappearing in a distorted perspective in the distance.

"What's the point of that? A big hole up in the wall?" I asked, unable to figure it out.

"It's a viaduct; we're under Brunswick Street."

"But, why have they got a hole up the wall? What was it?"

He bent down and picked up a stone, throwing it low and hard where it bounced again and again, leaving rings spreading across the mirrored flat surface of the water.

"Bloody hell, seven, it's a lake."

"Yep," he grinned.

"How do we cross it?"

"You can walk on it, surely?"

He may have been right as the ripples dissipated and the surface returned to glass.

"There's our boat," he said, pointing then walking off to the left, pushing a rotten wooden rowing boat into the crystal clear waters, ripples forming just before our feet, revealing the whereabouts of the shoreline.

"There's a few of them," he explained as he rowed below the arched vaults sailing above. "Water Street, of course. Then there's one under Castle Street; one under James Street Station; the Old Cains Brewery…"

"This is romantic brother," I interrupted, trying to divert talk away from actual places and memories above. I wanted to forget it all.

"Fuck off and don't say that," he snapped.

"Brother?"

"Don't call me that,"

"Brother, brother, brother, brother…" I continued, baiting him.

"Half-brother, not even that, now shut up, you're spoiling the ambience."

"Ah, brotherly love," I sighed, glancing up to find him looking away, ignoring me.

"Half expect the Phantom of the Opera to go bobbing past," I joked, filling the silence, but he continued to resist my attempts at humour as I looked down to see shapes writhing below, contorted bodies twisting as I waited for a hand to break the surface, grab me, drag me under.

A whimper escaped as the bottom of the boat scraped upon the rocks of the opposite shore.

"Get out," he instructed, still upset by my teasing.

"I'll get my feet wet…"

"Just get the fuck out."

We continued along straighter passages, tall stone walls made from massive stone blocks, rubble trickling through cracks where the ground had shifted. Rusted metal loops hung at regular intervals, their thickness eroded to millimetres as their iron streaked down the stone of the old dock walls that had been built upon, making them a distant memory.

We turned sideways, squeezing through a crack before coming to courses of red brickwork, beautifully built, even in this place.

"We're here," he announced.

"Where?"

"Here."

"Where's here?"

"The docks, warehouses, two storey basements."

"It's just walls…"

"In there," he nodded as we arrived at a rusted metal door.

"What's in there? Diddy Men? Jam Butty Mines? Father Feck?" I asked, spur of the moment humour betraying my nerves.

He remained silent, just nodding towards the door as I entered the empty warehouse, glancing between infinite lines of arches and columns until seeing a figure sitting next to a desk. The glow of a cigarette flared orange as he inhaled before exhaling a light blue plume of smoke. I was entranced, it seemed so long since I'd seen anyone smoke, it's orange tip cooling to a small point as it was lowered.

A nudge in my lower back prompted me to take an unplanned step, clumsy and noisy, causing the silhouette to look my way, stopping on me as the cigarette glowed bright again as he observed me.

"Ah, Peter," he declared, standing up, beckoning me towards him. Canty pushed me again, away from the walls and into the open as curiosity propelled me forward, overcoming any sense of fear as I felt like giggling at the game being played. I knew that I should be alert, fight or flight but my senses were numbed and I was floating forwards, natural urges held down by a cocktail of chemicals.

"Paul?"

He tilted his head back and laughed before returning his gaze upon me, his face cold and expressionless, "Not Paul, but yes, Paul to you."

I waited for a rush of anger as thoughts of Alf filled my mind, but my emotions were neutered, I remained standing, blank and empty, information without emotion.

He was wearing a dark suit, tailored and sharp, much more fitting than the tweed of the village.

"Not who you expected?" he asked, raising an eyebrow.

"Anything can happen in this place," I grinned, reaching forward to touch him, making sure he was real. "But, no. I didn't expect you. I don't recall us parting on particularly agreeable terms."

"Ah, the village bun fight," he replied. "No harm done but I had to step away, keep a low profile. It was that which made me look at you. I knew Nobbler was one to be wary of, ex-SAS, don't you know?"

"I didn't," I replied, my interest piqued as I remembered him alone in the darkness on the hill.

"Damaged, mentally, pushed beyond breaking."

"I know that feeling," I shrugged. "How are the kids?"

"Still mental, entitled, a fucking nightmare," he replied. "Like their mother."

"So they were real?"

"Unfortunately."

I grinned, recalling her hand touching my leg, feeling pity for him for a brief moment.

"What are you doing here? Developing property?" I asked believing we had fulfilled the usual etiquette, cutting to the chase. He pointed to a seat which I duly accepted, intrigued about the line my mind was taking with this tangent.

"A developer is what I am, but not what I was," he began as we faced each other across the table, surrounded by darkness in a pool of light.

"Black Magic Man in your polo neck?" I mocked.

"I was MI5."

"Oh, come on," I laughed, "and I thought I was living in a fantasy!"

"It's true," he shrugged, looking slightly taken aback.

"All this," I continued, waving my arms in exasperation. "It looks like some cheesy eighties spy film, the empty warehouse, the single light…I'd have thought my imagination would come up with something far better than this."

"We couldn't meet in The Waggon, could we?" he countered. "My past means I know everything about you, about the home, about the sex rings, the fighting, the…"

"Stop," I demanded as the conversation turned serious.

"…the church, your father, his murder, your real father…"

"Stop," I shouted, standing up, slamming the table with my fist.

"The depravity of human nature," he finished with a shrug, unimpressed. "I was part of the secret services…"

"Deep state?" I asked sarcastically, "Fantasy? Conspiracy theories?" I continued, my voice rising as anger sought release, realising I was losing control as spikes of emotion pierced through their chemical shield. I sat back down, trying to recompose myself, letting out a giggle, wishing the drugs weren't in my system.

"That are usually based upon a truth," he replied calmly. "There is a hard to perceive level of government that exists, regardless of elections."

"Very democratic," I tutted, shooing his words away with a waft of my hand.

"A strata of people above all of this who rig the world the way it needs to be. They are faceless, elite formations that ultimately, I came to learn, control nation states via their secret services, governments and people, protecting interests and preventing radical change by whatever means. Business as usual."

"Well they've fucked that up. It's hardly business as usual now, is it?"

"You've had a foot in both of these worlds, met some of the main players, though of course you won't have known who was fucking you at the time."

"You really need to work on empathy," I replied, shaking my head.

"Anyway, enough of me, let me tell you about your life," he announced.

"No big red book? Where's the curtain? Are they all going to come walking out? Hope not."

"I'm going to explain to you how your life is completely interwoven with what is happening in the world today. You have no idea how important you are, or indeed how your future actions may help right the wrongs that have been carried out."

It was unexpected. I felt like laughing. "Sounds like the start of a superhero movie. Important for who?"

"Primarily you," he replied. "But, through helping yourself, you could be helping others, children…"

"You?"

"Yes."

"I can't help anybody at the moment. I live in a hole."

"Which hopefully we can get you out of. You were taken into care after your supposed father was imprisoned for murder. I believe Canty has explained to you that your real father was actually the victim."

"Yes," I replied, waiting, refusing to speak and fill the silence that dragged on.

"You don't seem to be particularly upset about that fact."

"I'm not," I replied coldly, realising anger was the only emotion I'd ever felt towards this deception.

"You don't remember anything from before that time, do you?"

"No."

"Don't you find that strange?"

"I don't know," I replied with a shrug. "Doesn't everybody forget their childhood?"

"You went into a home where you were passed around and sexually abused, before you were transferred to The Pit, a different form of entertainment."

"Canty said my not-father sold me."

"He did, for a better life and the fact that he hated you, a walking-talking symbol of his wife's infidelity."

I recalled the blood spattered screen, the incandescent rage that could appear from nowhere.

"Of course, you can only sell something if there is a person that wants to buy, and they were interested in you."

"Who?"

"The home is where you ended up, when they decided that you didn't quite tick all of the boxes."

"What boxes?"

"It is in the nature of the psychopath…"

"Psychopath?"

"…or sociopath, as they prefer to be called, to make it to the top in society."

"Wait, you were telling me about my past, now you're talking about something completely different."

"The only difference between a psychopath and sociopath," he continued, ignoring my interruptions, "is that they take the next step and become homicidal, they are essentially wired the same."

"Are you suggesting I'm a psychopath?"

"Have you killed anybody?" he asked with a shrug, his smug expression suggesting he knew the truth.

"You killed Alf," I deflected, "and worked for the Secret Services. Surely that puts you in psychopath territory."

"Perhaps, but I did not kill Alf. It was his daughter-in-law, whom I was fucking."

"Greed," I mumbled.

"Boredom," he replied. "I had to do something, that village was boring as hell."

"Garden centre was pretty good."

"In the seventies and early eighties," he continued, "there were all sorts of programmes going on. Massive steps forward in neuroscience meant we could understand the brain like never before. Coupled with new assessment procedures, Bob Hare's lists, meant we could categorise personality types more accurately, and in your case identify psychopaths."

"I'm not mad."

"Neither are psychopaths," he replied. "Psychiatrists and psychologists were prodding and poking, studying brains of children like laboratory monkeys, talking of amygdalas and frontal lobes, biochemical imbalances and kryptopyrrole."

"I never went to anything like that."

"They came to you on the behest of certain privileged individuals. Social services was a magnet for young psychopaths, with their antisocial personalities and episodes of violence, their pathological lying, impulsivity and lack of remorse."

"But why? Why would they come to the bottom, the powerful, it doesn't make sense, they look after their own."

"You're right, they are entrenched at the top and look for ways to preserve that status for their psychopathic offspring. Psychopaths breed psychopaths, seeing their own character traits as the ultimate, thinking people like them should be the future as their illusions became embedded throughout society. They picked up appropriate children with their malleable minds and gave them a path, shaping their thoughts and belief systems to further entrench theirs."

"How altruistic."

"They were very successful, becoming top surgeons, generals, scientists, bankers, judges, you name it, they are there, climbing to the top and their sponsors taking the credit whilst reinforcing the myth of social mobility. There were a few fuck ups, where they did take the next step and their cruelty became visible, but that was mostly covered up."

"So, it's positive?"

"Only in particular roles. You don't want a psycho as Prime Minister, or in charge of the Welfare State for example, which is what we currently have."

"Surely not," I protested, painting their greying old portraits in my mind.

"There is no standard appearance, they don't walk around waving knives, they're perverted but functioning, appearing normal on the outside with their own brands of cruelty."

"They're sociopaths then?"

"Sociopaths is probably right, they are far worse. A psychopath can only ruin individual lives whereas a sociopath can bring down a whole country; You need to understand that they are the people who start the wars, set one people against another, punish millions with austerity whilst theirs reap the rewards."

"Lucky's not a psychopath."

"Of course he is, who else would keep getting back onto the ship? They are not always negative, they can achieve outstanding things."

"You're probably right," I replied, recalling his Nuremburg Rally, his need for adoration.

"So, we are now at a unique point in time. With each generation, their character traits have become amplified, and now with technology, social media, they have travelled beyond the village, meaning they have all come together, their voices heard on a global stage."

"Facebook gets blamed for everything."

"Leading us to the most basic, fundamental error of the whole experiment."

"Which is?"

"There is no longer enough room at the top. You cannot have that many psychopaths share the same space."

"It sounds like a horror movie."

"It is," he agreed. "They are individual, intensely competitive, they have no conscience, no empathy, an inability to conform to social norms; they're impulsive, taking what they want regardless of others, no guilt, remorse, inhibition or restraint."

"You're playing one of their tricks, labelling a whole demographic; the rich and powerful can't all be psychopaths."

"It's a small percentage, yet from their positions of influence their behaviour is so far reaching that they are reshaping society in their image."

"The people won't allow it, they are on the streets."

"They don't care. Look how blatant they've become with their politics, Brexit for fuck's sake, the City making a fortune as it sells off the rest of the country, leaders committing atrocities without remorse or comeback, assassinating critics and opponents, the Skripals, Kashoggi, Caruna Galizia, Corbyn…"

"Corbyn? It wasn't an accident?"

"Of course not, they'd lost control of one of the main parties, then the infighting, spitting bile at one another, death threats to their own, using the media to get the public behind them, turning them against each other."

"Riots, revolutions, you're saying this was all planned?"

"Not planned but inevitable, consequences of information, truths and fake truths descending on the masses, a society breaking down to be reconstructed," he shrugged. "The elites were unified, secrets safe but the world keeps turning and we are now at a point of change, a reformation if you like, where something new evolves from the old."

"Because of too many psychopaths?"

"There are two broad ideologies, but any alliances within these are completely unstable; on the one side is history, those psychopathic, aristocratic offspring, kept out of mental institutions by wealth, imperialist types creating a country run by privileged amateurs coming via the traditional routes, Clarendon boarding schools to Oxbridge, their classical art or ancient history degrees granting them high ranking positions in the Church, Military, Government, Civil Service, Treasury, Bank of England, Media, the City, whatever. For centuries they've stitched up the whole thing, enriching their establishment before retiring into the House of Lords. They are a state within the state, cronyist appointments beloved of third world dictators, just better hidden, rewarding themselves obscene amounts and justifying it with market rate, paid for with the degradation of the rest."

"The old boys networks are not too popular around here, we're the rest."

"But, they are pulling apart, by greed, as the psychopaths behave like psychopaths, and the plutocracy we have always been becomes exposed along with all of its lies. Their idea of nations is now blurring and they are trying to retain power by returning to the past, but globalisation has gone too far, the idea of distance and now countries disappearing."

"There are more walls going up," I argued, completely absorbed in the conversation, despite its surreal nature.

"That's how they retain power; we don't like strangers, nationalities, religions, races and we have no idea why, just what the media tells us, their extreme dogmatism leading to extreme violence. But, this flair up of nationalisms are the death knells of countries in their current form. It's a nationalism used to control the people, like religion, and they lap it up because they don't know what will happen once the nation disappears, so they feel afraid, like children looking back to myths and fables for safety and reassurance. It's a fear of the unknown, but it's already too late."

"Your saying countries will disappear?" I laughed.

"No, but they will be hollowed out, becoming pointless. It's already started, look around you, everything that we have built is being sold off: NHS, Welfare State, Council Housing, the commons, things created to look after the people transferred into private bank accounts, making us tenants in our own country."

"There is always a political solution. You sound like one of those populists you keep deriding, going on about new world orders, Bilderberg conspiracy theories."

"They don't have the monopolies any more, on money or information which is basically what a country is. Traditionally governments could avoid revolution by handing over just enough to allay the masses, but the offshores and multinationals don't give a shit and give nothing, meaning the politicians can no longer deliver meaningful change. They are devolving from rulers to merely admin, agents providing access to our taxes to real power."

"Who is this Real Power? Another superhero?"

"The offshore, a world without rules or boundaries, they're beyond countries now."

"A mystical realm, far, far away?"

"That's it, liberated from the state, residents of nowhere, coming from anywhere, draining out the assets of nations, lowering standards of living of entire populations, making everything beige. It's basically colonialism but the money pours out to nowhere."

"I suppose they're also psychopaths?"

"A high proportion," he agreed. "They're the new elite, only concerned with self-enrichment and survival of the fittest. They want a free market, no taxes, they don't give a fuck about a collective state. They're just money making machines, the new Cecil Rhodes, taking over then asset stripping entire continents."

"The country will still be here, its institutions…"

"As the money and wealth disappear, what is left is run into the ground. Look around, you must see that. The plebs stay onshore, living behind borders according to rules, paying their taxes, engaged in the day to day rituals and habits that keep them where they are, buying within their boundaries, away from the princes and princesses. Social medias now run their social reality, setting their horizons and ambitions, thoughts and prejudices, the lines within which they will live their lives."

"You talk about people as if they're mindless."

"That's exactly as they are viewed from upon high, sheep."

"Who are the good guys?"

"There are no good guys, just elites, psychopaths trying to either take the country back or accepting the new, hence the split. Whichever philosophy wins there will be no great redistribution, the poor will become poorer and the rich will get richer, whatever happens. Look through the flowery rhetoric and they either want to take us back to feudal fiefdoms or destabilise the world, destroy the old ways so they can profit from it. Freedom and democracy are now yesterday, totalitarian is the new black, setting up their own governments then mining them for wealth."

"The protesters believe in the country."

"But the foundations of the country are based upon fictions, lions, mermaids and unicorns that we all buy into though the wealthy use to suit their needs. The foundations are being undermined by truth, revealing the secrets, meaning it's not just money the country loses but also the moral high ground; they are being destroyed by their own corruptions."

"Then they will choose neither."

"They choose from whatever's on the menu."

"So, have you picked a side?"

"Yes, I'm with the new money all the way, it's one of the reasons I left."

"To become a property developer?"

"I saw the writing on the wall, and I'm just like them, greedy. I was protecting people that were stripping the country, I was repulsed and I wanted in. The commons is up for grabs, why shouldn't I get rich?"

"That basic human frailty, greed and the individual, destroying villages, communities…"

He grinned, "The Russians get blamed for most things, but in this case, for me, they are guilty. What happened with the Soviet Union is now a blueprint for what is happening here in slow motion. The bureaucrats and KGB stepped in and plundered it, the enlightened exiting offshore with their extreme wealth, never to be seen again."

"Inspiring."

"Communism died so capitalism doesn't need to behave anymore; money is the marker of success in this world at the cost of everything else. We can't resist, we are not moral, not vicars or priests, there for the benefit of fellow man, we are there to make money."

"And this will be your downfall. It's happening all over the world, they're burning super yachts in their harbours, trashing their Kensington Mansions…"

"No, it'll be my triumph, I'm on the right side. We don't need altruism any more, the tribe is dead, we've evolved past that. You don't advance by helping others, you achieve by climbing over them and pushing them back down. Technology and finance are the future, too nimble for them to keep up, destabilising countries further with cryptocurrencies and online business making it impossible to collect tax; countries cannot control multinationals, they'll take more until systems collapse and super wealth steps in, cleaning up, taking over government, education, culture, corporations."

"They won't allow it, the politicians or the people."

"Old school politics and politicians are obsolete, but what did they expect when they created a country so blatantly unfair? Whilst they cling on, building walls and threatening wars with their nations and armies, they will never be able to defeat information, data. It's virtual, without boundaries, with the ability to destabilise whole nations with the click of a button. New business is appearing and taking over. Apple is wealthier than Britain for fuck's sake."

"They won't fight wars for squabbling elites."

"They won't hand it over for free. Scary things need to happen for change to occur, and the current beneficiaries will resist it at all costs. War is a tool they have used time and time again, but can only come from looking backwards, not forwards."

"Why would they go to war, kill each other?"

"Because it's profitable and it is the everyday man that suffers. They'd massacre millions but keep the higher ranks alive; it has been like that since time immemorial. It's all just a big game to them, come, look at this."

We stood up from the desk and walked across the dusty floor. It felt good to stretch my legs and take a break from the intensity of the conversation, following in silence as he glided up a flight of steps into the next deserted level. I'd forgotten about his strange gait, floating across the village vestry as I listened intently for the sound of a footfall.

The next floor was identical but for daylight flooding in from small high level windows, lighting up the brick archways. He pulled a rickety old chair from a pile of interlocked wooden furniture, reminiscent of Degsy's barricade, which he placed under the window.

"Take a look."

"What is it?"

"Just take a look."

I climbed up cautiously, afraid of what I might find before glancing out across the river, above its frothy brown waves, finding the huge grey hull of a battle ship sitting anchored in the middle, a monolith with smaller grey craft buzzing around, travelling to and fro. It took me a moment to register what it was.

"What's that doing there?"

"It's where the military are basing themselves to minimise interaction with civilians and desertion. Most cities with a river have got one," he explained below me. "It's what we've been talking about, an ancient display of power, the HMS Liverpool pointing its guns at its own people."

"That's disgusting," I replied, hypnotised by the waves and their ever changing forms.

"It's history repeating itself, Churchill did the same during the transport strike in 1911, though it was the HMS Antrim."

"They don't show you that in the movies," I murmured before standing silently as my eyes followed the movement of the waves, my spirits rising in the daylight.

"They've also set up camp behind St. George's Hall, same as 1919, then yesterday, innocent protesters were shot in Manchester."

"Peterloo."

"History," he repeated with a nod. "It's like World War I, military tradition meeting new technology, but in this case, at least the technology isn't a machine, designed to kill."

"That is though," I replied, pointing to the crucifix in the sky.

"What?" he asked until he saw it looping in slow passive circles, like a child's toy. "Ah, a drone. The skies are also full of those,

surveillance of terrorists they say but it's only a matter of time…"
"Aside from the ship, isn't it good to see open space?" he asked, trying to inject a bit of optimism.
"It is," I agreed a little guardedly, trying to nip any positivity in the bud.
"Despite their evils, wouldn't you want to return to it? Freedom, the outside?"
"That's not about to happen is it?" I replied tersely, stating the obvious as I climbed down from the chair and hesitantly nodded back towards the stairs, a return to my future of darkness.
"You know," he said, as we retraced our footsteps to the stairs.
"Ultimately, they can't win, with their battleships and walls."
"Oh, why not?"
"Because they are in a double bind."
"Who?"
"The leaders. It's those human frailties you mentioned earlier, greed and the individual. They benefit from the same off-shore structures that make the globalised possible and when push comes to shove, a psychopath will always put themselves above the idea of a country. They may well kill millions to get to that point, but they won't win."
We returned to the desk in silence as I followed his erect floating body, checking the ground to ensure footprints were still being laid in the dust. He took his chair then gestured his open palm towards mine, though I remained standing.
"Well, it's been a fascinating chat but I'm afraid I must be going," I decided. "I have an important appointment with the hairdresser."
"You need one, you look like Jesus," he replied as my hand unconsciously brushed through my unkempt beard and hair. "We were just getting to the good bit," he continued with a splash of irritation.
"I've enjoyed it, really, I have, and we must…"
"There is a point to the conversation," he interrupted.
"Which is?"
"Context, you needed to understand what is happening in the big picture for you to comprehend what is happening in your life and how you are inexorably linked to this moment in time, the events in the world."
"I get it, I'm a psychopath, a reflection of my environment, a

microcosm of a psychopathic macrocosm."

"Yes, all that shit and more, but you still don't understand your life. You are more than that, you are special, made for these times."

"And you can tell me, I assume?"

"If you'll sit down," he replied, gesturing towards my seat once more. "You won't see me again, so perhaps you should hear what I have to say."

"You're a hallucination anyway, nothing to lose I suppose. So, why aren't I one of these populist psychopaths, one of the elites if I share their particular skill set."

"Not all with psychopathic inclinations will become the elite. They are all around us; think of that little Hitler traffic warden, or the checkpoints, they're full of them, revelling in their new found power. You could have been one of them. You went through the same processes, but you didn't make the cut."

"Didn't tick the boxes?"

"Before the home, they assessed you and you were not what they were after. You were a little bit more complex and the science was young, so your path took a different route, still in the service of the psychopaths."

"Fucking and fighting?"

"They needed an outlet for their eccentricities, shall we say, without comeback so they could function in real life. For every one person they helped there were probably twenty discarded but they didn't waste a single one of you. Plenty worked for the secret services over the years, doing their dirty work whilst you were used for pleasure."

"An outlet?"

"More of an inlet," he nodded. "They considered themselves above societal norms, often using classical civilisations as justification, as if they were something to aspire to. A painting of a boy getting bummed on a pot in the British Museum was all they needed, and you were very pretty."

"Thanks."

"They also convinced themselves that because of your psychopathic tendencies, your emotionless state, it was impossible to cause any psychological damage no matter what they did to you."

"They got that one wrong."

"So it seems."

"But, if I failed their tests, then I'm not a psychopath."
"What do you mean?"
"You said they discarded me, because I did not tick all of the boxes, so I'm not a psychopath."
"I said you were complex, you are certainly a psychopath."
"Oh fuck you."
"You're a narcissist."
"You're an arsehole."
"The magazines, tv shows, newspaper reports, massive screens shouting this is me, it's not a church or a club, it's me."
"What?"
"Addictive personality…"
"Thank you."
"I meant you suffer from addictions, you're a showman, completely dependent on the admiration of others, a need for stimulation, easily bored, cruelty, violence…"
"Rubbish."
"Priests don't get into fights at a village show; they don't attend riots, or punch drug dealers, shall I go on? A loner who struggles with authority, keeps breaking the law, as if the rules shouldn't apply to you, a God Complex, making you superior to the rest of us."
"I don't think I'm God,"
"No, but he speaks through you."
"Okay, so if I am a psychopath, then why did I fail? Why didn't they make me a top surgeon or judge or whatever. Why did I become trash, less than human, something to be abused?"
"Because of your split personality."
I sat looking at him as one side of his mouth curled up slightly.
"That's not true. The split happened because of the abuse. It's a coping mechanism, a way of hitting back at the world."
"The split was always there. There has always been two people in that head of yours, Jekyll and Hyde, Yin and Yang, the priest and the fighter."
"You're wrong," I protested.
"There is no dissociative reaction, yet you blame all your faults on your upbringing."
"I do have mitigating circumstances."
"But you decide how they shape you as an adult; as horrendous as

your experiences were, it was nature not nurture that decided you would be this way. You've always been like this, it's how God made you."

"I'm leaving," I said standing up.

"I'm not criticising you," he objected, holding out his palms, as if to prove innocence.

"Sounds like."

"I'm just explaining to you what you are. Like I said, psychopaths can be extraordinary. Look at what you achieved, even for a brief moment, where you took The Church, took the community; your average person just couldn't have done that."

"And look where it led me."

"You brought the religions together, under one roof, seeing them as equal, just different paths to the same, unknowable God."

"It's just logical."

"Of course it's fucking logical, but they hated you for it. You created the evolutionary step that religions must take, that perhaps God wants them to take, by removing the biggest obstacle to peace between them."

"Which is?"

"Power, exclusivity, and the wealth, corruptions and hatreds that stem from it. You were chosen to create a purer form of worship, you did it, you are the future."

"Why are we here?"

"Sorry?"

"Why are you here, talking to me? And don't say God sent you."

"As the elites fall apart, gaps form and secrets come tumbling out. They have skeletons coming out of their orifices and are doing whatever it takes to conceal their misdemeanours."

"Sounds painful."

"Oh, it is."

"The Chilcot report? The child abuse inquiries?"

"What do you mean?"

"Designed to fail?"

"No, no," he replied, appearing slightly amused and irritated by my naivety. "They're way beyond that. They are just to waste a bit more time, pacify the voters. Think of your list, the newspaper clippings, killing one by one, then the reporter, connecting the dots…"

"Migsy killed him."

"He was just a cat's paw, owned; he had no choice if he wanted his freedom."

"Then who?"

"The same people who have shaped every aspect of your life, made you a victim instead of a surgeon; created a whore, a killer; set up your charade of a father then killed him; planted an agent as your girlfriend, the mother of your child, who then aborted it."

"Judy?"

"Who is not really Judy; the same people who have now framed you for murder and taken your life away."

"Who?" I shouted, losing patience.

"We'll come to individuals later," he replied. "You are part of the fallout, a liability to be disposed of."

"Just when I thought my day was getting better."

"In this battle of information, you are bad news that must be eliminated. But, from where I am sitting, you are an asset, to be used."

"Used or eliminated, the future's looking bright."

"Used is perhaps the wrong word, let's say our interests overlap; they are on the other side, those that have been doing this, the opposition cleaning up their mess, which, perhaps, puts us on the same side."

"I'm not on any side."

"Yes you are. Look what they've done to you, the traditionalists, the establishment, your country, your church. They've buried you alive."

"One man…"

"Who speaks for the whole church, who align themselves with the nationalists, the old triumvirate who will tread on anybody to retain power."

"The government, crown and the church," I agreed, echoing Yoda's words.

"They're institutional loyalists, power, nothing else. The true message of God is long lost…"

"Oh, come on, what would you know of The Church?"

"They have aligned with the people who have done this to you; they are complicit in the whole thing, from beginning to end."

I flinched and glared at him. "The secret services were up to their necks in it. We were tools that they used to get leverage over…"

"I know, I know," he replied calmly, "I wasn't involved in any of that."
"But you know of it?"
"I've seen images of you as a child, videos of you…"
"Stop," was all I could say.
"I was as repulsed by them as you are, I can assure you. It was too much, too far, but, The Church knew about it."
"You're still not telling my why you are here."
"Would Jesus recognise this corrupted church?"
"It's not from the goodness in your heart…"
"What would happen if he knocked on the doors of Lambeth Palace?"
"It's got to be beneficial to you…"
"God and Jesus are actually quite far down their list of priorities."
I stood up to leave.
"Okay, okay, personally, they have come after you and eventually they will come after me."
"Why?"
"The same as you, for the things I know, and…" he paused.
"And?"
"For profit," he shrugged before reaching under the table and retrieving a folder. The hairs on my neck stood on end as he opened it up slowly, before removing a bundle of sheets, their layout, typeface familiar, sending the cold sensation running down my back.
I was defensive, "What are those?"
"You know what they are," he replied, without looking up.
"Migsy's folder."
"Some new entries," he smiled as he pushed the papers towards me. I kept my eyes looking forward, afraid to look down at the face looking back up at me.
"How can they be new entries?"
"There were a number omitted."
"Why?"
"Because it was a tool, used by the other side to get Jacko and Migsy to do their dirty work."
"And these are?"
"The faces they helped you forget, on their side of course."
"They couldn't make me forget."

"They don't have to remove all memories, sometimes the mind blots them out if they are particularly painful. You'd be surprised how malleable the young mind is. They deconstructed then reconstructed you, omitting certain memories, I'm giving them back to you."

"I don't think I want them."

"The man who has ultimately killed all of your contemporaries, denied your truths, has put you in this place, and will ultimately kill you is in there."

"And you want me to?"

"Kill him, yes," he replied. "He is extremely powerful and would be a major obstacle removed."

"You talk of good and evil, then in the same breath, ask me to help your side take over, plunder…"

"You can't change anything. Massive wheels are turning, an evolution that will happen with or without you, but you can do something for yourself."

"And for you?"

"Like I said, we are on the same side."

"Which one?" I asked as curiosity, held high on a scaffold of chemicals, was overcoming my fear.

"Top," he replied.

I flicked my eyes down then straight back up, catching an outline then a little bit more with each glimpse, daring myself, afraid to stop on it for too long. Eventually my eye paused long enough to catch his features, to construct a face as my mind collapsed and nausea raced through me. I screamed as he ran through my mind again, his cruelty, the pain, the perversions. I felt a stinging on my cheek, then a voice echoing in the distance. I was leaning back, lolling, floating, the walls were white, the ceiling was white, my hands restrained by straps, then another blow to my cheek, whip crack, "You're okay, Peter…Peter."

"You remember him?" he shouted through the haze. I didn't know if it was a question or an instruction as he shouted again, "You remember him?"

"Yes, but who is he?" I replied, emerging from the white.

"One of those hereditary bastards," he replied, pointing to the paper before me. I looked again, this time holding my gaze as I read the familiar text.

"He looks like the grand master of a cult, all handshakes and regalia," I murmured.

"Isn't that exactly what they are?"

"He's even got evil in his name," I said, as I read it for the first time.

"He is pure evil, but has been protected."

"We knew him as Little Lord, because of his tiny cock."

"Perhaps that's the reason why…"

"He was so cruel? He used whips, razorblades and wire, he wanted blood…" as I saw fountains of red.

"The Pit was his idea."

"He used to flay them. He started with fingers, then took limbs, eyes, he cut Swanny's tongue out," I recalled as the new memories ran like a film reel, as a tear journeyed down my cheek.

"He should have been sectioned many years ago. He's Jack the Ripper, Josef Mengele…"

"He bled to death. It just kept pouring out of his mouth…" I continued, as the memories kept coming. I looked across the room to see him standing there below an arch, naked and erect, with a crowd forming behind him, remaining in shadows.

"He's still doing it, to others," Paul whispered.

"What?"

"Illegal immigrants, their children…"

I felt bile rising, the burning acid in my throat as I kept reading.

"He's in the House of Lords."

"So, you see why he deserves to die?"

"Yes," I murmured, struggling to form words.

"You see why he deserves to die?" he shouted, slamming his palm on the table before reaching across, shaking me by the arms.

"Yes," I yelled back at him, all humour and sarcasm gone as anger flared up for the first time in millennia.

"There's more," he said, nodding down towards the pile of papers laying in front of me. I glanced across at His Lordship with the crowd of shadows standing behind him, waiting to step out into the spotlight.

'Tonight Matthew, I'm going to be…' Peter whispered, his first whisper for so long.

"Who are they?" I asked, turning back.

"Look."

"I don't think I can."

"They are the ones they omitted, from your folder."
I flicked through rapidly as my head filled with memories and my
body with pain, looking at their features, then and now, maps of
where they live, where they work, their daily routines.
"There's a lot of clergy in there," I observed.
"Didn't you think it was unusual, that there were none in the
original folder?"
"Didn't really think," I replied, feeling foolish. "So, what? Am I
supposed to take sides, exact revenge on these and forget about the
others."
"No, you do as you like, act out God's will. They have all
committed sins against you and other innocents, and you deserve
justice. They are evil."
"Repay no one evil for evil," I said quoting Romans,
"Vengeance is mine, I will repay," he replied, also with Romans.
"God talks through you, now perhaps he will move through you.
It's up to you how you square it with your God, it doesn't have to
be revenge, you are helping others."
I felt breathless for a moment, at the idea of God moving through
me, dispensing judgement and justice. It made sense, for I was
never really in control, an observer in my own body.
"You've shown me this, but I'm still a wanted murderer, living in
shadow."
"There are ways around that, if you are prepared to help. God
willing, we can give you your freedom and you can walk the streets
again, though in a different guise. But, there are things you must
commit to."
"Go on."
"You need to come off the drugs, which we can help with. You are
blocking out your true-self."
"And?"
"We don't want you, we want Peter, so step back, let him take
over."
I glanced up at him as shock registered on my face.
"You thought I didn't know?"
"How?"
"We know everything. Like I said, you're story is completely
entwined with what is happening out there. You yourself are
multiple truths, alternative truths in a post truth world. You are

unique, you are the world; as it goes through this nervous breakdown, so do you; you feel everybody becoming split, like you, between the real and the virtual. Don't you stop to think why?"

"Because I'm cursed."

"Because you're blessed, with insight, with an ability to become somebody else when bad things happen or need to be done. Peter protects you, don't you see? In the darkest places he takes over, like a guardian angel, sent by God, this is your truth."

"I can't..." I mumbled.

"All the things that happened to you, the path that God set out for you was for a reason; for this, here and now. You had to go through them, to survive them, to reap God's vengeance, removing evil from the world. Your cause is just, they defiled you as they continue to defile others..."

"Stop," I whimpered.

"You must be exhausted..."

I felt the energy leaving my body as the words left his lips. "When Peter does things, it isn't me."

"But it's Peter that we need right now."

"I can see him, what he's doing. It's like I'm watching a film, but I'm powerless to intervene."

"He has no qualms about killing."

"I can't allow him to do that," I replied, shaking my head.

"For the greater good? You have a responsibility, to protect innocents. You have God given abilities."

"God would not condone killing."

"You have read The Bible?"

I sat in silence, my head heavy, hard to lift as it hung over the desk.

"It'll only be for a short period." he explained in a calming voice. "When the world settles, there will be a need for moral guidance, more so..."

"I need to think," was all I could say. I was numb.

"... and that is when you can return, with an uncorrupted religion. Surely that is why God made you as you are. This is a trial, exile, where you redeem your sins and you emerge different, a resurrection to carry out the words of God, '*Happy are those who are persecuted for righteousness' sake.*'"

"Beautitudes? Our Lord is talking through you?"

"A prophetic vision which you choose to believe in or not, Our Lord doesn't do emails."

"How can I believe you?"

"Because I am not really here. How can I be? I'm Paul from the village."

I lifted my head and looked around, Canty was standing there, his silhouette materialising from the column as if he'd emerged from the brickwork.

"Before you go with your brother, I have one more," Paul revealed, saving the best for last as he placed another page onto the desk. It was Yoda.

"That's not true," I said, pushing it back to him.

"I'm afraid it is. Have you ever wondered what his actual role is in The Church?"

"He's retired."

"He does their dirty work, an enabler, he has no official role."

"It's not true," I repeated. "He wasn't there."

"He's carefully stage managed your life since you were sold to them…"

"He saved me."

"He put you in there, then took you out again," he replied sharply. "You're Stockholm Syndrome written large. They were part of it, the whole network."

"So why did he bring me back here, to create something remarkable?"

"Because you were going to leave and they wanted you close, though they could never have anticipated what you would create."

"Why?"

"To kill you of course. He's dying, he needs to tie up loose ends before the next life, and you're a loose end."

"He was never there, he wouldn't…"

"Just because he didn't actually fuck you, doesn't mean he didn't fuck you. He was your handler, your interface between worlds. Anyway, I've given you the information and it's up to you what you do with it. God willing, I can give you freedom, a life, justice, if you choose to take it but there is a price."

"Vengeance?"

"Vengeance," he nodded in agreement.

I looked down at the table then back at him. His features contorted, he turned into Alf. "I'll send you a gift, to prove my integrity."

I was awoken on the sofa by the familiar pangs of withdrawal, the
first contractions of my new birth as I reached down into my bag,
scrabbling around, poking into the corners with the old crisps but
the tablets were gone, probably finished.
"Not sure what you've been taking so we need to find out if it's a
predominantly physical or psychological addiction," Canty
suggested from across the room. "Do you know what you're
addicted to?"
"Everything," I replied sitting up and looking across. "It'll be all of
it: panic attacks, cravings, sweating, freezing, shitting, puking, it's
gonna be great…"
"Better open the windows then," he joked.
"How long have I been here?" I asked, glancing around at the new
figures packed around me, silent, standing room only, as if in
mourning which gave me some hope.
"Eternity," he replied, evasive as always. "Are you sure you want to
do it?"
"I have to."
"I've got all sorts of tablets here if you can tell me what you're on.
It'll make it easier."
"It's a trial that I have to go through."
"You could have seizures, heart attacks, strokes…" he advised,
reading from a pamphlet.
"It's God's will."
"Back on God now are we? You were a minotaur last week."
"God never left. I'm being tested. You see, all of this is me, the
underground, the darkness, it's me in physical form. I haven't left
the world, I've been looking within myself, shown my truths."
"Right," he murmured, as he continued reading labels.
"The dark passageways, rooms, memories, capsules of history,
truths revealed, about my past by my past, like gospels explaining
what I am." They looked agitated around me as I continued, "the
bodies and bones, my brother…"
"Half-brother."
"…revealed to me, my real father revealed to me, my truths,
visions, revelations."
"I got you a television."
"I was lost, confused, afraid inside of myself as I wandered around
that maze in darkness. But, I've come to understand it, understand

myself and now a truth is becoming clear."

"Yep, delirium is on there," he replied. "Do you want a cup of tea?"

I stopped my eulogy as the contractions intensified and I curled up on the sofa, joined by the imperceptible approach of the pain, slowly intensifying in gentle waves, each receding before returning stronger, reaching in that little bit further and taking another piece of me. I welcomed it this time, every shitting, pissing, puking second as it had a purpose. I was being tested as Our Lord decided what to do with my soul, joyously embracing the palpitations, trembling and twisted thoughts that cross-examined me, trying to break my focus, probing for weakness as I lay prostate, incoherent, awaiting the final decision as my body and mind contorted, life leaving me before flooding back then washing away again.

Canty was there, on the periphery, caught up in the waves as he disappeared before returning when the pain was hitting a peak; A stuttering image, flickering stills as he came in, hands covered in blood, reminding me of who and what he was, cursing at the smells of bodily waste waiting for him, tainting his hole in the ground as he emptied the buckets and refilled the bottles. Lucozade, always fucking Lucozade.

Despite my state, I only recalled him losing his temper once, replying to my incessant pleading, begging, to put Lucky on the screen, on the radio, standing up before sitting down again, reining in his anger, deep breath, "Fuck off, I'm watching Gogglebox."

He'd leave, but I was never alone as the others closed in around me, bending over, putting their sneering faces into mine to a backdrop of sound and flashing images from my window to the world, Lucky on the screen, this time talking about bypassing government with a network of Citizen's Assemblies. It was all part of the test, a judgement, my past being assessed, reactions gauged as a rare smile briefly touched my lips at a glimpse of Stan and Elvis sitting either side of him, but my smile was of distant nostalgia more than true feeling; their problems seemed miniscule now, pointless, in a different world.

Other scenes replaced them as Our Lord showed me the world the sinners had created. Images of brutality, clashes and firebombs, mass movements of the poor, an exodus of sinking boats and crowds at borders. There was finger pointing rhetoric, fear mongering to a backdrop of famine and fighter planes, emaciated innocents with no concept of the distant politics that was killing them. I felt nothing for their reality as I acquiesced, handed my life over to something above the human condition.

Then, there it was, the gift, dragging me from my internal journey as scenes of the village played out before me. An image of Ted filled the screen, in his robes, his portly frame striding across the fields followed by a crowd, a congregation, familiar faces behind dusted off placards with Nobbler a shadow in the background. Then, there she was, Meg, smiling, with the wind blowing through her hair, the strength of feeling surprising me as the camera paused on her for a second making me panic, emotions supposedly neutered.

I stood for the first time, taking baby steps towards the screen as it showed Alf's son and daughter-in-law being led away, arrested for his murder, the developers shocked at the turn of events and wishing to distance themselves, cancelling the project. There were muted celebrations, the clinking of plastic cups from a hastily produced bottle of sherry on a hill side as the wind blew through them and they reminisced about Alf. Then they were gone, followed by scenes of mass arrests as terrorists were escorted from Nottingham's Market Square, but my mind was in the village, its cast of characters meaningless to most, but these events deeply significant to me.

'We need to get to work,' Peter said, his voice strong as I moved away from the screen.

∞

"You're leaving tonight," Canty said.

"Why?"

"They're still looking for you here."

"Where to?"

"Over the water," he replied, "Or, under it."

"What?"

"The Wirral. Then we can get you above ground and away."

"How am I going to get over there?" I asked. "There's a big river and a warship in the way."

"You'll drive through the tunnel. There's another road below the actual road deck with a Morris Miner waiting for you."

"A Morris Miner?"

"Well fucking walk then," he replied with a shrug. Our conversations had become bullet points since I'd emerged; I was different, no longer vulnerable and we both understood that as we circled like two alpha males locked in the same cage. Peter hated him, revealing a jealous side, a brother vying for my attention.
I packed my small bag quietly, almost automated, the way I operated these days. I was purely functional, just facts, science, feeling like I was in a waiting room, an airport, a non-place where I just had to exist, eat, shit and breathe, as I drew closer to the massive events just over the horizon, where my new reality would define me, where I would find peace as I finally shed my past. There was still much to be explained, the how's and when's but I was relaxed as it was already written. All I had to do was follow the path laid out for me, passing each test that was presented.
I looked around without fondness at my innate scrawlings covering the walls and floors, evolving from politics to a new religion as I lowered myself into the ground for a final time, switching on the goggles then walking without thinking in what had now become routine. I knew myself, the twists and turns of these winding passageways and where they would take us; we were heading towards the river, in silence, as I watched his back move before me.
"I need to go back, make sure we are not being followed, Migsy's down here," he said as he stopped at a junction, leaning over, pulling me into an embrace.
"You're leaving me?"
"You're in God's hands now, brother."
"But…"
"Here," he said handing me a phone. "It's got internet and everything. My number's programmed in, call it when you get there."
"Internet?" I smiled.
"You've come through, I can trust you," he replied, pulling me in close as my spirits lifted; it felt like I was moving forward again.
"You know the way and you have my number, I'll see you on the other side."
"You will," I replied, feeling optimistic as the next steps in God's path were revealed. I'd been at the bottom and was now ascending as he acted in the world, through me.
I moved quickly, the tunnels now as familiar to me as the streets

above as I travelled through time, pausing to take one last look before continuing forward, down the old railway tunnel until I reached the old docks, dragging my hand along their stone walls, trying to get some feeling from the people who had placed them there. My pace accelerated as I got closer to the crack, squeezing through then continuing to the ventilation shaft, and then the car.

'You can't drive,' Peter reminded me as I stopped, a mild panic starting to rise as I had overlooked the obvious, but it didn't matter, a smile touching my lips, knowing everything would work out.

"Hello Peter," a voice appeared from the darkness ahead, a voice I recognised, freezing me to the ground as anger tore through me.

"Judas," I hissed, before turning, screaming, "Judas," at the darkness behind me, towards Canty, flying into a rage as I spun back around.

"Where are you?" I shouted, before that unmistakable click, shock washing through me as I realised my life was over before it truly began.

Panic overwhelmed the rage as I scanned the area in front of me, the old dry dock walls, crumbling, with dark impenetrable recesses all the way along punctuated by piles of rubble, where retaining walls had failed, providing further opportunity for concealment.

"Armed. A nice way to greet an old friend," I said to the shadows, but there was no movement, only my voice echoing back to me.

'Turn, run,' Peter whispered, the first time he'd ever said those words. There was important work to be done, something bigger than us.

"Where to? He fucking sold us," I shouted, clawing at my face, trying to get to him before starting to shuffle backwards, watching the shadows in front then turning around, finding nothing as my head switched continuously from front to back. I was getting closer to the crack in the rock, to the point where my mind was steering, telling my body to turn and run until movement caught my attention, a smooth movement as a gun, an arm, then the bald head of Migsy emerged from a recess in the wall, followed by Yoda, miniscule behind him.

"Alright Migs," I said, filled with anger as I stuttered, wondering whether to launch myself at them or stand my ground.

"What was the price?" I asked.

"Sorry?"

"What was the price, to lead me here?"

"Your phone brought us here," Yoda said, moving in front of Migsy, towards me. "You've been gone for a month; we thought you were dead."

"Sorry to disappoint," I replied. "What do you want?"

"To bring you with us. You can't stay like this, Peter."

"I know all about you," I said, my finger trembling as it pointed at him.

"Doubt it…"

"He put us in the home," I said, glancing up at Migsy, "to be raped."

"Don't be ridiculous," Yoda groaned, shaking his head slowly.

"You've been controlling everything. I know about the tests, the psychopaths, how you manipulated my father, how you…"

"Your psychosis is the reason I helped you."

"They tested me; they did tests."

"Of course they did, that's normal in care."

"It's why you bought me. I was sold, to be tortured."

"Where did you get all of this nonsense?"

"My brother."

"You don't have a brother."

"My half-brother, The Nightman," I said glancing up at Migsy. "That's why you kept me away from him, created all those stories, isn't it? Isn't it?" I screamed.

"Another fucking psychopath," Yoda shouted back. "He went through the same thing as you, both fall out from a punch in a pub, you just took different routes. Is that how you have been living down here? Locked in with that animal?"

"He explained the truth to me."

"Whose truth, yours? Feeding your illusions about abuse and violence before setting you off on this self-destructive path? To do what? Where the fuck are you going?"

"I don't know, God is showing me…"

"All the work we did, putting you back together, you're coming apart again."

"God came…"

"God has shown you nothing. You're a psychopath, you always were."

"The home made me like this," I shouted.

"'The wicked are estranged from the womb: they go astray as soon as they be born, speaking lies.'"
"You're quoting fucking Psalms at me now?" I shouted. "You're corrupted, you're church is corrupted, you have no right to say those words."
"It's you that's corrupted," he replied angrily. "You always have been."
"Religion has been betrayed; Jesus has been betrayed, by you, The Church, seduced by wealth and power."
"Power is either something you do, or something you let others do to you. We make no apologies for our allegiances."
"Politics is atheist; you can't be both belief and disbelief; the church of the rich and the poor. You've abandoned them."
"That's a myth, look around, atheism is in the past. Russian politics is now Orthodox, Indian politics, Hindu, the Yanks can't drop a bomb without mentioning God, then the Muslims, don't get me started on the Muslims. Religion is back at the forefront, we have chosen power and the powerless will fall in line eventually, they always do."
"You've abandoned them, your congregations are on the streets."
"Power is religion, the mob is not."
"They'll reject The Church, you're oppressors."
"Nonsense, they'll come to us and we can share austerity together, until the next world, where everything will be tickety boo and they'll be on top."
"As long as they have obeyed the rules? Be pious and you will get your revenge in the next life?"
"Hope - it keeps them in place. It's how it's always been, allowing the country to operate."
"It's Christian Fundamentalism, God oppressing..."
"We are a key element of a successful country that needs its poor, an army, a workforce. They don't need to progress in society, they can express themselves in The Church, still become leaders, without damaging the real world."
"Listen to you," I giggled, "Seduced by money and power. Building your walls, entrenching your wealth…"
"Reinforce people with money and take from those without; it's the way the world works. Would you rather the institution just vanished?"

"That word, institution…"
"Where have you been getting these ideas from? The Nightman
doesn't do politics."
"Paul, from the village."
"What?"
"Paul, from the village. That's not his real name, he's former secret
service…"
He started giggling, trying to hold it in before it forced its way out.
He leant back and laughed, the sound taking me back to better
times, mung dinners and dog shit reporters, before Peter started
boiling within, furious.
"Do you know how that sounds?" he asked. "Do you understand
what you've been saying?"
"It's real," I shouted as he continued sniggering. "Do you mock
when you read about visions in the Bible? Or are they an
unquestionable truth?"
"Did an angel come and release you, Peter?"
"It's how Our Lord reveals himself, and spreads his will amongst
us. It was impossible, an experience beyond reason, beyond
science."
"An angel called Paul?"
"Did you come here to kill me?" I asked, tired of his mockery.
"We came here to help you, to bring you in."
"Going to give me my job back?" I asked, sarcastically.
"They've turned their back on you, after you debased the whole
religion."
"You sound like those placard waving Grandmas, standing
outside."
"That's not to say we learnt nothing from you," he continued.
"Opening a chain of nightclubs?"
"No, but we realised that we have to evolve, allowing slightly
different interpretations in different areas, depending upon the
demography. As long as we retain power of each then everything's
fine, doesn't matter what interpretation of The Bible they want to go
with. We may even pitch a few against each other, gives them a
cause, boosts attendances and income as they compete to be devout.
So, you see, you do have a legacy, though nobody but us will know
anything about it."
"Did it have to be this way? Could I not have continued?"

"You're too inflexible, too principled, too vocal, too belligerent."
"So what? You're taking over? You and Crab Scratch with your Jew's Harp?"
"Ah, miss that kid," he mused before running his tongue across the broken tooth, a smirk crossing his lips. "Father Williams is reclaiming his parish. Lily has dropped all allegations and the Father has successfully completed the remediation process."
"No, they wouldn't back down, they were telling the truth."
"You're right, but, like we've been saying, money and power win out in the end. That's what these people need to understand, it'd make their lives much easier."
"They took a deal?"
"No, we just stretched it out so it became unaffordable. She wouldn't let go you see, and now she'll die a very bitter woman."
"The people will never accept him."
"They'll be scattered once things settle. There'll be a new flock for him to guide, then, in a year's time, we'll sue Lily and Danny. We have to send out a message, prevent this sort of slander happening again."
"It wasn't slander, it was truth."
"So?" he shrugged.
'Kill him,' Peter whispered, discarding the bigger picture for immediate satisfaction.
"Easy," Migsy warned, cocking the gun, recognising the body language. I'd let him get to me.
"I won't go to prison, my life has taken on greater meaning."
"What meaning? What are you going to do?" Yoda asked. "Come with us and you'll get the care that you need; go alone and you'll last five minutes, you'll be taken away."
"Out of your control."
"You couldn't handle prison. You've said it yourself, you're too fragile, we can make sure…"
"I'm not coming with you," I insisted.
"You're unravelling, we can fix you, we've done it before."
"You brainwashed me, made me forget things, I'm susceptible, to religion."
"How can it have been bad? We did what was needed to bring you to God, to give your life meaning, a direction. It may have been difficult but you were difficult, a stubborn, hard faced brat whose

life was only going one way."

"It could have gone any way, I didn't get a say in it."

"It's in your genes. Your father was a psychopath, a life in prison, now here you are, ready to take his place, believing the lies that fit your narrative, manipulating…"

"You're twisting it, like you always have. My father wasn't in prison, and you know it."

"You need to ask yourself at what point are we mad, what step on the path? Look at yourself. What's imaginary? What's real?"

"That's quite a statement from the clergy," I laughed, scoring a cheap point.

"You'll end up in a secure unit at best, a psychiatric ward."

"There are much bigger plans for me."

"You are coming with me, one way or another."

"How? How's that going to happen? You're going to shoot me Migsy?" I asked, looking him in the eye. There was determination there as he held my gaze. "Wrap me up in plastic and put me with Mary and the rest of our friends?"

A frown creased his forehead, "I've no idea what you're…"

"You killed Mary" I said. "You killed the others, friends, blaming it on The Nightman."

"I didn't kill Mary," he replied. "Though I did kill the others. There's a price, for doing business."

"So, if the home didn't happen, why are you killing them?"

"Because they were nothing to do with the home, they were drug dealers," Yoda replied. "You'd never met them, your mind just creates these intricate webs."

"You killed Bob Sponge because he was joining the dots."

"But the dots didn't point to the home, they pointed to the drugs trade, and back to Migsy," Yoda explained. "You put the dogs onto him. You killed the reporter, you gave Migsy no choice."

"Then why would he show them to me in the first place?" I asked, "Before becoming your bitch."

"He was playing with you, tying you in knots, creating a bogeyman."

"The Nightman? My brother?"

"You haven't got a brother," Yoda repeated.

"Then why are you creating fantasies to keep me away from him?"

"Because he's evil, psychopathic, simple as that. Anything good anybody tries to do in that place he's there, taking. There would have been no church, he burnt it down for fuck's sake…"

"I can handle evil," I replied.

"You can't, like you said, you're susceptible, to conspiracies and anything negative, then you pull things down from the inside, destroy everything you have built. You do it every time, every placement, then move on. It's a fault line, within you."

"You're twisting, evil…"

"I've been nothing but good for you," he protested.

"You killed my father," I said interrupting him, knowing it would irritate him. "That's evil, psychotic, though of course he wasn't my father, was he?"

"Of course he was your father," he shouted.

"Liar!"

"Let's say that's true, which it's not. What harm did it do to you, having a father?"

"Because nothing in my life is real," I replied. "It was manufactured, by you."

"Surely it was him that suffered for his sins, not you."

"I don't know who my real father is, and you have to ask what harm did it do."

"Everything has been done to help you, from love."

"And this is love?" I asked, turning to Migsy. "Why are you even with him, pointing a gun at me?"

"Because he can do what I cannot."

"Oh, you mean…"

"Because I love you so much. Prison will destroy you, I can't let you go through that."

"So you'll kill me?"

"If I need to," he replied. "I know you don't believe in the direction The Church is going, but above all of that, us…"

"At least you're consistent," I interrupted, "Jesus was executed for his words and actions, for challenging the true power behind religion."

"You're aligning yourself with Jesus now?" he smirked.

"Always," I replied, before glancing back at Migsy. "Our shared histories and you change allegiance like the wind. What has he got on you? What was the price for freedom?"

"You," he replied, raising an eyebrow, his hand steady.

"You'd pull the trigger," I asked, trying to read him.

"Yes," he replied calmly.

"After everything they did to us, you'd still kill me?"

"Our lives overlapped, that's it," he shrugged.

"That's it?" I repeated.

"He killed Jacko, he's not going to give two shits about killing you," Yoda chuckled.

"You?"

"Yes," Migsy replied with a shrug. "He was blocking my path to the top, he understood."

"What do you mean, he understood?"

"Because I told him, before he died."

"I wanted to take him to hospital, the doctor said no."

"The doctor was busy killing him. We told a little white lie."

"Come with me, Peter," Yoda said, holding out both of his arms, willing me into his embrace.

"I can't," I replied, repulsed by the idea.

"We're coming to the end. Please, come with me, Peter," he beseeched, his tone demanding.

"Never," I replied, shaking my head, believing in God's intervention.

"I beg you one last time. Look behind all of these miss-truths, these fabrications."

He stopped talking as a tear ran down his cheek, though I could see through his acting.

"Let me show you something," I offered, wondering who the act was for as a look of irritation, then suspicion creased his features as my hand moved slowly towards my bag.

"Peter," Migsy warned.

"It's a sheet of paper," I replied, fingering the zip, glancing down.

"What is it?" Yoda asked, an urgency in his voice, off balance for a change.

"Just a piece of paper," I replied, "one of many," as I slowly removed it from the bag, its rustling the only sound in the cavernous space. Yoda appeared agitated, recognising the potential threat of a document, words, as I kept my movements slow, meeting with silence as I held it out before me.

"Where did you get that?" Yoda demanded, his response removing any lingering doubt as he recognised its format.

"Paul, from the village," I replied, "the one you had a good laugh at."
Migsy's eyes had moved onto him for the first time, questioning, the slight frown re-appearing as the first cracks of doubt pushed through.
"You?" Migsy whispered, unable to hold his tongue.
"I wasn't involved in any of that," Yoda protested.
"So you know what it is?" I asked.
"No, well yes," he stammered.
"You were a facilitator, a pimp…" I shouted, now sure of my words, sure of the truth.
"No, this is a fabrication, a fake."
"It's real, they're all real," I replied, reaching in and pulling out more of the clergy,
"They're fucking with you, somehow…" he shouted, as panic pulled down his calm veneer.
"You gave us to rapists, to power, your holy trinity…"
"Shoot him," he demanded, turning to Migsy. "He's too far gone."
Migsy looked back to me, doubt on his face for the first time, looking like a child again as he raised the gun towards me, slower this time.
"Who paid you, to kill the others?" I asked, sinking the frown deeper into his forehead.
"Don't know," came the reluctant reply.
"You don't know? You're better than that for fuck's sake."
"There are contacts, anonymous, password protected…"
"I told you, don't let him in," Yoda insisted, but I was in, and Migsy was engaged as his eyes locked onto mine.
"It's always been like that, the price of business," he continued with a shrug, deflating before me as Yoda's lies collapsed with him.
"It's one of them. You've been working for one of them, from the home."
"No," he mumbled, as doubt continued burrowing.
"This one," I said, holding another sheet of paper before me, the identity concealed, the Little Lord staring back at me, still creating panic, apparently contagious as Yoda's mask slipped completely.
"Kill him," he shouted, reaching up, jumping like a child as he tried to grab Migsy's arm, but curiosity was buying me time as he remained focused on the sheet.

"Show me," he whispered quietly, the fear seeping through as I turned the paper slowly, looking around it, feeling a pang of pleasure at the split second of recognition, then guilt as his face slackened, body buckling as he held Yoda off, deaf to his hysterical rantings. "No," was all he managed to say as Yoda started to slap him.

"They made us forget."

"He's getting to you," Yoda screamed, fear now tinting his voice. "We had a deal, it's the only way we can help him."

"Victims killing victims, covering his tracks, it's perfect," I continued softly, pummelling him with truth.

"You're going to prison," Yoda threatened, looking comical, jumping, pointing a threatening finger.

"I know why you're doing it," I added, "but he'll kill you too."

"You're both going to prison, I can promise you that," he continued, ignoring me, regaining the upper hand as Migsy looked down at him. "We agreed, I'm your only way out."

"I need your help Migsy," I pleaded, trying to get him back. "He's got to do this, he's in the folder, you'll be next."

"There's only one way to help your friend," Yoda argued.

"We need to get him," I said, jabbing at the paper, trying to bring him on board. "You and me, we'll get all of them."

"There's no other way," Yoda added mournfully, the grabbing hand now gently placed on his forearm. "If I don't walk out of here, the information will be sent. You'll be away for the rest of your life."

"He's one of them," I pleaded, as the gun was lifted slowly towards me. "You remember what they did to us, he's one of them."

But, Yoda's words were getting through, his argument more pervasive, Migsy's instinct for self-preservation stronger than his urge for revenge.

"Sorry," Migsy replied, mask back on, job to be done.

"Migs," I murmured as the room erupted in sound, as Migsy's face collapsed inwards in slow motion, deforming before blowing outwards in fragments of liquid and flesh, his eye still focused on me as he fell backwards. I dropped down next to him, hoping to catch that moment as life left his body but he was gone.

"God," I said, feeling awestruck, relieved that it had come to an end, that he had to bear it no longer before instinctively moving into shock and grief, shouting "No," as my face contorted, fingers turning to claws, my body starting to buckle beneath the weight of grief, forcing me down, before realising I didn't have to do it any more, then standing up straight, my heartbeat slowing as I let out a giggle, I felt indestructible.

"Don't," came from behind me, as I glanced down at Yoda on the ground, living next to dead, his hand touching Migsy's gun still held in his stiffening fingers, eyes looking past me in shock.

"Second time I've had to do that, brother," Canty said as he appeared next to me.

"Sorry, I was distracted, I just automatically go into role play."

"You need to shake that off,"

"Years of habit. Did you have to kill him?"

"He's too easily turned."

"What was all this?" I asked, glancing across at his gun still fixed on Yoda. "I thought you'd betrayed me."

"It was a test," he replied, "to see if you can do what has been asked of you."

"He said my phone…"

Canty grinned, "My phone, your SIM. As soon as it was switched on they were after you. I knew they'd be watching."

"But how…?"

"The SIM? Off Willo, in the park. Good move that one, otherwise we may have been reunited earlier."

"He came past covered in blood," I recalled.

"He didn't want to share," Canty shrugged.

"He's evil," Yoda hissed from the ground, his voice regaining strength.

"Which one?" Canty laughed, more of a cackle.

I felt a moment of pity as I looked down on Yoda, but Peter stamped that out quickly. He was shaking now, starting to stammer, but it was anger that was driving him.

"Evil," he kept muttering.

"Can you do what has been asked of you?" Canty said, handing over his gun. It felt heavy in my hand as I looked down it, through to Yoda who was kneeling in the pool of blood, next to Migsy's corpse.

"Shoot me if you want to, I'm dying anyway, riddled with it," Yoda cursed, waving me away with a flick of the hand,

I paused, my finger stroking the trigger, applying tiny pressure, tiny pressure, *'Kill him'* Peter shouted, but I couldn't, I still loved him, despite the despicable things he'd done to me.

"Not my style I'm afraid," I said, handing back the gun.

"He can't do it," Yoda mocked, an unpleasant smile contorting his features, "He's too fucking weak."

"I'll do it in my own way," I replied. "A bullet is too quick, with no chance to repent. And, I'd like to spend a bit more time with him."

Canty shrugged, "Whatever you prefer, there's a reward waiting for you when you've ticked this one off your list."

"Another field?"

"Better than that," he replied with a grin.

CHAPTER 6

RESURRECT-

"So are you going to tell me how you did it?" I asked, sat on the sofa drinking beer, eating nachos, waiting for the twenty four hour news cycle to return to Anfield.
"Very simple," he replied, reaching over, grabbing a handful. "They always over complicate these things in the movies, swapping faces, all that sort of shit."
"There's a body, so there must be a victim."
"There is."
"Who?"
"I only do the sinners," he deflected, "you know that."
"Who?" I asked again, impatiently. I'd been pleading like a child for the last week, after he'd presented my reward for my first kill; it was beyond expectation, nullifying any lingering remorse I'd felt for Yoda.
"Knockout," he replied with a sigh, then a grin, enjoying the moment of revelation, examining my face for a reaction.
I was initially shocked, but felt no remorse, remembering the person he was, the worst type, the cowardly often the most cruel.
"He was making some kids life hell in a Hertfordshire village, doing his big-I-am county lines thing. But," he shrugged, "now he's not."
"But," I paused, "it doesn't make sense."
"What doesn't?"
"How can I be dead? How can I disappear?"
"We disfigured him. He was in pieces."
"But, a simple blood test…"
"You're asking why aren't we scraping off your fingerprints? Pulling out your teeth? Fiddling with your DNA, all that stuff?"
"Well, yes."
"We just hacked into the records, put your name to his information and now you're dead. How does it feel?"
"But, in the village…"

"They think he's moved on, glad to see the back of him. We killed him in a different county, there's no comeback."

They'd discovered my body last week, Canty joyously unveiling my murder on Breaking News, putting an abrupt end to the multiple nationwide sightings reported each day. It was a relief to me, that I was dead, dismembered, my body parts and memories spread over a mile of riverbank near Ross-on-Wye, discovered by a group of anglers, Keith, Bobby, Peter and Billy, who'd sobered up quickly when Billy's dog delivered a forearm. It was my life of torment, scattered in the fields. I was reborn, something new, for whom the past does not exist, an eternal now.

The press framed it as a gangland killing, talking silhouettes revealing secret contracts, but conspiracies spread rapidly, #underclass labelling it an establishment assassination, my death symbolic of the depths power would stoop to protect their position. I was becoming canonised, immortalised by the people as my face appeared on banners, becoming a myth, an outlaw, a freedom fighter taken from them. The government was now teetering from the upswell of emotion, an #underclass reinvigorated, the riots intensifying as cities were re-ignited, engulfed in fire and smoke by crowds of Gilets Jaunes with their flash jackets and seventies headbands. Lucky was in ascendancy, riding on the wave of anger as a good populist should, word of my death curtailing his moderate tone, his words from the lectern now laced with fury, sending the powerful scattering to assume a conciliatory position in this complex, fast moving game of chess.

Breaking news bounced along the bottom of the screen, '*Gamekeepers turned Poachers: Accountants revealing hidden monies of clients to avoid prison sentence,*' distracting me momentarily from my own funeral which was being televised, shots from a helicopter revealing massive crowds filling the cemetery and Stanley Park opposite. Peter had allowed me this moment, to say goodbye, a tear running down my cheek as I watched my history come together, walking past journalists and prying television cameras, some pausing for a photo, as if in line for an award as they walked into the sandstone crematorium.

"You tried to shoot me last time we were there," I said, glancing across at Canty sprawling across the room. He'd been working hard, taxing the newcomers trying to get a foothole in the city's

clandestine trades, tentatively stepping into the space left by Migsy.
"Wish I bloody had," he mumbled.
"Can't believe you didn't go to your own brothers funeral."
"Half-brother," he grinned.
This was God's work, of that I was sure, making me wonder if this
is what happens, your life flashing before you, a retrospective for
assessment at the gate. It was wonderful, pure nostalgia as I
watched the cast of characters, my closing credits, a smile touching
my lips at a defiant new Ted, fully robed against instruction, his
body shaking with emotion, cheeks flushed red, blubbering as he
was held upright by Roy and Pin. A little piece of me wanted to
explain to him, relieve his grief but the dead stay dead, it was
Peter's future now, I had lived my life.
His congregation followed behind, a crowd of familiar faces:
Marion, Nobbler, Margaret, Alan, Pauline, Noddy, Andrew,
Scarlett, without her horses; I could picture their journey up here,
the whole village coming together, relocating for a day, a charra of
packed lunches, scotch eggs and trays of beer, laughter and loud
chatter behind coach windows covered in condensation, with an
empty seat left for Alf.
A frown crossed my face as Bishop Gordon appeared from the
crowd but he was short lived as Meg appeared in black, walking
behind them, nostalgia turning to grief for the first time following
my death as I bolted upright in alarm, then sunk back with a smile
as I spotted Discharge, one step behind, a lion stalking prey though
she seemed oblivious to the danger.
"More STD's than a game of scrabble that one," I mumbled.
"You had feelings for her, didn't you?"
"Yes," I replied, after a pause. None of it really mattered any more.
"There is a reason for that," he grinned.
"Which you're not going to tell me."
"When the time is right," he replied, handing over another can of
beer and the bowl of popcorn which was now empty, just kernels
remaining at the bottom.
"I wish I could be there," I sighed, it felt like a state occasion as
characters from my previous placements streamed past, some
barely recognisable, older versions of themselves, their conservative
middle aged appearances at odds with their actions and memories
of youth. Amongst them were old flames that had never truly

ignited, passing with no idea of each other or their place in my evolution, talking with the university group, Cheesy, Stoke, Reg, Spence, Marshall and Miner.

The majority of the crowd was made up of my beloved congregation, however, all of whom deserved to be in The Chapel; but only the Knowalls, and a select few were making their way through the scrum. Lucky was at the vanguard, jaw fixed, striding through in a determined gait, sporting a black headband and a raised clenched fist, like some western sadhu committing to an eternal pose. Elvis and Poison Ivy were immediately behind him, Elvis head to foot in gold with a new gold tooth. Stan followed, his face twisted by emotion.

"He's not crying about you."

"What's he crying about then?"

"Boots have started selling Viagra, he's skint."

The Jim's walked in size order, like a row of Russian Dolls, Big Jim grabbing hold of Mekon Don who was readying to launch himself at the reporters. Next, the flaming orange hair of Red Molly came into view, vivid against the black, revelling in revolutionary fervour. Striding behind her came a formation of Golden Girls, the grey arrows, Anna, Ginny and Margaret, a joint hanging out of her mouth, stern faced, telling the reporter to "Fuck Off," as he approached with a cheerful demeanour.

Willo walked alongside, deep in conversation with Plato, lighting a spark of happy memories, real friendships, before being extinguished by recollections of Judy and deceit.

I laughed as they stopped by the microphone, caught in traffic as they filed into the crematorium, completely ignoring the reporter who was far too polite to get anywhere,

"What is the point of consciousness? Does it make us more successful in the game of survival of the fittest?"

"Of course it does, we're cock of the Earth."

"And what good is that doing life? We're destroying it. No other creature is doing it, just us with our consciousness."

"What's your point?"

"My point is, for the natural world, consciousness is a negative. Grass multiplies very well, as does bacteria. It appears the more conscious the creature, the more dangerous it is; natural selection is natures suicide."

"Consciousness ensures our success."
"Consciousness ensures our destruction."
I felt another pang of regret, wishing I was there amongst them as
they moved on, their voices fading away. But it was faint, the dying
twitches of the deceased. "God gave us consciousness," I'd have
shouted, to a barrage of abuse.
The camera was distracted as the floating figure of Gabe came past,
a moving monolith in a black flowing gown focused steadfastly
forward whilst Libby staggered drunkenly in her full Yoga regalia
in front, behind, then alongside him. The erect figure of Stretch
followed, he'd brought a barn owl for the occasion.
The doors closed and the camera panned back, revealing the crowd
outside becoming organised, the wandering reporters splitting them
into identifiable groups, different strands of my life interweaving,
creating a collage, a living fabric, particles and waves as a festive
atmosphere was breaking out. There was Tom with Moat, the actors
performing on a quickly set up stage; then the dance troupe in full
get up, performing in front of Crab Scratch mumbling into a
microphone.
"Prawn crackers," I mumbled to myself with a grin.
"Got quavers," Canty replied, pointing over towards a plastic bag in
the corner, oblivious.
Mo and Fuck Slap were there with regiments of children bobbing
their heads along to the music, each wearing a black armband,
orders drilled in, behaving immaculately, letting out a unified gasp
as a ball of flame was blown into the air above their heads by the
performers. The astronomers walked by, then Shaun with his art
group in tow, all carrying beers which I traced in a line back to
Callaghan who'd set up a bar, Tejel and Jamie the Tiler quickly
erecting food stalls next to him as James the Legal Eagle was
downing beers like the bar was about to run dry.
It was a greatest hits show, Miriam weaving her magic from another
stage as a bunch of balloons floated left and the giant puppet dog
Xolo came from the right, tail wagging as it cocked its leg to pee on
the crowd, a show of solidarity from an art troupe in France. Flags
were flying as impromptu dancing started, red and blue smoke
bursting from canisters and flares, filling the air. It was like the
sixties again as young radicals appeared in their Gilets Jaunes and
headbands, with a list of no's painted on banners – no war, no state,

no religion, no private property. The camera, caught up in the
pandemonium, paused on the lone figure of Smiler, massive,
tattooed and apparently lost, drifting past a group of gymnasts who
were making their way to replace the dancers.
It was looking deeper into the groups that provided most joy, for
they had dispersed from their factions, the barriers between them
dissolved, irrelevant, their identifying garments the only clue,
signalling them as Syrian, Muslim, Sikh, Jew, Rasta, Hindu or Hare
Krishna. Even the Cornermen and Rip had made an appearance,
circling along the periphery, a buffer between the uniformed ranks
of the police and military, waiting on the fringes for the inevitable.
I felt a sense of relief watching, they didn't need me anymore.
Margaret was still smoking her joints, Elvis putting on his Lycra, the
singers still singing, the dancers still dancing, but there had been a
plan, God's plan, my whole life story now making sense as I stared
at the screen, displaying images of what I'd created, a coming
together of diversity in joy and chaos, within a smooth space, free
from the rules and stratifications of power.
I was being shown the truth, God's blueprint for the human
condition, away from the corruption of authority in all its guises
and dogma; a path which did not lead to anarchy as they
threatened, but the other way, towards love, joy, togetherness,
towards Our Lord. It was an instant of revelation as the story of my
life fixed seamlessly to this moment: there were no coincidences or
accidents, it was written, my fate pre-destined, everything in it had
a purpose which I only now understood, shaping me for this
moment and the next stage.
I am fourteen thousandth generation human. I am all of the old
stories, their mystics, myths and their gods. I am one, all, chosen
from the seven billion souls that walk the planet. I came in the flesh
to suffer, a corruption, an innocence born of a perverse, dishonest
affair and from the point of conception had a fault line running
through me. In addition to our original, my first sin was a personal
act, a kill within two hours of birth, delivering judgement as my
mother bled to death, torn, punished for her deception and
adultery. *"Behold, I was shapen in iniquity; and in sin did my mother
conceive me," said Psalm 51:5.*
This fault line rent my personality in two, a blessing that they could
not understand so they labelled me psychotic. But I was God,

holding up a mirror, an amplification of the darkness and light in all of us, both created by Our Lord, each with its own purpose. Perhaps Yoda had seen it as he purchased me for The Church, bringing me to its tarnished version of God and its truths, lies, loves and fallacies.

My constant questioning of Our Lord, about justice, the meaning of my early years seemed childish now, but my ignorance was understandable, only recognisable when set within the context of the path my life had taken to this point. I had to experience suffering beneath those people, bear witness to their truth, for how can there be grace and righteousness without suffering? Our Lord had shown me their evil at a most personal level, allowing me to understand how they were capable of doing the same to entire populations through their social structures. It was their corruption, their usurpation of positions of power that was causing misery throughout the world, force feeding their values which the haves would blindly adopt and try to emulate. I knew them, I always had, sent visions, hallucinations to remind me of their existence, their evils, and now, as my life was reframed with understanding, I could see the devil and my retribution would be just. *'Fracture for fracture, eye for eye, tooth for tooth,'* said Leviticus 24:20.

I glanced at the television, seeing Danny and his Mother wandering, their faces fixed, looking older, worn down, medicated, another timely reminder.

'They are still doing it,' my better half screamed in rage. *'They devils are still torturing them.'*

Following these lessons, my life had become a pilgrimage, moving from the abuse of the home, through the wilderness of villages and towns, the loneliness of cities, gathering wisdom and understanding. The lessons were the people I'd met, the words and actions of the faces I recognised walking before me on the television screen, discovering the overwhelming goodness in the hearts of most people, despite the forces bearing down on them from above, shaping them towards evil.

Our Lord had then brought me to this nonconformist place, where I'd unravelled the works of power, the distant oaths and allegiances of the politicians, money and organised religions, returning this small pocket of society to God's design, joyful and chaotic, communal, for where else could it come from if not the poor? But, I was not immune to the temptations and deceptions around me, the frailties of human nature. I'd become the focal point, an ego receiving the applause, forgetting the purpose of my works until Our Lord removed me from The Temple where I'd lost myself and my humility. I was not a Priest, I was a con-man, inauthentic, a lestai, cast into my personal darkness where all the myths were true; the dark was something to be afraid of, there were monsters under the bed, in the wardrobe, in every corner of my mind as the nightmares would come and overwhelm me. I was tested, through conscious and unconscious, by goodness and evil, as multiple realities and truths were revealed, as Our Lord showed me myself, man, the universe, one and the same, made from the violence of collapsed stars, a cataclysm beyond comprehension.

I glanced across at Canty, who I now saw in a new light, as a tiny part in the whole thing, a stepping stone. He was an agent of power, no different than Yoda, relevant, though at the same time irrelevant in the scheme of things, to be disposed of if necessary.

"Did you take your tablets?" he asked, sounding like Yoda as he sensed me looking at him, his eyes still fixed on the television screen.

"Yes" I replied, a lie, I hadn't taken them for days.

"Big day tomorrow," he continued.

"Big day," I replied in agreement before switching my attention back to my funeral, looking at the faces that didn't matter anymore.

'For I know the plans I have for you, declares the Lord, plans for welfare and not for evil, to give you a future and a hope,' said Jeremiah 29:11.

CHAPTER 7

ASCENS-

As time catches up with us, I sit in an anonymous bar in an anonymous town, looking biblical, all long hair and trailing beard, one of those you see sitting alone, staring ahead, into the middle distance, muttering the occasional word, lost in memories. You glance then look away, worried that you might attract their attention, that they may try to speak to you, wondering how they ended up like this whilst telling yourself that you never will.
Now you know.
I'm sitting patiently, thinking of Yoda and his last days, the moment he exhaled his last breath, looking for a feeling, but there is nothing, just clear recollection, emotionless, rational thought; the psychopath equals pure science.
This freedom, or version of freedom, was reward for my first murder, though I didn't strictly kill him, I'd just allowed the cancer a free run without medication hindering its pain and progress. He was already far gone, riddled with the malignance God had placed within him, a corruption for the corrupt. In truth, it was cowardice on my behalf, perhaps a sliver of humanity remaining inside preventing my pulling of the trigger. Canty on the other hand saw its opposite, a barbarous act, exacting revenge with my own brand of cruelty, prolonging his agony; As Yoda said, I am weak.
Most of the time I was talking at him as he lay unresponsive and unrepentant, referring only once to his order to kill me, "I couldn't bear to see you put into their system, I love you too much."
So I spoke, endlessly, my words like the scrawlings on the floors and the walls, a constant flow of narrative, about how my new life was framed, its meaning, my visions, revelations, *'He does not come into judgement, but has passed from death to life,'* said John 5:24, his only reply a dry laugh and sarcasm.
"Add messiah complex to your list of ailments, all hail the new messiah," he whispered.

"All hail the new messiah."
"All hail the new messiah."
"All hail the new messiah."
He was trying to provoke anger within me, but I knew the tricks
this devil played, my thoughts remaining pure, emotions non-
existent.
"I'm the opposite of a messiah," I'd argued, trying to draw him out.
"I don't want to form a new church, I want to take people away
from organised religion. They cannot find their own path to God
whilst institutions have power."
I waited for a response, but there was nothing, so continued with
ponderings on religion, provocative sentences delivered to tease out
a reaction, but he also knew this devil, remaining silent, unwilling
or unable to fill in the spaces which were becoming longer as time
passed by.
"They've got to move away from the organised church."
Silence.
"For individuals to worship God in their own way."
Silence.
"It's a corrupted, man-made path, defined for everybody."
Coughing then silence.
"But, once you get away from the organised religions, is it still
religion? An individual, unconventional path to God?"
Silence.
"Maybe it's more spiritualism, though that seems to step towards
shamans and yoga teachers."
Silence.
"The pathless path."
Then he'd start singing the same song on repeat, his response to my
endless questions, his counter attack in our curious battle of wills as
we tried to piss each other off.
"Oh, the crystal chandeliers light up the paintings on the wall, the
marble statuettes are standing stately in the hall…" he crooned,
Charlie Pride, stuck in a loop, the same lyrics, again and again,
perhaps taking him back to a happier time, in a happier place.
I missed the angry little bastard before he'd even died, his
conversation, his company, Ice Road Truckers and Mary Berry, the
time before, living in ignorance before realising it was all a lie.
We'd laid for weeks, locked in the darkness together, without

bodies, just minds.

It was only towards the end, as he was drifting in and out of consciousness that he'd confessed the truth in his own way, stubborn to the last. I remembered it word for word as it justified everything, the sound of his straining voice rattling, whispering the words as he realised Hell was near.

"I often thought about what motivated them to do it, the powerful," I'd began, expecting to be rebuffed with nothing, or a snappy, "Fuck off, leave me to die in peace."

"Could they not stay in their safe, ermine lined enclosures?" I'd continued, sensing a change in his breathing. "Why did they have to risk it all?"

"They risked nothing," came his reply from the pitch black.

"Did they not have enough from life?"

"They take what they want, consequence free."

"If it was just about sex, then weren't they in a more advantaged place than most to get it?"

"You're asking was it a primal urge, or were they just entitled? Both."

"Maybe it wasn't just about sex," I continued. "What if, when you reach the top there is nothing, it's empty behind those high walls, those gilded cages where appearance is everything."

"I don't get it, speak properly," he admonished, "you sound like a fucking fortune teller."

"The loneliness of sitting there when you've got everything, finding this is all there is, needing something else," I tried to explain. "They see the meaninglessness of existence from the pinnacle, power and wealth. But, from the top of the mountain, there's just emptiness. Maybe it's anger that propels them? Frustration, feeling conned that there is no happiness there, a heaven on earth, driving them towards something perverse."

"They are just perverse, I can assure you. Don't provide them with any metaphorical alibi, they don't see the world as you do. They are power, they do what they want, without consequence."

"Maybe it's all relative then, a moral relativity?"

"Scientific theories never work well when applied to people. It's why the world is the way it is now, so many words coming through, people splitting as they cling to one or the other, so many different relativities where there just used to be one, The Church."

"Perhaps from their frame of reference they were doing nothing wrong. Maybe there is no right and wrong, just interpretation from each perspective, what is morally acceptable is relative."

"You're right, but it's nothing to do with relativity, they just don't give a shit; Caligulas that think they own the world."

Next time he awoke the walls were back in place and he denied everything, his only words reminding me that I was a cunt and a psychopath.

As we got closer his body gradually started buckling, twisting, contorting as the soul started to separate from matter. I could smell that familiar smell, of decay, of putrefaction as organs started failing, the pain expanding exponentially as he begged me to kill him, further corrupting his soul.

There was no dramatic ending, he just slipped away, already buried in a cavernous stone room at the heart of the maze. I remembered my words as life left his body and his spirit descended to Hell, disagreeing with the right to die, death becoming economics, a subject completely unremarkable as he finally submitted, his heart and lungs just stopping, now silent and still, mouth open, eyes closed. I stood up and looked down on him, waiting for whatever emotion may appear, but there was nothing, just the closing of a chapter as I bent over and kissed him on the forehead. I was complete.

I check my watch and look at the worn, two day old newspaper, lying on my table, grubby around the edges. A grin comes to my lips as I see a photograph of Jayne on the front cover, looking exquisite in black at my funeral. She'd caught the eye of the nation, the shock reverberating around social media, as if such beauty couldn't dwell in these parts. Now they were trying to claim her as their own, the illegitimate daughter of a disappeared Lord, they said, as her face appeared next to his. 'He's still alive' she'd claimed, making me grin a second time at all of these truths, real or unreal, it really didn't matter.

Canty had disposed of Yoda near the remains of the old kilns under Limekiln Lane, before giving me my reward, a new life, becoming somebody else, free but controlled. My current incarnation, or incarceration, was Brian Diggle.

"Brian Diggle. What sort of a name is that?" I'd asked, as Canty handed over the documents. "Shouldn't it be a bit more anonymous? John Smith or something?"

"Just made it up," he shrugged.

It was Canty who'd asked me to come here, to receive the reward
for my next kill, even though I hadn't committed it yet. I was in a
village close to the city, but far enough away to be unrecognisable
beneath all of the hair. I was twitchy, on edge as The Little Lord was
waiting for me, chained up naked in the darkness of The Pit, where
my mind kept travelling, the anticipation almost unbearable.
Capturing him had been surprisingly easy, climbing over the wall
onto the estate, then finding him standing alone, in the middle of a
salmon run on his own private stretch, his obese form striding over,
full of anger and arrogance as he spotted me on the bank, a
trespasser.

It was amateurish for I was an amateur. I'd attempted to hold him
down and incapacitate him with GHB; Fortunately nobody saw his
demented figure in the solitude of the fields as he became excitable
and slightly euphoric for almost an hour before he slipped into
unconsciousness. The police were already searching for him, no
doubt confused by the erratic paths taken through the long grass,
scanning downstream and the surrounding forests, assuming the
river may have taken him, though fully aware that something else
may be afoot in the current climate.

He'd be awake by now, hopefully outraged and angry, a Gammon
ready for combat, for I was going to give him a chance, an identical
opportunity to all of those children he sent down there to fight for
their lives. It would be slow, he had to feel what they had felt,
understand the savagery and fear that completely envelopes you
with the realisation that you are going to fail, as you lose control,
co-ordination, as the mind crashes and we become animal. He
wouldn't die like that, none of them could, their minds having to be
clear so they understand and have an opportunity to repent. Then,
God could judge whilst I'd scatter his body amongst the others in
the Nonconformist's Graveyard, unidentified, anonymous; it had a
beautiful symmetry which his victims may enjoy. *'For the wages of
sin is death, but the free gift of God is eternal life,'* said Romans 6:23.

"Top up love?"

"Sorry," I replied, jumping slightly then looking up at the stocky
owner who had appeared from behind the counter, her forearm taut
and muscular as she held out her heavily patinated tea pot.

"It's bottomless tea between ten and eleven with a Full English," she continued, as if I should know. "You've got ten minutes left."
"Go'ed," I murmured, then, "thanks," as the stewed tea poured into the cup, a thin sheen of scumbergs floating on the top.
It was almost time, eleven o'clock he'd said, as I glanced at the table number, checking again that I was in the right place for his carefully stage managed plan. He'd been wary, sensing something but not sure what as the padlock clicked behind The Lord's sleeping body, laid out in a slightly cultish manner, a star on the ground in the middle of the circle.
"Isn't it funny how they're called Lord and we call God Our Lord?" I'd asked as he looked at the specimen through the bars in admiration, like a new arrival in the zoo, "How they align themselves with The Almighty."
He seemed relieved that he'd arrived unconscious, providing a window of opportunity to delay the job as he fished for hints about my line of thinking. It was chess again, an inflection point, having completed the deal, both fulfilling promises. He wanted me to walk his path as he delivered his sales pitch, full of arrogance about future business, his sentences peppered with 'Brother' as he explained how I would remain free to carry out God's work.
'A resource to be used,' Peter mumbled.
He was right in many ways, our interests were aligned, the folder was to be my life's work, but another route had been chosen, our lives destined to touch for the briefest of moments before spinning off into different directions. They held the keys to my freedom, or so they assumed, but their hand was a busted flush, for God had provided a man lying beneath a tomb stone, as yet unborn, waiting for life to be breathed into him. Migsy had set up my account, housing crypto-millions which I'd buried alongside documents and history beneath a headstone, meaning Brian Diggle's life will be short and eventful, soon to disappear as I become another, burying this biography of Peter McKay as his closing chapter, a fitting final resting place, awaiting discovery sometime or never to provide a means of explanation.
Meanwhile, God is communicating with me, instructing me which soul to deliver next.
The visions that scattered have started to return, just one this time, the General standing next to the counter with its display of pre-

mixed sandwich fillings, an augmented reality, a perverse Pokemon
licking his lips as he fondles his genitals, salivating in anticipation
for what is to come, as am I.

*'Consider the ravens: they neither sow nor reap, they have neither
storehouse nor barn, and yet God feeds them,'* said Luke 12:24.

It's time and I glance up at a movement, a dark silhouette slowly
emerging on the other side of the frosted glass of the front door,
pausing then moving again, solidifying, becoming definite, a shape
that I recognise. I push myself back into my chair then stand up,
leaning forward, placing my hands on the table, my mind reeling,
the science of the psychopath overwhelmed by ghosts in the
machine, by the visceral fighting back - beliefs, emotions, thoughts
and desires, all unmeasurable, immaterial, fleeting and real. It
seems they did hold the cards after all as doubts fill my mind, as I
make out the dark hair cascading over her shoulders, her gentle
curves as her hand becomes real, stretching up towards the door.
Meg was the only one that could reach into me and grab my heart,
the only one.

'It's a test,' Peter shouts, but my mind is careering ahead, thinking of
the life we could have together, away from the village, away from
The Church as the door begins its inward journey along a swinging
path. Then time stops, and I finally understand, it hits me like a
sledgehammer, that love exists.

The door opens fully and she stands in the doorway as I lurch to a
halt. Her posture is slumped and her hair carries grey, her skin
creased by the years, as if she in the future. My mind is stuttering,
it's a vision I'm grasping to understand as hope becomes its
opposite; it's not her and I freefall into a chasm as the door slowly
returns on its trajectory, the bell ringing as it swings closed behind
her.

Peter is fury, screaming, *'What trick is this?'* But, the noises blur into
one as she glances at me then pauses, a crease forming between her
eyebrows and I look at her again, her eyes still fixed on me. There's
something familiar, an energy, gravitation, then I'm rising to my
feet as her mouth slowly opens but no words come out. She takes a
tiny step forward, still no sound as her hand reaches out and clasps
my arm, it feels electric as we fuse together, then she gently
whispers "Peter?" in a voice I've never heard before but one I've
always known as I stagger past the table sending my tea cup

crashing to the floor. I raise my hand to touch her, not daring, holding my trembling finger an inch from her lightly powdered cheek, still wondering if she is real. She places her hand on mine and I touch her soft skin before the word comes to my mouth, a word that I have never spoken before, "Mother."

I am a reflection of my environment, on the cusp of something else, all of us, on the cusp of something else, if only they would stop dragging us back. The lights flicker, the walls are white, the ceiling is white, I am bound.

www.ingramcontent.com/pod-product-compliance
Lightning Source LLC
Chambersburg PA
CBHW051505030726
47592CB00006B/2110